PRASE FOR A.

PRAISE FOR *THE GOOD LIE*

"Ambitious and twisty . . . Great bedtime reading for insomniacs and people willing to act like insomniacs just this once."

—*Kirkus Reviews*

"This kinky tale is compulsively readable."

—*Publishers Weekly*

"A blend of serial killer story, court cases, and even romance, this is a tricky story that will keep readers going."

—*The Parkersburg News and Sentinel*

PRAISE FOR *EVERY LAST SECRET*

"Deliciously, sublimely nasty: *Mean Girls* for grown-ups."

—*Kirkus Reviews*

"Torre keeps the suspense high . . . Readers will be riveted from page one."

—*Publishers Weekly*

"A glamorous and seductive novel that will suck you in and knock you sideways. I love this story, these characters, and the raw emotion they generated in me. I devoured every word. Exceptional."

—Tarryn Fisher, *New York Times* bestselling author

"Raw and riveting. A clever ride that will make you question everyone and everything."

—Meredith Wild, #1 *New York Times* bestselling author

A
FAMILIAR
STRANGER

OTHER TITLES BY
A. R. TORRE

A FAMILIAR STRANGER

A. R. TORRE

THOMAS & MERCER

Text copyright © 2022 by Select Publishing LLC
All rights reserved.

Published by Thomas & Mercer, Seattle

www.apub.com

Amazon, the Amazon logo, and Thomas & Mercer are trademarks of Amazon.com, Inc., or its affiliates.

ISBN-13: 9781662500121
ISBN-10: 1662500122

Cover design by James Iacobelli

Printed in the United States of America

To Tex Thompson. I hope one day to be as literately awesome as you.

I just want to start off by saying that love wasn't what caused all this. The murder, the double life, the lies . . . None of it was triggered from a lack of me loving my husband.

It was from a lack of him loving me back.

—Lillian Smith

Everything I told David on the day that I met him was a lie.

I did that a lot back then. I didn't have a single notable thing about me—about Lillian Smith: writer, mother, wife—worth talking about, so I often invented a life, a persona, of someone better. Someone who rolled out of bed with a purpose. Someone unpredictable and exciting, and . . . hell. Lust-worthy. Someone whose husband would gaze at her in awe, and shower her with affection, and never stay late to work if he had the opportunity to spend just one extra moment in her presence.

Those people—those women—do exist, you know. In my job, I've dipped my toe into their lives. I've spoken to their friends, their families, their coworkers. I've summarized their lives, which are always extinguished too short.

The day I met David, I was thinking about extinguishing my own. Would Mike even notice? How much time would pass before he realized I was gone?

Dinner, probably. That would be the first tell. No poorly cooked meal set out on the table. He'd be annoyed. His handsome face would settle into those hard, disapproving lines. A terse text would be sent, one heavy in blame. A call would be made, for delivery or pickup, and the problem would be solved. My husband loves to solve problems, which is probably why he married me to begin with. Other men choose women they can't live without. Mine chose a woman who was unlikely to live without him.

It was a hypothesis proven true by the sleeping pills I had been stockpiling, *just in case*.

So yeah. By the time David Laurent crossed my path, I was a disaster of the most boring variety, a woman so yawn-worthy that when David smiled at me and I introduced myself, I lied.

I picked the most exciting woman who had recently died, and I stole her spirit. I stole her story. I stole her life.

And it felt really, really good.

TWO MONTHS BEFORE THE DEATH

CHAPTER 1

LILLIAN

@themysteryofdeath: Three women go to Vegas for the weekend. A trophy wife, an internet coach, and a struggling single mom. One of them won't make it back home. Who will die?

I posted the tweet, then pushed my grocery cart forward, pausing at a display of laundry detergent and scanning the bottles for the hypoallergenic brand that my husband preferred. Rising to my toes, I grabbed the pale-green container and pulled it from the shelf, wincing at a twinge of pain that resulted from the action.

Mike had hidden my pain medicine, though he'd acted innocent when I asked about it, his face adopting that blank, wide-eyed look I hated. He'd followed up the denial with a suggestion to use the high-dose ibuprofen, which I was supposed to switch to a week ago, but which barely cut the edge off the pain.

I wedged the green detergent jug between a bag of chips and a pack of toilet paper, then parked my cart to the side of the aisle and picked up my phone. There were already a dozen responses to my tweet, and my mood lifted as I scrolled through the replies and liked the more entertaining ones.

- christopher23: single mom, choked to death on a Chippendale's sparkly thong lol

- ncarolinamom: trophy wife. Shot by a hit man hired by her ugly and cheating husband.

- imahoney: @ncarolinamom ikr? I agree on the trophy wife. hot ones always die first in the movies

- bornblonde247: In the MOVIES. This is real life, you idiots. I vote the internet coach. Was making a #blessed social media post while crossing the Strip and got ran over by a taxi

I returned my phone to my purse, a smile crossing my face. My followers were witty, if not a little macabre. But hey, so was I. When I started the account, it was because my family and friends had grown tired of playing my death-guessing games. Where they'd rolled their eyes, the internet had embraced me. My Twitter account was up to ten thousand followers and steadily growing.

I'd wait another hour, then add a series of hints. If no one had solved the mystery by the end of the day, I'd unveil the truth, paired with their obituary. I wasn't sure how often the obituaries were clicked on, but as an obit writer myself, I felt like the inclusion added a certain punch of class to the game, and acted as a dignified nod to my profession.

I had a set of guidelines, designed to protect the game. I always changed enough facts so an internet search wouldn't spoil the fun, pre-reveal. And I rarely used my own obituaries, to keep any followers from figuring out who @themysteryofdeath really was.

Sometimes, though, I just couldn't help myself. I had a stack of obits in my drawer that were flagged for future tweets, ones that deserved more eyes than just the *Los Angeles Times* readers. I had a sneaking suspicion that most of our subscribers only used that section of the paper to line their kitty litter trays.

"Oh my gosh, Lillian!" The familiar high-pitched trill sounded shocked, as if running into someone you knew in the grocery store were unheard of, and I hid a sigh as I turned to face my husband's secretary.

Heather was dressed in a red pantsuit that clung to her thin thighs, the jacket buttoned just under her lace-cupped cleavage. She held a green shopping basket in one hand and beamed at me with undisguised delight. "I'm *so* glad I ran into you. I was just asking Mike about you yesterday! How's your shoulder?"

"It's fine." I rubbed the joint out of habit. "Doctor says I just hyper-extended it."

"Well, if you need *anything*." She let the sentence hang there, and I tried to ignore the open proposition. "You know, I'm a licensed masseuse."

No, I didn't know that. I tried not to grimace at the news. If my husband's model-worthy employee hadn't been tempting enough, let's add in a set of talented, pleasure-inducing fingers. "Thanks, Heather."

"Oh no, thank you! Having those days off last week was heaven. Did you enjoy Santa Barbara?"

I nodded automatically while I tried to figure out what she was talking about.

"I wasn't sure about the hotel," she continued, oblivious to my confusion. "I mean, it's a Ritz, so of course it *should* be nice, but the reviews were iffy. Mike said you liked it?" She gnawed on the edge of her bright-pink bottom lip and peered at me in concern.

"The Ritz-Carlton?" I clarified, while my mind raced through what she was saying. Mike had been out of town at a continuing-education course last week. But in San Francisco, not Santa Barbara—at least, according to what he'd told me. "Yes, it was fine. Really nice."

"Oh good." She blew out a relieved breath that smelled faintly of peppermint. "Well, if you need anything, just ping me."

"Thanks, Heather." I watched as she wobbled by in heels that had to be four inches tall.

An upscale vacation, without me. My gut twisted at another piece to the puzzle of my husband's suspicious behavior. I added it to the stack, which was beginning to tilt from the weight.

I needed to just face what was happening, but my heart couldn't take it. Not yet. Maybe, somehow, there was an innocent explanation.

CHAPTER 2
LILLIAN

On light obituary days, I visited the dead. I always started at the north end of the cemetery, where the freshest graves were, and worked my way up and down the rows, putting a daisy stem on each name that I knew.

The last one I visited was always Marcella's.

I put the remaining daisies at the base of her headstone. It was a simple one—not as ornate as some, but substantial, especially for such a small grave. The engraving was simple.

MARCELLA PRAWN
DEC 15, 2002–MARCH 1, 2010
MAY YOUR LAUGHTER AND SMILE CARRY YOU INTO HEAVEN.

I liked it. That line was the final one in her obituary. I'd been tempted to use it since, but it had felt wrong, like wearing a dress you'd stolen from a friend. I did that once in college. Jenna Forester left a Betsey Johnson at my house, and I knew it was hers, and I should have given it back, but I didn't. I wore it to Whiskey Bar on a weekend that she was out of town, and felt like a thieving bitch the entire night.

I sat with Marcella for a minute, then continued to the older section, where I found her father sitting underneath a tree, his eyes closed, legs splayed open, the hem of his cemetery uniform exposing some of his hairy, swollen belly.

I waited for a moment before interrupting him, my mind comparing this version of Lenny with the man I'd first met, more than ten years ago. When I had gotten the predeath obituary order for a young child, my heart had ached at the request. The little girl was in hospice and wanted to contribute to her own obituary, a unique but not impossible request. With my stomach in knots, I'd rung the doorbell to the hospice center and been greeted by a man with a stern, almost military bearing, his face lined in stress and fear.

Since that time, Detective Leonard Thompson had lost his job, his purpose, and his health. Now the cemetery groundskeeper, he watched over his daughter's grave, consumed an unhealthy amount of alcohol, and begrudgingly allowed my friendship.

"Hey." I crouched beside him and patted his shoulder. "Lenny."

He jerked to attention, then relaxed when he saw me. "What?"

"You know, one day you're going to get fired for sleeping on the job." I sat beside him and dug in my backpack, bringing out the extra chicken salad sandwich I'd packed. "Hungry?" I placed it on the thigh of his faded black cargo shorts.

"Don't you have someone else to bother? A puppy that needs rescuing?"

"Puppy rescues are only in the afternoon." I withdrew my own sandwich, along with a can of Sprite, which I set in the grass beside him. "Right now, it's lunchtime."

I took a big bite of my sandwich and chewed, holding his eye contact. His beard needed trimming, the wiry nest now past his collarbones. "No onions, right?" I nudged the edge of the sandwich bag, which was still lying on his leg. "See? I listen."

"I said that I *like* onions." Lenny glared at me as he grabbed the green soda can and wedged a dirty fingernail under the tab.

"Shush, you did not." I used my tongue to dislodge a piece of salad that was stuck to my gums. Turning my head, I watched as a mower attendant drove down an adjacent aisle. "Who's that?"

"A new guy." Lenny brought the soda to his lips and took a long drink, then belched. "Won't last."

"It does take a hardy sort," I said solemnly, and earned a rare Lenny chuckle.

He bit into the sandwich and I did the same. Chewing slowly, I caught him watching me.

"What's wrong?" he asked, and considering that he was probably seeing two of me, his gaze was remarkably sharp.

"Nothing." I took another bite, and stifled a groan as he set down his sandwich and glared at me, waiting. "It's my husband," I admitted, after swallowing my bite. "I think he's cheating on me."

"Husbands typically do."

I laughed despite the anxiety in my chest. "Thanks, Lenny. Very reassuring."

He lifted both shoulders in a shrug. "You catch him in a lie?"

"A few." San Francisco hadn't been the only one. There had been an expensive cologne gift he'd lied about, scratches on his back that had looked suspiciously like nail marks, and an overall detachment from me that seemed to be increasing. Three months ago, I'd considered confronting and leaving him.

I'd abandoned the idea by morning. Was protecting my personal pride worth ripping apart my family, especially when Jacob was only two years from graduation?

And maybe Lenny was right. If most men cheat, why trade a known for an unknown?

"I cheated on Marcella's mother." Lenny wiped at the edge of his mouth with one dirty knuckle. "Didn't do a great job of hiding it. I didn't really care if she found out. It was my lazy way of getting out of the marriage, of making her take that step. Is he being sloppy about it?"

That was a hard question to look into, mainly because I was afraid of what I'd find. "*Sloppy* isn't a word that ever describes Mike," I hedged.

Lenny chuckled, and I knew he could see through me. "Just think about it."

I didn't want to think about it. It was one thing to view Mike as being selfish and wanting to have his cake and eat it too. It was a bigger, uglier situation if he didn't want my cake and was plotting his way out.

I didn't know if it was the former or the latter, but I did know one thing about my husband, and that was that he thought everything through. If Mike was planning to leave me, I needed to be prepared, because he would have contingency plans on top of contingency plans and the risk was high that I had already been set up for failure.

CHAPTER 3

LILLIAN

My mother used to say that she'd cut the balls off any man who ever cheated on her. It would have been funny, except that my mother was just crazy enough to do it. Every time she made the reference, whatever man she was dating would invariably shift uncomfortably in his seat, his legs crossing to protect his sacred treasures.

When I married Mike, she conveyed the threat to him, her eyes flat and watery from three Bloody Marys, the edge of a nipple peeking embarrassingly free of her yellow formal dress as she leaned over the wedding reception table and stubbed out her cigarette on the rose-decorated china. Smoking was forbidden, as a hotel employee had mentioned twice already, but that was my mom for you. Rules, as with income taxes, common courtesies, and speed limits, didn't apply to her.

When I was young, I was ashamed of her. Now, with my fortieth birthday looming . . . I almost envied the reckless disregard she had for other people's impressions. She wanted something, she took it. She found something entertaining, she did it. She disliked someone, or something they did, she let her opinion be known.

I had fought so hard to avoid any similarities to her, but maybe, beneath the foul language, slutty outfits, and afternoon martinis . . .

maybe there was something valuable there. Something that would have distinguished me from the bland individual I had become. Some color.

God, I could use some color. Right now I was so boring I was falling asleep on myself.

I left the cemetery and decided to swing by the *Los Angeles Times* office. I hadn't visited the El Segundo office in almost three months, and I rode the elevator up to the editorial floor with a bit of nostalgia as I thought of our previous downtown location, which had been the home of the *Times* for over eighty years. Now we were in a building that had gone out of its way to avoid any uniqueness or beauty. Mike was convinced the company was on its last legs. Print, in his opinion, was dead—and if my morning e-book purchase was any indication, he was right. Still, I'd hold on to the feel of newsprint as long as I could, especially when my name appeared weekly in eight-point font on its obituary pages.

I stopped in the bullpen, where my in-box was crammed with junk mail, a few interoffice memos, and a bright orange Post-it from Fran, my boss, that read "Come see me." The Post-it was attached to a three-week-old death notice on a local pastor, and I tossed both into the trash.

I cleaned out my in-box, then glanced into the editorial pen to see whether any familiar faces were there. A bunch of strangers with graphic tees and colorful hair hunched over the glass desks, their attention on their phones, and the sense that I was working at a legitimate news organization grew fainter. I headed for the elevator and tapped the call button.

"You new here?" A guy with a backward cap and a Lakers jersey stopped beside me and gave a half wave with a Styrofoam coffee cup.

"No." I tried to swallow the know-it-all look that used to get me beat up in math class but . . . come on. *New here?* I was an original. Hell, I had been here during the *Tribune* purchase. "I work remotely."

"Ah, right on." He stuck his hand out. "I'm Rick. I cover the fantasy football picks."

His palm was there, unable to avoid. I shifted uncomfortably in my flats, then shook it, trying not to grimace at the contact.

He kept my hand captive and tilted his head, reading the lanyard badge that hung around my neck. "Lillian Smith. Editorial?"

"Yep." I pulled free and stared at the elevator panel, wondering what was taking so long.

"Written anything I might have read?"

"Not unless you read the obituaries." He smelled like mustard, and the fact that he was close enough for me to catch the scent proved his violation of my personal space.

He hesitated at my response. "Like, this week's?"

"Any week."

"Ohhh . . . You're the celebrity obituaries girl." Understanding dawned, along with that sympathetic look that had followed me ever since I'd been served with a restraining order.

"I was. Now I'm just the obituary girl. No celebrities." I smiled to take the bite off the words. According to my husband, I'm still snippy about the demotion.

"Well." He let the word hang in the air. "Seems like a cool job."

Oh yes, so cool. I struggled not to roll my eyes at the statement because, after all, it had been. Two years ago, I'd been a favorite of the newspaper's executive board, the quirky obituary writer who had lunched at the Ivy and chronicled every dead celebrity for the last twenty years. I'd even had the high honor of being asked to speak at Jacob's middle school career day. When I'd mentioned meeting Janet Jackson for her brother's obit, the entire auditorium had gasped in awe.

Last year, I hadn't even been invited to the newspaper's Christmas party. This loser, in untied tennis shoes and sporting a wallet chain, had probably attended, while I'd spent the evening at Sam's, downing expensive eggnog and lamenting my downward trajectory in life.

The elevator chimed and I waited as a group stepped off, easing my way around the flow before darting in. The sports guy hesitated, and maybe my failure carried a stench, because he stayed in place and lifted his coffee cup in parting.

I pulled out my phone in avoidance of a response and opened my Twitter feed, but the hint I'd posted on the way to the office had only two replies.

Shit. I was failing at everything.

CHAPTER 4

LILLIAN

My husband cut his meat with the slow speed and precision of a surgeon. Placing his fork, prongs down, on his plate, he picked up his napkin and smoothed it across his lap, then reached for his glass of red wine. "Jacob? How was school?"

"Fine." Our son slouched in his seat, his purple prep school polo crooked on his large frame. He poked at the small breast on his plate with suspicion.

Mike glanced at me. I tried to see if there was a hint of unhappiness in his dark brown eyes. He gave me a kind smile and I sighed, useless at reading him.

"What about French class?" I tried to at least help lift the load.

"Fine. What *is* this?" Jacob used his fingers to pinch off a piece of the meat.

"It's chicken," I lied. Jacob's increasing pickiness was rejecting everything as of late. "The other kids in French, they're good?" I pressed, and tried not to think about Heather's mention of Santa Barbara and what or *who* my husband was doing there for three days. Three days. Someone could fall in love during that time. Plan a divorce. Impregnate a woman. Interview for jobs.

"Yeah, Mom. They're fine. And we aren't kids. Some of them are already eighteen." He put the piece of duck in his mouth and tentatively chewed. "This doesn't taste like chicken."

"Eat it," Mike ordered.

"I just want to make sure," I said quickly, "because we can't change your schedule again. Not with the semester—"

"I'm not going to have any issues with anyone in French," Jacob said dryly. "No one will come near me, so you don't have to worry about it."

Mike's and my gazes connected again, and I was reassured by the protective look that passed between us. He might be distant, but Jacob would always be our priority, and Mike wouldn't disrupt his family. I believed that—I had to believe that.

Mike picked up his fork and pierced a wedge of potato. "That'll pass, Jacob. It just takes time."

"Whatever." He pushed his plate away. "This is lamb, isn't it?"

"It's duck," I said, annoyed. "You've liked it before."

"Well, I don't now."

I forced myself to take a deep breath and waited for Mike to interject, but his attention was on his phone, which had buzzed with a notification.

"I'm going to my room." Jacob pushed away from the table and grabbed his plate and dirty silverware. "Thanks for cooking, Mom."

I watched as he carried the items into the kitchen and dropped them with a loud clatter beside the sink. A few years ago, we could have ordered him to stay at the table, but now, the chances of being ignored outweighed the chances of being obeyed. As a parent, you could lose only so many arguments before you lost them all.

The school had learned that lesson with Jacob the hard way, with him and another kid ending up in the principal's office with blood and bruises. If it hadn't been for a sizable donation in his name, Jacob would have been expelled. If the kids were ignoring him in French, maybe that was a good thing. In high school, being ignored was a thousand times better than being focused on—at least it had been for me, an acne-ridden girl with a stutter.

Jacob's steps pounded up the stairs and I sighed, pushing my own plate away. "I don't know how to handle him."

Mike finished chewing, then wiped his mouth with one of the blue linen napkins we used for everyday meals. "He's seventeen. He's dealing with hormones and high school. When I was that age, I was either trying to screw or fight anyone that spoke to me."

Normally I would have smiled at the comment, so I did my best, my lips stretching painfully as I picked up a wineglass and hid behind it. "You did not. You probably made a pros-and-cons list first."

He shrugged. "Maybe in my head."

I folded my napkin in half, then in half again. Underneath the table, my socked foot jiggled against the wood floor. I was itching to get into the office, to finish the outstanding obituaries on my docket. This afternoon, two new orders had come in, both with tight turnarounds.

But jumping straight into work would break one of my husband's unwritten rules. Postdinner, he expected the dishes to be washed immediately, then loaded into the dishwasher for an extra sanitary cycle. The leftovers would be transferred into the Pyrex cubes that neatly stacked our fridge. Scraps would go into the food disposal, recycling into the bag, trash into the compactor. It would be an hour before I could escape to the more exciting life of someone else. Someone whose spouse had probably been loyal.

"Dinner was delicious." Mike took a long sip, finishing off his glass. He would restrict himself to one, while I . . . I would quietly finish off the bottle during the cleanup. "Thanks for cooking."

I could see the next line coming, like a closed-captioned reel that was ahead on its timing.

"I've got to head to the office. Better push off, before it gets too late."

At times, with certain phrases, there was a hint of the British accent that Mike had carried when we first met. He'd been born in London and moved to the United States with his mother when he was thirteen. The posh accent had slowly faded, diluting into the bland Californian sound that Jacob and I carried—but it popped its head up at times, nurtured strongly by Mike, who I suspected preferred and missed the more haughty slant.

Now I warred between wanting him out of my hair and wondering where he was really going. "Why don't you just log in from here?" He used to do that. We'd even set up my office so he could work remotely during the months that traffic was hell or there were blackouts downtown.

"No, the file that I need is at the office. This client is in Hong Kong, so I'm dealing with that time zone." He quickly tapped his fork tines across his plate, piercing and collecting a mixture of carrots, mushrooms, and onions.

He wasn't looking at me, and this was the husband I'd been dealing with for the past year. Stiff posture, no eye contact, and a flimsy excuse that would take him away for hours at a time. The man in complete control still had minute tells, and I'd learned most of them.

Swallowing his final bite, he folded his napkin in half and placed it beside his plate, then rose. Collecting his plate and silverware, he passed Jacob's empty chair and paused by my seat. I lifted my chin and he bent down, skipping my expectant lips and pressing a kiss on my cheek. "I'll be back in a few hours. Don't wait up."

Don't wait up. The three most telling words in a marriage.

I stayed in my seat as he washed his hands at the kitchen sink. In standard Mike fashion, the practice took a solid minute, followed by the selection of a fresh hand towel from the stack. His dress boots clicked across the tile, and he lifted his key fob off the hook by the interior garage door.

"Night," he called out.

"Night," I said dully, lifting the bottle and refilling my wineglass.

Maybe I should have gotten in my car and tried to follow him. I considered the idea, but the thought of it sounded exhausting, especially given the dinner cleanup, plus my writing, which were all waiting for me.

So instead I was a good little wife. I stayed in our three-bedroom house with the white picket fence. I cleaned the kitchen and put away the food, and sat in my office and wrote until I finished my assignments and sent them in.

And then, sticking to my role, I took a sleeping pill, washed it down with the remainder of a second bottle of wine, and went to bed.

CHAPTER 5

MIKE

My wife was beginning to suspect something. I could see the sharp pinch of her stare, the way she repeated my words back at times, as if she were tasting the flavor of truth versus lie.

Unfortunately for her, she wouldn't find anything. It was cute, really, how easily I manipulated and deceived her. It gave me a sense of reassurance, knowing that I was able to protect her, to guide her choices and opinions and make her life easier. If only she knew how many of her "decisions" were ones that I orchestrated with simple A plus B equals C manipulations.

I would find a place for her suspicions to land. A mistake "accidentally" made, one that revealed my supposed secret, and she'd fume and she'd accuse and I'd roll over and show my stomach. She'd think she had won and that I was defeated, and our marriage would go on to live another day. This house was my castle and she and Jacob my sheep, and everything would happen as it should because intelligence was the gravity that pinned all the pieces onto the board. While I might not be the handsomest or most athletic man in the room, I'd always been the smartest and would, as always, win.

CHAPTER 6

LILLIAN

I woke up with Mike behind me, one of his hands on my hip, his mouth half-open in a snore. Curling around, I burrowed into his chest and inhaled deeply, suspicious even while foggy with sleep. He smelled like his dandruff shampoo and soap, and I pushed off him, frustrated at the blank slate.

Closing my eyes, I listened to the clicking hum of the fan and the unsteady drone of his snores. His sleep apnea was back, and I was supposed to wake him up when too long of a pause occurred between snores, but I listened to the pauses and buzzes and imagined, in the moment before I fell back asleep, what would happen if he just suffocated and died.

We had cushy insurance policies on us both. I would pay off the house and Jacob would attend whatever college he wanted, and I could move out of Los Angeles—God, I was over this city—and to a small town (maybe Montana?) where traffic stalled behind Amish wagons and strangers waved hello, and I could jog alone at night without fear of being raped or killed. I reached over and poked Mike hard in his ribs, and he grunted and rolled to his left side.

The snores stopped.

When I woke up the second time, the room was filled with morning light, and the house was quiet. I checked my phone for emails, then flipped on my police scanner and started a fresh pot of coffee. As the coffee dripped and the scent of ground beans filled the room, I opened my new e-book and started reading where I had left off in chapter 2.

The book was called *How to Catch a Cheating Spouse*, and the second chapter was focused on paranoia versus justified suspicion. It seemed that I had a heavy amount of both. Which was all fine and good, but not worth the $12.99 I'd paid. I skimmed the next few pages, then rose when the pot chimed.

As I added cream and sugar, a familiar code came across the scanner.

A dead body, found. Setting down the Garfield cup, I turned the radio up, then grabbed my pen and my work notebook. Writing down the details, I glanced at the sunshine clock above the family organization board that hung by the pantry. I pulled out my travel mug and poured my coffee into the stainless-steel vessel and screwed the lid onto the top.

I tried not to be excited by a death, but this moment, before I found out the details, before I knew all the answers—it was like a shot of adrenaline. I loved it.

———

@themysteryofdeath: Monday morning in a high-rise office building. A group rides the elevator up to the top floor. Among them: a maintenance man, a business exec, an admin, and a new middle manager. One of them won't live until lunchtime . . . Who will die?

Edward Schwartz (the business exec) was found in his high-rise corner office, slumped over his desk from a heart attack. Unless we got lucky and someone placed an obituary order, this would be an unpaid job, but

I didn't mind that. I was a sucker for the aftermath of death, whether it came with a paycheck or not.

This man, as I soon discovered, had already been on his way out. "Four tumors," his secretary told me gravely, her eyes perfectly lined in charcoal liner and clear of tears. "Doctors said he only had a few months left."

I noted the details, then sat in the parking lot and scrolled through the man's social media. A car pulled into the spot next to me, and I thought of Edward's vehicle, which was probably on the executive level in one of the assigned spots. If the photos on his Instagram were any indication, it was a Porsche 911. How long would it suck up an expensive downtown spot before it was moved or sold in an estate auction?

According to his bio stats, the man was single. He was either childless or ignored them in his social media posts. The chances were high that there would be little family, if any, to mention in the write-up.

Single adults were one of my biggest challenges. Anyone could write glowing and loving tributes about soccer moms and hardworking fathers. People like Edward Schwartz needed a creative pitch and someone insightful and diligent enough to figure out whether their lives held anything more than paychecks and peroxide blondes.

Sometimes they didn't. Sometimes you scraped away the top layer of a prick, and underneath was just more of the same. I was only twenty minutes into Edward and I could foresee a seven-layer dip of selfishness and conceit. His secretary of seven years had been practically cheerful at her boss's demise. Either she was an asshole or he was.

My phone rang while I was scrolling through Edward's LinkedIn profile. I hit the button on the steering wheel and put the call through the Fiat's speakers. "Hey."

"Nora Price died," Sam said, jumping straight to the point. I winced at my best friend's news.

"No," I groaned. "How?"

"Apparently she had cancer. No one knew."

Shit. Nora was easily the most famous Black comedian in the world and had never failed to make me laugh out loud with her quick wit and sharp humor.

Two years ago, before Griswell Axe supposedly committed suicide—a death and obituary that led to my demotion and police record—I would have already been on the phone with Nora's publicist. The *Times* would have had me on a first-class flight to New York to meet with her wife and children, pen in hand, ready to properly chronicle her life.

"Are you there?" Sam's smooth voice deepened with concern. The man could have been a phone-sex operator. I'd told him that the night I met him, at an open-mic performance at a comedy club. He had paused for a beat, then told me we were going to be best friends. I'd laughed it off, but he'd been right. Sam was always right, either by wisdom or forced design. It was one of his most annoying traits.

"Yeah, I'm here. Just . . . caught off guard. I really loved her."

"Look, I'm headed to a showing in Calabasas, but wanted to see if you were down to hit happy hour later? Oyster House?"

"Yes," I said immediately, my gaze darting to the car's dash clock. "When?"

"Five?"

"I'll see you there." I ended the call and pulled up the obituary order for my afternoon appointment. It was for Taylor Fortwood, a middle-aged woman who died in a car accident earlier that week. It was a paid obituary, hence the family interview, which was scheduled for one thirty. I weighed traffic at this hour, then fastened my seat belt.

Nora Price. It was crazy, how quickly someone could be gone. No one would miss Edward Schwartz, but there would be memorial events, foundations, and nationwide mourning over the five-foot-two comedy icon. I pushed her out of my mind and pulled up Twitter, adding a hint for my followers, who had already decided that the maintenance man was definitely a goner.

> @themysteryofdeath: Hint: with more money often comes more problems.

That clue was a bit obvious for them, but hey. The stress of perfectionism could be deadly.

CHAPTER 7

LILLIAN

It's important to examine why you are trying to uncover their cheating. Is it to solve and heal problems in your relationship? Or are you setting them up for justification for your own mistakes? —Chapter 4, How to Catch a Cheating Spouse

In Los Angeles, coffee shops were the dating pools—singles edging around each other in line, sending bedroom eyes across small tables in crowded cafés, and sucking seductively on vapes in the shade of a palm on Hollywood Boulevard. Because of that, I typically walked into a shop on a mission, my shoulders steeled in defense, a permanent *hell no* stamped across my forehead to ward off men and the occasional panhandler.

"One venti pumpkin spice latte, with almond milk and two Splendas." Voice crisp yet kind.

Card swiped.

Tip added: 25 percent.

Coffee collected.

Seat captured.

Headphones on.

Laptop out.

Fingers furious against the keys.

I wasn't a particularly attractive woman. But in Los Angeles, you had to wear armor or you were devoured, and your armor was either that of the huntress or that of the hunted (me). Nice women in between got eaten.

The recently divorced (and deceased) Taylor Fortwood was a huntress, one with six boyfriends (according to her sister) and a two-story living room that could hold my entire house. I had perched on her fabulous red leather couch, sipped a pineapple chai latte served by her butler (yes, a *butler*), and flipped through a photo album that showed the successful calendar buyer on dream vacations and at celebrity encounters, and lounging with snow leopards alongside two sheiks and a Bentley. Taylor hadn't been much prettier than me, but she had brimmed with confidence and life, the energy radiating out of every photo and each perfectly chosen piece in her home.

Even her death—a simple blown tire that had led to a fishtail that had careened into oncoming traffic and resulted in a fourteen-car pileup—had been dramatic and impactful. When I died, it'd probably be from an infected toenail, and my obituary writer would struggle to fill the requisite three paragraphs.

As Matchbox Twenty crooned through my headphones—Taylor had toured with them in Germany her sophomore year of college—I reviewed my rough draft of her write-up, which was already pushing six paragraphs, and that was highlighting only the most exciting moments of her life.

Thirty-seven years old. Two years younger than me, yet a million times more interesting. I saved the draft and closed the laptop with a sigh. Slipping the headphones off my head, I took a long sip of my room-temperature coffee.

It was a moment of vulnerability, heightened by a glance around the shop to see what I had missed. And there, sitting just one table over, was David.

If he had been beautiful, I probably wouldn't have fallen. I would have snapped my gaze back to my table, forced my face into cool disinterest, and worked my headphones over my ears. But David wasn't beautiful, at least not in the manner that graced magazine covers and cologne ads. He was thin and scruffy, his chin and jaw covered by a wild beard that curled over his lips and matched the tufts of hair that peeked out from the sides of his baseball hat. He wore tortoiseshell glasses and a white T-shirt with board shorts. I stared at the shorts and wondered what grown man wore a bathing suit on a Thursday.

"They come in women's sizes, if you're interested."

I lifted my gaze to his face and blushed. "I'm not interested, thanks."

"Oh, the bitter sting of rejection." He cupped his hand to his chest, wounded.

"I have a feeling your shorts will recover." Why was I still talking? I should have been standing up to gather my trash and put away my laptop. I made a conscious move to lift the green coffee cup with my left hand, clearly exposing the diamond wedding band. Would he notice? Did he even care? Maybe this was just friendly conversation between two adults. I was too out of practice to know.

"I haven't seen you here before." He leaned forward, his elbows resting on his knees. He was a few years younger than me. Maybe thirty-five. Maybe as young as thirty-two. His voice held an accent, and my ears played detective with the sounds of it.

I cleared my throat. "Well, you wouldn't have. I'm not normally in the area. I'm traveling through on business."

On business. I warmed to the unexpected lie. But what business? Maybe he wouldn't ask. And anyway, wasn't I leaving? I should have been leaving. *Stand up, Lillian. Stand up right now.*

"Ah, business." He gestured to the computer. "Let me guess. Insurance sales."

"That's a very specific guess, but no." Shit. I needed a business, and my mind grasped wildly at straws.

"Divorce attorney?"

My good mood sank, and I fought to keep the smile on my face. "Not even close." I grabbed my crumpled napkin and stirrer and he groaned.

"No, don't do the clean-up-your-table thing. Please. If I don't get it right on the next guess, then I promise that you can leave." French, definitely a French accent.

I laughed despite myself. "You're not going to get it." And how could he? I didn't even know it.

"Is it bigger than a bread box?"

"What?" I laughed again, and I was being too loud. Two tables over, a teenager shot me an annoyed expression and rattled her bracelets.

"Twenty questions. It's a game. I ask you twenty questions about an item, and if I don't figure out the answer, then I lose. The bread-box question is fairly standard," he explained, "though the game is normally not about a job."

"I'm a calendar buyer." I don't know why, of all the possible lies, that one came out—except that Taylor Fortwood was still heavy on my mind, and I was still amazed at the idea that selecting calendars for stores to stock was a real job.

He paused, then gave me a rueful look that admitted defeat. "Well. I would have needed more than twenty questions for that."

"I know. I hate to set someone up for failure." *Okay, Lillian. Stand up. You have your trash, your cup in hand. Stand, slide your laptop into your bag, and go. You've been friendly; now it's time to leave.*

"I'm David." He extended his hand.

I hesitated, then slid my palm into his. "Taylor."

And just like that, my fake life began.

Some women careened into deception with reckless disregard, but I slid, on my bottom, slowly down the hill, bumping along and using my feet to stop myself if I started to get out of control. That first day, it was just an introduction and a simple lie about my name and occupation.

David went his way, and I went mine, and no one was harmed in the transgression. It was my butt hitting the grass, my legs jutting out and pointing down the hill, my mind deciding whether I wanted to push forward and begin my descent.

It was nice, having someone smile at me. Pay attention to me. Laugh at my witty remarks.

It was nice, wearing the skin of another woman, even if I was the only one who knew of her intricacies.

Maybe that was what my husband was keeping from me. A search for another life more exciting than our own.

CHAPTER 8

LILLIAN

Two hours later, I held my purse over my head and jogged through the Oyster House parking lot, cursing at the rain, which increased in ferocity as I got closer to the double doors.

I escaped into the interior and shook the rain off my bag, looking for Sam. The Oyster House was a tetanus-worthy dump with a sliver of a beach view. Their draw was in their cheap gulf oysters and ice-cold beer served in frozen mugs. I moved through the crowded tables and spotted Sam at a booth by the bathrooms. I was late, but he was used to that. He considered tardiness a sign of disrespect but always delivered the criticism with a smile.

"Hello, my love." I bent over to receive his standard kiss on each cheek. "Sorry for being late. You know. Traffic." I waved a hand in the general direction of the 405.

"No worries—it's given me a chance to scope out the local talent."

"Any hot surfers?" I asked and stole a sip of his beer.

"No, just suits and tourists."

Sam, who had a weakness for shirtless and sandy athletes, was on a yearlong dry spell. I'd been supportive. I'd played matchmaker. I'd analyzed dating profiles and social media messages and listened to a dozen bad-date recaps, which had been entertaining but dismal. Another reason to hang on to my neurotic yet stable husband, even if he was hiding something from me. As chapter 2 had pointed out, it might not be a woman; it might be a gambling debt or drug habit. It was pathetic that I was almost hoping for those—though my husband, a man who had read the owner's manual on our new microwave before using it, would never gamble or use drugs. Sadly, he was above such weak activities.

A woman, though . . . Was he above that? According to my new book, affairs were often more than just carnal need. They were about receiving attention or fighting insecurity. Which . . . after twenty minutes of quasi-flirting with the man in the coffee shop, I could almost understand. The attention of a strange man was intoxicating. I kept thinking about the way his eyes had been pinned on mine, as if he couldn't wait to hear the next thing I said.

I tried to refocus. "You act like you couldn't be with a suit. Trust me, there's nothing wrong with bedding someone with a high attention to detail."

He raised a brow. "Says the woman whose husband hasn't tapped her calculator in . . . months?"

"Easy," I said sharply and gave him a warning glare.

"Sorry." He raised his hands in surrender and stepped into the one subject I really didn't want to talk about. "How *is* your other half?"

"Umm . . ." I looked around for a waiter. "Not great. I mean, Mike seems fine. But like you said"—I reluctantly met his eyes—"he's been distant. It's like there's a wall between us and I can't figure out what it's made of."

He winced. "I'm sorry, sweetie. Have you given any more thought to—"

"Don't say it," I warned. "Please. That was a weak moment, fueled by Jäger." While tucked into Sam's side at our Fourth of July barbecue, I'd shared that I was thinking of leaving Mike. We'd been alone in the living room, the rest of the party outside by the firepit, and I had been feeling uncharacteristically emotional and irritated by Mike, who had spent most of the evening chatting up our buxom new neighbor—a conversation he'd sworn was only in the interest of securing a new client.

"Maybe the Jäger was telling you something."

Telling me to leave my husband? Not likely. I shook my head. "No. I just . . ." I thought of Taylor Fortwood. "Sometimes I wonder what would have happened if I'd chosen a different path in life."

One without a husband and child. God, the words were so horrible. Could he hear me thinking them? I reached out and grabbed his arm, hoping to distract him from the last thing I'd said. "Tell me I'm crazy, please."

"You're not crazy." He leaned forward and gave me the same slightly crooked grin that had carried me through the last five years. "You're normal. I know you don't want to hear it, Lill, but you're one hundred percent normal."

I returned his smile, but inside, a part of me cracked in dismay. *Normal.* How incredibly boring.

CHAPTER 9

LILLIAN

@themysteryofdeath: A wealthy woman, an anxiety-ridden teen, and an elderly man get stuck in an elevator together. Three months later, one of them will be dead. Who will die?

I parted ways with Sam at six thirty, avoided most of the traffic, and was at home by seven, in my pajamas by eight. Mike was working late, and Jacob was parked with his homework at the dining room table. I poured a glass of wine and escaped into the cramped utility room that housed our washer and dryer.

We'd purchased this house during the market crash, when Jacob was a toddler and Mike had an insurance settlement check from a car accident that had permanently damaged the sight in his right eye. Over the last fifteen years, we'd renovated the kitchen and master suite. This room was next on the to-do list—only we'd been saying that for six years, and I was still using a shuddering old machine and stacking clothes on a rusty hot-water heater.

Taking a generous sip of wine, I checked my tweet, curious whether anyone would get the sly reference to a *Saturday Night Live* skit that

Nora Price had been in three months ago. So far, it was going completely over their heads.

I raised the washer lid and pulled clothes from the hamper, checking pockets and then pushing them into the opening. My yoga pants went in, followed by two golf shirts, Mike's pajama pants, and some underwear. As I went through the pockets of his khaki pants, I tried to justify the business card that I'd withdrawn from the back pocket of my pale-blue skinny jeans just fifteen minutes ago, before I put them in this basket. David Laurent's card, which he had passed on "just in case" I ever needed anything.

I had accepted it out of sheer politeness, planning to toss it into the trash as soon as I got out of eyeshot. Except that I hadn't.

It wasn't too late. Right now, I could go upstairs, withdraw it from the pajama drawer I had hidden it in, and throw it away.

In the front pockets of Mike's khakis, I found a five-dollar bill, a receipt, and some change. Dropping the collection on top of the dryer, I tossed the pants into the washer and dug deeper into the basket.

The next pair of pants had nothing, and I pushed them in, then unscrewed the top of the detergent bottle. Pouring in the measured amount, I thought of the obituary I would be writing for Nora Price if my prior station in life were restored.

The comedian deserved something witty, a sharp dissection of the life of a sister, daughter, and *Saturday Night Live* regular. It needed to be both celebratory and mourning, a mini-memoir of her journey and the funny and influential moments that had marked her forty-nine years.

Whatever. I shouldn't care. It was out of my hands, and the obit was no doubt assigned to Janice, who would craft the important tribute with the care and skill of a toddler with a fat scented marker.

I added a capful of softener, then dropped the lid closed. As I turned to leave, my gaze caught on the crumpled receipt next to the five-dollar bill, both still sitting on top of the dryer.

Gain access to his bank records, phone records, and find a way to track his movements.

I had made it to chapter 3 of the book, which focused on how to properly spy on your spouse. While it all seemed fairly obvious, most of the suggestions were impossible for me. I had spent our eighteen-year marriage oblivious to everything Mike did. He had his bank accounts; I had mine. He had a company cell phone; Jacob and I shared a family plan. I had tried, unsuccessfully, to log in to his bank account using our anniversary, his common pass codes, and the last four of his social but crapped out. What I did have was our joint credit card statements, but those had been pristine.

I grabbed the receipt and uncrumpled it, both hopeful and fearful that it would incriminate him in some way.

It was from a steak house in Malibu. Two filets mignons. One bottle of wine. Dessert. I sucked in a breath at the dollar amount at the bottom of the receipt. We hadn't spent that much on dinner in years. Only on special occasions, if that. Mike was tightfisted, and I was always happy with a salad and a glass of house wine. I checked the date. Tuesday night, at 7:32 p.m. I fished my cell phone from the pocket of my flannel pajama pants and did an internet search for the restaurant. It was small and upscale, with views of the ocean and attached to a boutique hotel. The exterior view of the hotel was familiar to me—I'd passed it whenever I felt like driving the forty-five minutes to Sam's ritzy area of town.

I closed the browser and opened my text messages, scrolling back in my history with Mike until I got to Tuesday night.

Two texts. One at 6:22 p.m.

Won't be home until late. Client dinner.

Typical. I opened the second, two hours later.

Have to stay the night. Clients want to show me the project in the morning. Will call you tomorrow when I'm on the road back. Make sure Jacob studies for his econ test.

Oh, that's right. Mike had been in San Diego that day. I had spoken to him around lunchtime. He'd been meeting with bankers on an apartment-complex purchase. When he'd texted me about staying the night, I had wondered, for a flash of a second, whether he'd go out for a late-night drink.

This was so much worse.

I stared at the receipt, which proved that he hadn't been in San Diego at all. He'd been right here in LA. Just twelve miles away, with two different texts showing his thought processes. First—making plans for a late night, wife-free. And then, just after dinner—the decision to stay away all night. Who was she? How had she convinced my husband to spend an entire night with her?

Or maybe he—my meticulous planner of a husband—had been the instigator, the aggressor, the seducer.

I gripped the edge of the washing machine and felt my stomach heave. This was, I reminded myself, not the first clue. After all, just earlier this week, in the grocery store, Heather had told me about his trip to Santa Barbara. I had known, then, just like with the clues here and there, that it had probably been another woman, and here was another domino, set in a line, next to the others.

Nothing to freak out about. My shrink, the one I'd fired after the restraining order was issued, floated through my subconscious, her voice soothing and melodic. *Nothing to freak out about, Lillian. Let's just take a breath. A deep, deep breath.*

The expensive e-book was unnecessary. I knew what this was. It was time for me to stop making excuses and giving him the benefit of the doubt. I had married a cheater, and the chances were, he was lying to me tonight. *Working late.* He was probably with her now.

God, my mother could never find out. She'd be giddy at this news. She had never liked Mike and always preached about the impossibility of male monogamy. Maybe, in this one thin section of life, she was right.

Inside my chest, a sharp pain snaked underneath my breast, and if there was a physical pain associated with heartbreak, this was it.

———

I paused beside Jacob, who was hunched over a worksheet full of equations, his pencil tip scratching along the page. Kissing him on the top of the head, I ignored his groan of protest. "I'm going to bed."

"Aight." He flipped over the pencil and erased something.

I climbed the stairs slowly and trudged down the hall, past Jacob's room, and entered our bedroom. It was dark and quiet, the red digits of the clock glowing beside Mike's side of the bed, the dark-blue comforter neatly stretched over the large king, three rows of pillows in neat order.

I was not a pillow woman. In fact, I hated the tassels and rough surface of the gold embroidered design. Every single time I made the bed, I grew annoyed at the extra, unnecessary action of lining up each row of pillows, just because Mike liked the look, liked the order, liked the preciseness of a well-put-together room. If I left him, I'd switch to feather pillows, big giant fluffy ones that I would leave in disarray, my sheets in a tangled knot, half the blanket hanging on the floor.

I laughed, and it was a sad sound, drenched in self-pity because while I wanted to be a woman like Taylor Fortwood, this was proof positive that I wouldn't. This was proof that, in my most rebellious and inspirational fantasies . . . messy bedding was the end result. And not from hot sex, but just from a general laziness to conform to my husband's exacting standards.

I took two of Mike's sleeping pills and crawled under the blanket and curled into a tight ball on my side of the bed.

The problem was, while I could daydream about undignified bedding and a life of reckless disregard, I couldn't leave Mike. The idea of divorcing, with Jacob in his junior year, with almost two decades together . . . What did my life look like without Mike? Who *was* I without him? My identity was rooted in being a wife, a mother, in having his support, his feedback. When I'd tossed out the idea to Sam last summer, I hadn't actually meant it. It had been a throwaway statement that I would never have acted on.

Let's just take a breath, Lillian. A deep, deep breath. My lungs obeyed and my body relaxed as the pills did their thing, and within minutes, I was blissfully dead to it all.

CHAPTER 10

LILLIAN

I woke up with dried drool on my cheek and a kink in my neck. Carefully rolling onto my back, I gauged the light in the room. It had to be midmorning. Nine, maybe even ten. Mike's side of the bed was unmade, and I wondered what time he had come home. *Working late.*

My phone was on the floor, and in last night's distraction, I'd forgotten to plug it in. I scraped my fingers along the thick rug until I reached it.

My battery was at 4 percent, and I had a missed text from Jacob at 11:22 last night, wanting to know where we kept double-A batteries. Nothing to give me any indication of what time my husband had returned home. I plugged it in.

Turning on the shower, I stepped inside and stood under the spray, which was lukewarm and growing hotter. I put my hand against the white subway tiles, remembering the first week in this house, how Mike had put his hand over mine, his chin against the back of my neck, his slick body against mine, the water muting the sounds of my moans as we had christened the space.

Maybe that was the issue. Our passion was gone, and all the friendship and respect in the world couldn't make up for that loss. When he looked at me, there was no heat. When we kissed, no life. When we did make love, it was short and rudimentary, a trade-off of orgasms before bed.

A year ago, I'd given myself a makeover with hair extensions, tighter clothes, and higher heels. I wore low-cut tops and makeup and went to bed in skimpy silk shorts and almost-sheer tank tops. I put in an embarrassing amount of effort, hoping it would restart Mike's interest.

It didn't. I gave it exactly thirty days, then removed my extensions and returned to my flats and makeup-free look. Through it all, Mike had remained a cruise ship, set on autopilot. Plowing forward, undeterred by weather or circumstance.

I turned my face into the water and held my breath as it beat on my cheeks, lips, and forehead. Lifting my chin, I gulped in a fresh breath, then went back in.

The book said that I should record any evidence and continue to gather more, building an unquestionable case before I confronted my spouse. Accusing them too early, it said, would cause them to cover their tracks and ruin any chance to uncover more of the truth.

I didn't want more of the truth. If anything, I wanted less of it. The idea of waiting and trying to catch Mike in lies sounded agonizing, and I was not a woman built of patience.

I had to confront him. Otherwise, I'd go mad.

CHAPTER 11

LILLIAN

Mike worked at a financial firm in Pasadena, in a low four-story building surrounded by palm trees. I parked in the visitors' lot shortly before noon and stared across a grass median at his silver Volvo, which was parked in the Employee of the Month spot.

I didn't know he had been named Employee of the Month. The last time that had happened, we'd gone to dinner at one of those hibachi places and celebrated. Jacob had produced a rare laugh when the chef flipped a shrimp into his mouth. Mike did three sake bombs and got drunk, and held my hand when I drove home. It was a sales-based award, one that came with a hefty bonus. We'd used the prior one to pay off his car. What had he used this one for? Was it what had funded the expensive steak dinner? The hotels where he had conducted his trysts? Was he buying her flowers? Gifts?

I turned the air higher and forced myself to stop thinking. I picked up my phone and sent a text to Mike.

We need to talk.

It was a little dramatic, but the situation warranted it. I waited, my attention stuck on the screen. He responded quickly.

Why?

Annoyance swelled, and I could already sense how this would unpack. Maybe I shouldn't have brought this to his work, but I was here and the text was sent, and I couldn't put it back in the box now.

He sent another question mark, so I typed back before I lost my nerve and drove away.

You know why. Come outside. I'm parked in the guest lot.

Not my most mature and finest moment, and I'd lost the element of surprise, but I was also hoping he would just confess and save me the trouble of a shaky and unresearched accusation.

My cell phone rang.

I sent his call to voice mail, then—in a bold and uncharacteristic move—turned off my phone and set it in the cup holder. If he wanted to talk, he could come outside. Screw any meetings. Screw any calls. I was his wife, dammit. Oh God. The tears were already building, leaking out the edges of my eyes.

I stared at the building. *Come on, Mike.* This was me, hanging from a ledge, asking him to grab my hand and pull our marriage to safety.

He could come down three flights of stairs and out to my car, or he could stay inside.

I gripped the steering wheel tightly.

Come on, Mike. Save us.

CHAPTER 12

LILLIAN

It took five excruciating minutes. Minutes in which I flip-flopped between an emotional outburst of tears and a sharp fury that dictated I follow my mother's lead and cut off his balls while he slept.

I wanted him. I needed him. I didn't know how to exist, how to function, without him. How could he break up our family?

I hated him. I was bored with him. I wanted passion and excitement, which were the antithesis of him. Forget him dumping me—I should have left him years ago.

By the time the front door of the building swung open and Mike walked out, I was teetering on an emotional tightrope and close to falling off. He crossed the lawn slowly, his dark tie held in place by his left hand, his glasses on instead of his contacts. The wind whipped the legs of his charcoal pants, and his pale-blue dress shirt still held the iron creases along his forearms. He met my eyes through the windshield and held them, and I could see the wary uncertainty in his step as he crossed over a low border shrub and approached the passenger side of my car. He opened the door and lowered himself inside, then quietly and carefully closed it.

A beat of silence lingered. Stretched. My hands were trembling, and I tucked them underneath my thighs to hide the weakness. "Tell me why."

He didn't move, didn't speak, and his lack of reaction told me everything I needed to know. He was guilty. The only question was how long this had been going on and to what depth his emotional investment extended.

My chest thickened and I pinned my lips together and prayed he couldn't see the vulnerability on my face.

"I don't have an excuse, Lill. It was just . . ." He paused. "A series of bad decisions."

Outside the car, a leaf blew across the lot and stuck to the windshield. "Who is she?"

At his silence, I twisted in my seat to face him. "Who *is* she?" I repeated, my voice growing stronger.

He paused, and I knew this face, this quiet look, his pupils minutely tick-tocking, his breathing quiet and calm. He was thinking, calculating, a dozen thought processes shifting and moving into place behind the scenes. I had seen this process a hundred times, and watching it, I realized my mistake.

I had shown one of my cards—chosen a question that alerted him to how little I knew. If I didn't even know who she was, how could I know the extent of his deceit?

He swallowed against his tightly buttoned collar. "How did you find out?"

Shit. Could I lie? Could I backtrack and find higher, more confident ground? I searched for another path and failed. "It doesn't matter," I snapped. "I know about it all. Santa Barbara. Tuesday night. You aren't as smart as you think you are." I blew out an angry breath. "Why? What the fuck—wasn't I enough?"

He shook his head. "Stop. It doesn't have anything to do with you, Lill. It's just sexual. A mistake. It didn't mean anything."

It's just sexual. What a stupid and hurtful statement. I balled my hands into fists and hit the steering wheel so hard that my forearms vibrated in pain. "Who *is* she?" I repeated, my voice rising. "Someone younger? Hotter?" *God, I bet she's waxed.* Probably cellulite-free, with no responsibilities and stupid enough to find his OCD tendencies cute.

"It's no one you know," he said quickly. "And she's our age. Not hotter. She's just different." He didn't say all the things a husband in trouble should say: *No one is as hot as you. Lill, you're beautiful. You're perfect.* Instead, he just sat on the statement, a period of silence at the end of the inadequate sentence.

"You're a pig." The words broke out of my chest with jagged edges, and to my horror, I started to cry.

"Lill . . ." He reached for my hand and I moved it away. He twisted in his seat, facing me. "I'll stop it. Right now. Immediately. I promise."

I couldn't believe that he wasn't making an excuse, that there wasn't an explanation. In the book, they said that the cheater's first instinct was to lie, to cover their tracks, but he was just rolling over and admitting to it all.

"Look." He captured my hand and squeezed. "I'll stop it. It's done."

"You should have stopped it on your own." I yanked free. "I should have never found out about it." Wouldn't that have been better? Blissful ignorance. It was sad, but that was all I wanted. To have never noticed anything, to have a husband who had stayed attentive, stayed around, and conducted this fling without me ever growing the wiser. "You were sloppy, Mike. You've ignored me." My anger grew and its focus on his careless cover-up didn't make sense, but it was still there and raw and bubbling out around each word. "I loved you," I spat. "I still love you."

"Oh, Lill," he said sadly, and his features broke in a way that I hadn't seen since my miscarriage. "I'll always love you. This was nothing, I promise. It was me being selfish. And it's over. Please, please believe me when I tell you that it's over. I'll end it today. Right away."

He cupped my face and stared into my eyes, and my heart sagged in relief and resignation because that was all I wanted to hear. "Jacob—" I said weakly.

"I'm your husband and his father, and I swear to you that I'll do a better job of both," he said firmly. "Okay?"

I nodded. What other option did I have? He was a husband and a father, and I was a wife and a mother, and the two roles were intertwined and my life had no other substance.

I flinched at the thought. Was it true? Without my marriage and my motherhood, I had nothing else? My job . . . There was that, however bleak last year's demotion was. My Twitter account . . . God, I couldn't look for purpose in a social media profile.

Was the bulk of my existence, my happiness, balancing on him?

I looked at him in horror and flinched as he smiled, his thumb smearing a falling tear across my cheekbone. "It's okay," he whispered. "Look at me. I promise that I'm yours. All yours. I won't fuck up again."

I had to change this life. I had to find a better, braver, more independent me before he chewed this version into pieces.

CHAPTER 13

MIKE

I wasn't lying to her. Sacrifices needed to be made, given whatever she'd discovered. She apparently hadn't found much out, since she didn't even know who I'd been with. But enough risk was already present. She knew about Santa Barbara and Tuesday night. Just those two puzzle pieces could unravel everything, if someone wanted to dig deeper.

Thankfully, my wife wasn't a digger. She was a bare-minimum type, one who took the easy road, so I'd give that to her. A big, wide, beautiful road called Happy Married Life. I'd be the perfect husband. Loyal. Trustworthy. I'd grovel and court, and do all the things necessary to distract her from "the affair" and remind her of our love and family.

She didn't have other options, so she'd fall back into place. There would be some bitchiness, some punishment, some frigid shoulders and sharp words, but Lillian was a creature of habit and comfort, and the alternative—a forty-year-old divorcée—was not a path she'd want to tread.

But yes, sacrifices would need to be made, which was why I returned to the office, picked up the phone, and made the call. I kept it brief and unemotional.

I ended it.

So there. That was done.

CHAPTER 14

LILLIAN

@themysteryofdeath: A scooter pulls out in front of a truck driver on a quiet island paradise, in sight of a Yorkie-walking teenage girl. Within seconds, the lives of all three will change. Who will die?

I scrubbed burned cheese off an oven grate and stared at David Laurent's card, which was propped in front of the sink, against the pale-blue glossy backsplash. I should call him. We could grab lunch. I could slip into Taylor's world, pretend that I was just back from a calendar-buying trip to Florida, and tell him that story about how she—I—hitched a ride through the Everglades on a park ranger's airboat when her—my—car ran out of gas. Maybe I'd wear that low-cut top that Mike had ignored. I could spend an hour flirting and laughing my way out of heartbreak.

All it would be was a lunch. It didn't have to be anything more.

I picked up my phone and scrolled through the Twitter responses.

@greengoblin: scooter rider. obviously.

@ryanswife9: that's why it isn't the scooter rider, @greengoblin. She never does the obvious one.

@jessbessandtess: Maybe she's doing the obvious one to throw us off the scent

@planktonsboss: Truck swerved to avoid the scooter, hit the dog-walker. #micdrop

They were off base, and I tried to think of a clue that would be accurate but wouldn't completely give away the answer—that the truck hit the scooter, the driver thought he'd killed her, and he'd pulled over and shot himself in guilt.

"Something's different." Sam spoke from the doorway of the kitchen, and I looked up from the phone to see him leaning against the frame, his arms crossed over a tight yellow golf shirt. "What is it?"

I smiled, surprised to see him. "Hey. I thought you were in San Francisco this week."

"The client flaked. Decided to move south instead of north. We're going to look at homes in San Diego tomorrow."

Placing my phone on the counter, I picked the grate back up and resumed my scrub. Dammit. I should have soaked it first.

"What are you doing?" Sam came to stand beside me. "Is that part of the oven?"

"Yeah, I'm deep cleaning." I shook my hands above the soapy water, then dried them off, dropping the dishcloth in front of David's card before Sam could notice it.

"Why?"

"Good question." I blew out a breath and turned to the small round table between the kitchen and the living room. Pulling out one of the chairs, I sank into it and watched as he circled the table, eyeing the spots before carefully pulling out the one that Mike normally took. Sam hitched up the thighs of his dress pants before sitting down, and the care that he took with every movement was infuriating. For once, I'd like to see him trip over a cord or snort up soda or have a piece of spinach in his teeth. He would never be in my situation. He would have seen Mike's affair—or was it *affairs*?—from a mile off, plotted and planned a contingency plan, and found a way to seduce and marry the prospective mistress before she ever found her way to his husband.

Meanwhile I was . . . I didn't know what I was doing. I was sitting here, scrubbing Mike's kitchen, while I trusted his promise that he would break things off with this woman. I should have pressed for her name and insisted that he call her right then, while I was still in the car, and heard their conversation for myself.

But I hadn't wanted that. I hadn't wanted the proof that she was real. I liked the blank slate that came to mind when I tried to picture her. If I figured out that she was our new neighbor, or his HR director, or the dental hygienist that always flirted with him . . . I would obsess. Research her. Follow her. Practice my accusations and confrontations until the moment when opportunity and weakness intersected and I did something that I could never take back.

"Lill?" Sam leaned forward, and his expensive watch clinked against the freshly polished wood surface of the table. "You're freaking me out. Are you okay?"

"It's Mike." My words were slow and measured, carefully controlled and void of emotion. "He's cheating on me."

Sam looked down at the table and ran his fingers along a grain of the wood. "With who?"

"I don't know." I let out a strangled laugh. "I don't care. He says it's over."

"Do you believe that?" He lifted his gaze, and I could see the struggle to hold back his true feelings. Sam had been in my life for almost six years. He'd lived through more than a few ups and downs in our marriage, and acted as my counselor on each occasion.

"Yeah, I do. He was . . ." I started over. "He knows what's at stake. Between Jacob and me, he has too much to lose. And he told me it was just sex. If that's true . . ." I rubbed my eyes, relieved to see that they were still dry. "He'd be stupid to risk our marriage for that. Even if we are a little . . ." I tried to find the right word. "Disconnected right now."

"This isn't a recent thing, Lill. You were complaining about Mike two years ago. Did he say how long he's been cheating on you?"

I shook my head, not wanting to think about the possibility that this was a long-term relationship. Sam's input wasn't helping, and a wave of annoyance flared at his unannounced drop-in. I needed to do a better job of defining our friendship boundaries. Maybe it was time for me to ask for my house key back. Was it possible to draw a line here and block any further opinions on my marriage?

"I've got to get back to cleaning." I stood up. "I'd take off, unless you want to grab a toothbrush and work on the grout lines."

"You're avoiding this." Sam stayed in his seat. "You need to leave him, Lill. Otherwise he's not going to learn. He'll behave for a little while, but then he'll do it again."

He might have been right, but I had already considered and discarded that path. Maybe in a month or two, I'd be open to it, but I couldn't wrap my head around that momentous a decision now. I needed to defrost the freezer, reline the cabinet drawers, and then wash the blinds above the sink. Those were things I could do—things I could handle—now.

I turned the faucet on high and picked the oven grate back up. Fishing the scrub pad out of the cloudy water, I attacked the grime with fresh vigor. Silence stretched after Sam's comment, and I ignored it, focusing on a spot of burned crust that was starting to break down from my efforts.

Sam's chair dragged back against the tile, and he came up behind me and squeezed my shoulders gently. "Okay, I'll leave you alone." He kissed the top of my head. "Call me when you want to talk."

"Thanks. Love you." I turned to give him an apologetic smile, but he was already heading for the door. It closed behind him with a gentle click, but his last opinion hung in the air long after he got in his Range Rover and drove away.

Was he right? Was it just a matter of time before Mike cheated again?

SIX WEEKS BEFORE
THE DEATH

CHAPTER 15

LILLIAN

A week passed and my hurt turned to anger. I ignored Mike, who was suddenly home for dinner each evening, his leftover work performed in his office, attention poured on me at night. I rejected his advances, and began to notice the bags under his eyes, the slight recession of his hairline, the annoying way he held his food in his mouth for a moment before swallowing it.

Was he who I really wanted to spend the rest of my life with?

What's crazy is that the sex with the other woman wasn't what was making me mad. It was the money. The expensive dinner had been a hint. What else had there been? Hotel rooms. Roses? Gifts? Was he paying her rent, while we still had Jacob's future college bills hanging over our heads?

It was a stupid thing to care about, but that's what I had been obsessing about. *How much had he spent on her? How much had she been worth to him?*

"Good morning."

I turned from my spot at the kitchen window to see Jacob rounding the bottom of the stairs, his school uniform on, his hair still messy from sleep. He needed a haircut. His dark locks now curled along his purple collar, and I was pretty sure the shaggy style was an intentional move to piss off his father. I could get on board with that. I set my coffee on the counter. "Hungry?"

"I'll get some cereal." He opened the pantry door and reached for a box of Froot Loops. "There's some light that came on in my car. The uh . . . the engine light."

"You tell your dad?" I pulled a bowl from the cabinet and set it at the bar, then retrieved a spoon for him.

"Not yet. He'll probably tell me it's the oil change thing I was supposed to do last week."

I took a seat at the stool next to him and watched as he shook out the brightly colored rings. "He's probably right."

"I heard Nora Price died."

"Yep."

"I wish you still did the famous people."

"Yeah." I picked up the coffee cup and warmed my hands on the smooth ceramic. "Me too."

"Remember when you did Robin Williams?" He perked up. "Or Michael Jackson? And you took me with you to Neverland Ranch?"

Yeah, probably not my finest parenting moment. I was saved from a response by my phone, which dinged with an email notification. Opening it, I swiped past the new message, which was a junk email about bedding. Scrolling down, I saw an email from Fran at 6:45 a.m. At first glance, the time would have been worrisome, except that my editor was from New York and liked to remind everyone of that fact with annoying habits like sticking to an East Coast work schedule, even though she'd been in Los Angeles for almost a decade.

The email was short and to the point (another New York holdover).

Reminder: Employee review today at 10am.

Shit. I glanced at the clock. No time for a shower. I carried my coffee to the sink and poured it out.

"So why did you stop with the celebrities?"

I turned on the hot water and made a face he couldn't see. We had shielded him from the mess last year, avoiding any mention or discussion of the Axe twins in his presence. He hadn't seemed to notice I'd stopped doing celebrity obits, his attention glued to video games, card games, and wiping his browser search history. I glanced at him, surprised to have his full focus, an honor I hadn't received in years. "Ummm . . . one of my interviews went poorly. It was supposedly a suicide, but there were too many clues pointing against that. I thought the woman's twin sister was in jeopardy, tried to warn her."

"Wait, you're talking about the coffee twins? The hot ones?"

I rinsed out the orange mug. "Yeah, I'm surprised you know who they are."

"The dead one was in *Maxim*. Trent has a poster of her up in his game room."

Of course he does.

"So you went, like, superspy on them? Damn, Mom. That's cool."

Oh yes, very cool. It was *so cool* when I had sneaked past Brexley Axe's security and interrupted her dinner party to warn her about the possible threat and show her my research. It was *so cool* when she had swung a bottle of wine at my head and screamed for someone to help. It was *so cool* when I tried to run and was tackled by a three-hundred-pound bodyguard and hog-tied with handcuffs. If I'd gotten any cooler, I'd be in prison right now.

I set the cup upside down on the drying rack. "I've got to run upstairs and change. Have a good day at school."

He leaned in as I kissed him on the top of the head, his spoon rising to his mouth, attention back on his phone, the hot twins already forgotten.

"Love you," I called as I left the kitchen and started up the stairs.

He grunted through a mouthful of cereal in response.

CHAPTER 16

LILLIAN

While waiting outside Fran's office, my ankles crossed and tucked under the stiff chair like a kid outside the principal's, I read the news on my phone. There was an article about a lawsuit the Marina del Rey boat owners were filing, and I fished David's card out of my purse to forward him the article. He had mentioned keeping a boat in their slips just outside the coffee shop.

I started to write the email, then realized my mistake. I couldn't send him something as Lillian Smith. Not when I had introduced myself as Taylor. I swapped methods and picked up the card, looking for his cell number. There was only a WhatsApp number, and I recalled him tapping it as he handed it over and asking me if I'd used the messaging app. As Taylor, I had laughed, because of course I had. And honestly, I did use WhatsApp, with Mike, who had always been paranoid that Apple was somehow reading (and cared about) our text messages.

I opened the app, checked to make sure my username on it was still just my phone number (no Lillian reveal there), and started a thread to him. I pasted the link, then composed an accompanying message that was as unflirty as possible.

Thought you'd find this interesting, though you probably already know all about it. - Taylor (from the coffee shop)

Before sending, I read it twice, testing the tone in my mind. It was good. Not suggestive or flirty. Appropriate for a married mother. Though . . . would Taylor send something different?

Yes, of course she would. Taylor would send a flirty pic, probably one from an exotic vacation, along with a fun message, not a boring article. I opened my camera roll and scrolled through the albums. Thanks to Mike's fear of flying, most of our vacations were in dull locales like Bryce Canyon or the Sequoia National Forest. I opened our Lake Tahoe album and found a photo of me floating in an inner tube. It was by a spit of island, and the waters around me looked straight out of a Caribbean brochure. In it, I was wearing a red one-piece and white sunglasses and was laughing at something that Mike had said, right before he snapped the picture. I copied it and attached it to a new text to David.

You taking your boat out soon? I'm floating here—no, that was stupid.

Just wanted to say hi. Also dumb.

Hey coffee twin. How's Fresno?

Not bad. We had laughed at our identical coffee orders (pumpkin spice with almond milk), so he would be reminded of who I was, and the picture would help. He lived in Fresno but spent half his time in LA, one of the few items he'd shared while he was busy asking questions about my fascinating life. I—

"Lillian?"

I looked up to see Fran standing beside me, one freckled hand on her hip, today's outfit a brilliantly loud orange pantsuit set off by blue

Birkenstocks and a yellow scrunchie that did a poor job of containing her auburn pin-screw curls. "Hey, Fran."

"Come on in." She held open the door, and by her brisk tone and pursed lips, I could sense how this was going to go.

I hesitated, then stepped into her office. She closed the door behind me, and the click of the lock was as sharp as a guillotine blade, snapping into place.

CHAPTER 17

LILLIAN

That evening, I rested my chin on the bar top of Perch, my beer so close that the curved glass gave me the viewpoint of a goldfish. "She's such a bitch," I said morosely. "It's the New York in her."

Sam squeezed my shoulder and gently pulled me upright. "Hey, at least you weren't fired."

"Might as well have. She spoke to me like I was a child." I puffed out a frustrated breath. "I don't know what she expects, with the garbage leads they give me. Like, what the fuck?"

What the fuck? was Jacob's newest catchphrase, and I was warming to it. It rolled off the tongue in a reckless fashion that appealed to my Taylor Fortwood side, which I was thinking of embracing. My coy message to David had been a smashing (Taylor seemed like she would have said *smashing*) success, and we'd texted back and forth a dozen times, with plans to meet for a second coffee later this week when he was back in Los Angeles.

While secretly messaging a man was a relatively tame rebellion in the general scheme of things, it'd given me an almost giddy high, one I had needed after my bleak employee review.

"Okay, but she *isn't* firing you," Sam confirmed, smoothing down the silver skinny tie that intersected the middle of his pale-purple dress shirt. He looked like he was ready for a photo shoot, and I had the sudden urge to run my hand through his perfectly coiffed hair and mess it up.

"No, but they've been laying off people. I can't help but feel like the whole review was just documentation for when they fire me." I propped my sandal on the closest barstool and looked around. Okay, so Sam was properly dressed. I was the one who was sticking out, my pale-blue capri pants and cardigan great for a lackluster employee review but about three rungs short for this martini and olives crowd. I watched a woman teeter by in four-inch heels and a minidress that showed way too much thigh. Was this the type of place I'd have to frequent if I were single? Could I avoid serious effort and still lure in a keepable guy? A guy like David?

". . . which raises the question of contentment." Sam paused and crooked a brow at me.

I'd zoned out. I nodded as if I knew what he was talking about.

"You feeling okay?" Sam peered at me with concern.

"I'm fine." I glanced at my watch. "I can't stay here long. Jacob has a thing at school that I'm supposed to go to." An assembly for parents to discuss the growing drug use problem among students. Talk about a yawn fest. "One more drink. Maybe two."

"Fun stuff. Is Mike meeting you there?"

"Not sure." I pulled a short menu from a glass holder in the middle of the bar. There were only four items, and I couldn't pronounce any of them. "I'm starving. We should have met for dinner."

He ignored my dietary needs. "Have you guys discussed it any further?"

It. The Affair. The giant prickly bomb that Mike and I were skirting with increasing efficiency.

"No." I brought the glass to my lips and took a long sip of the beer. "Let's change the subject. Tell me a story about a boy."

A ghost of a smile crossed his lips. "That old game?"

He used to always have stories about boys. Executives from dating sites. Stuntmen wanting ranches in the desert. Waiters who passed him their numbers on a napkin. Actors looking for one-bedroom apartments they couldn't afford. All wooed by Sam and often with disastrous and entertaining outcomes. I hadn't heard a story about a boy in years. But I'd take any he had, even if it was an oldie.

"Hmm." He tilted his head, and I wasn't surprised he had a drawerful of heartbreak stories. I'd always been a little smitten with him myself. "Okay, remember when I had that blue convertible . . ."

I drank my beer and listened to his story, and when the bartender paused in front of us, I ordered another. Soon, I was laughing.

That was the great thing about Sam. He could make you forget everything.

CHAPTER 18

LILLIAN

I woke up on Sam's red sectional, a couch button biting into my cheek, my left leg hanging off the side. Rolling onto my back, I stared up at his tray ceiling and watched the sun-framed shadow of a palm frond move over the wood inlay. Why was I here? What time was it?

I slowly propped myself up on my elbows and looked around. Everything was in perfect order. A stack of books with a skull weighting them down. An ivory cashmere blanket, folded into thirds, hanging off the side of his saddle leather chair. Above the fireplace, two white eels swam lazily in an aquarium around black coral. "Sam?"

Swinging my feet to the floor, I grimaced at the pain that shot through my right temple. Where the hell was my purse? I leaned forward and looked along the leather shag rug, then under the coffee table. I was also missing my pants. I thrummed my fingers against my bare thighs. Tilting to one side, I looked down the long hall that led to Sam's bedroom. The door was ajar, the light off. I needed to find out what time it was and where my purse and phone were. What had happened last night? We had been drinking at Perch . . . and then . . .

I stood and lurched unnaturally to the right, one foot stumbling over the other as I tried to stay upright. I sank onto the couch. Maybe I should lie back down, just for a few more minutes. Did I have any appointments today? What was today? Had I made it to Jacob's school meeting?

I closed my eyes and listened for Sam's car or footsteps. He would take care of everything.

———

"Damn, you're trashed." Sam shook my shoulder a little more aggressively than was needed. I moaned and tried to push him away. "Seriously, Lill. It's almost ten."

I opened my eyes and almost mewed at the sight of the Starbucks cup in his hand. "Please say that's pumpkin."

"It's pumpkin."

I sat up and reached for the cup with both hands, humming in appreciation as I took a tentative sip to test the temperature, then a long glug. "You're a saint."

"And you're a mess." He gently separated a strand of hair that was stuck to my cheek from drool. "What do you have today? Anything this morning?"

"What is it, Friday?"

His lips pinched together. "Yes, Lillian."

"You don't have to say it like that. My head is a complete fog. How much did I drink last night?"

"With me?" He sank back into the couch and propped an expensive monogrammed slipper on the coffee table. "Maybe three, four beers. I have no idea what you took in after you left."

I twisted to face him. "After I left?"

He adopted the slow and annoying cadence of someone speaking to a dunce. "After you left the restaurant, I put you in a taxi and you went home."

"What?" I had no recollection of that. No recollection of anything past Sam telling me a story about a valet at a gay bar . . . I strained to think, to capture another memory. I had seen someone there at the restaurant. Someone I knew. Who had it been? "So how did I get here?"

"You called me about an hour later and needed me to pick you up from Ladera Heights. I told you to take a taxi, but you said that you didn't have enough cash. And you refused to take an Uber because you said Mike would see the charge."

"Why would I care if Mike saw the charge?" This made no sense. "Where'd you pick me up from?"

"Near Fox Hills. Shitty area. I hit a pothole that fucked up my alignment."

"Why would I be in . . ." I paused as a horrible gear clicked into place. "Was I by the mall?"

He picked up his own coffee cup. "A little more to the west. You were at a gas station, sitting on the *curb*." He said it like I'd been bare-assed on a skid row bucket. "Probably ruined your pants. I put them in the wash for you."

"Thanks." I squeezed his knee, unsurprised by the gesture. Sam was the ultimate caretaker. He'd probably given me two Tylenol and a glass of ice water before telling me a bedtime story. One day, he'd make a great father, but until then, he was all mine.

My mind detoured around The Ways Sam Was Great, because there was only one likely reason for me to be in Ladera Heights, near the mall, at that exact station that Sam was mentioning—*I know that gas station*—and it was because Fran lived two blocks inward, in a Pepto-Bismol-pink house with twin plastic flamingos in the yard. I knew because I'd fed her cats for two weeks, a few years ago, when she was in Costa Rica. I knew because once, after feeding those scrawny Siameses, I'd bought cigarettes at that gas station. There, hit with an immense craving for nicotine, I'd convinced myself that one or two cigarettes wouldn't hurt anybody.

So why had I been there last night? Maybe Fran had called me and wanted to smooth over her employee review with a glass of merlot and those smelly French cheeses that she always gifted the *Times* editorial staff for Christmas. "Where's my phone?"

"I left it next to you." He reached behind me and patted the cushion, then ran his hand down the back crack. It wasn't there. "Here, I'll call it."

I found it just before it rang, the thin case wedged between the arm and the cushion. "Got it." I unlocked the screen and went to my call log. No missed calls from Mike. What kind of husband wouldn't notice—or care—if his wife didn't come home? Or maybe I had come home. After all, I'd had to get to Fran's somehow. Had Mike given me a ride? I tried desperately to remember something, but came up blank.

Yep, there was my call to Sam, at 11:42 p.m. Before that, nothing. No call from Fran. I checked my texts and discovered the same. "What'd I say when you picked me up?"

He ran a hand across the thigh of his linen pant leg and flicked at a piece of something. He stayed silent, and my concern grew. "Sam?"

"You don't remember anything about last night?" he finally asked.

"No," I snapped.

"You were drunk," he said reluctantly. "And upset. At least, you were upset when we parted. But at the gas station, you seemed . . . satisfied."

Satisfied? What was that supposed to mean? At my blank look, he sighed. "I should check on your pants. They should be dry by now."

"Like, sexually satisfied?" I ventured.

He broke out in unexpected laughter, a bout that stretched so long that I glared at him. "It's not that funny," I sniped.

"Oh my gosh." He caught his breath, his laugh wheezing to a halt. "You took what I was saying in the completely wrong context. It's my fault for trying to beat around the bush. Ignore *satisfied*. You seemed *vindicated*. That's a more accurate word."

Vindicated. Dread closed like a vise around my stomach. I didn't like that answer at *all*. The idea that I was lurking around Fran's neighborhood at midnight was already an unsettling thought. The thought of me emerging victorious and villainous did not bode well for whatever I'd been up to. "Did I say anything?"

"Well, before you vomited into my messenger bag, I asked what you'd been doing and you smiled." He shifted uncomfortably, and I stifled the urge to remind him that I was the good girl in our pairing, the one who always told him to slow down when he was driving, and that a homophobic asshole at the bar wasn't worth arguing with. This drunk, vomiting weirdo he was describing—that wasn't me. That didn't sound like anything I would actually do, yet here I was, in my underwear, looking at the record of a phone call that supported that exact action.

"I just smiled?"

"It was this creepy evil grin." He grimaced. "And then you said that you were 'righting wrongs.'" He lifted his hands in surrender. "Whatever that means."

"It doesn't sound good," I said dully.

"Well, no offense, Lill, but you're not exactly a masked vigilante. Worst-case scenario, you probably left a strongly worded Post-it Note on someone's windshield who parked too close to a fire hydrant."

I almost smiled at that, the scenario accurate.

He stood. "Look, I've got a listing appointment in an hour. Let me grab your pants from the dryer, and I'll give you a ride to your car."

I nodded as he headed to the laundry room. Returning to my phone, I opened my email. Any optimism I'd gained disappeared at the latest email in my in-box. It was from Fran, and the subject line was all I needed to see.

Lillian Smith: Termination.

CHAPTER 19

LILLIAN

Fran's email was short and also sent to an address I didn't recognize—probably HR—with four CCs, including me.

> Lillian Smith is no longer employed with Los Angeles Times Communications LLC, effective immediately. Please disable her database access, key fob, parking card, and company email account.

I was still staring at the screen when Sam returned, my blue capris in hand. In my peripheral vision, I could see them hovering, and reached out and blindly felt around until I found them.

"What's wrong? You're super pale." I felt his hand on my forehead. "Temperature feels normal."

"I was just fired."

"What?" He sat next to me and I listed to the left until I hit his shoulder. He put his arm around me and pulled me against his side.

Twenty-two years. Two decades. I'd been with the newspaper longer than I'd been with Mike. It felt like everything in my life was splintering apart. I let out a groan.

"Hey, it's okay." Sam smoothed a hand over my hair, then wiped a tear from my cheek.

No, it wasn't. I was a happily married wife; then I wasn't. I was a respectfully employed writer; now I wasn't. What did my life look like without my job? What did *I* look like?

"You can get another job." Sam pressed a kiss on the side of my head. "Lillian. Hey. Stop crying."

Oh God. I *was* crying. I clamped my lips to stop the small mewing sounds that were bubbling out. I hadn't been this emotional over Mike's cheating, and what did that say about my mental state? Sam went to stand and I clung to his shirt, my cheek pressed against his scratchy linen top.

"Just let me call Mike. He'll come and pick you up."

"No." I surfaced from the grief long enough to find my voice. "*Don't* tell Mike."

"Why not?"

"Just, promise me you won't." The thought of Mike knowing about this failure . . . Talk about a deep knife in the wound of my already damaged ego. First, I couldn't keep a husband; now I couldn't keep a job. "I'll tell him later, when I'm ready. I need to talk to Fran first. See what's going on. Maybe she'll hire me back." Even part-time, even as a freelancer. Hell, I'd grovel and beg and do sales calls if I had to.

Well . . . maybe not sales calls.

"You have to be honest with him, Lill. This is a big deal."

No, Sam was wrong about that. Mike hadn't been honest with me for months, maybe a year. He'd always wanted separate finances, so we had them. He'd wanted separate lives, so we lived them. I had enough in my savings account to cover my half of the bills for a year, which was plenty of time for me to find another job. So why did Mike need to know what had happened? "Sam, I swear on my child's life, if you tell him, I will strangle you with that stupid necklace you're wearing." I glared at him.

He laughed. "It's a bolo tie."

"It's ugly."

He ignored the insult. "Mike's not stupid. And look, I hate to say it, but we've got to leave if I'm going to make my appointment."

Right. Because he had a job. *Still* had a job. Unlike me, who should have spent the day writing the Clark and Dentlinson obituaries, which were due by two. Who would write them? Janice? Screw her. I let out a sob and Sam's shoulders sank.

"Come on, Lillian. You have to pull yourself together."

"I'm fine," I protested hotly, even as my voice cracked and broke on the words. "Just give me my purse and we'll go."

He rose. "I'm sorry. I would cancel my meeting, but it's with the pier project."

The pier project? A good friend would have some idea of what he was talking about, but I was blank. I worked one foot, then the other, into my pants.

Okay, I could do this. I just needed to get to my car and get to Fran and find out what was going on.

That brilliant plan stalled out in less than fifteen minutes, in the parking lot of Perch. I sat in the passenger seat of Sam's car and went through my purse contents for a second time. *Shit.* My keys—a giant round ring packed with tools and mementos—weren't there.

"This is crazy," I mumbled, my anxiety rising. "My keys are missing."

Sam looked toward the bar, which was closed until dinner. "Think you left them in there last night?"

"I doubt it." I groaned. While Mike always considered me to be absentminded, the truth was, I was fanatical about my keys and my purse and had never lost either. "Do you have time to take me home? I have a spare set there, and I can get a taxi to take me back here."

"Sure, it's on the way." He shifted into drive and waited for me to fasten my seat belt. "By the way, I told Mike you were staying at my place. Last night, I mean. I called him after I picked you up."

Ah. The mystery of why Mike hadn't reached out to me was solved. I should have known that Sam had reported in—he and Mike were bosom buddies when it came to taking care of me. "You should have just taken me home."

He chuckled and pulled forward. "Yeah, you were *not* down with that idea, and you know I always follow drunk Lillian's instructions."

"Drunk Lillian has not made an appearance in quite some time," I defended myself. When I did used to get drunk—and there had been a period, a few years ago, when I had gone through a bit of a phase— my personality had certainly harshened under the influence of alcohol. I didn't believe it until Jacob filmed me, sputtering and bossy in the kitchen one night, insisting that brownies must—from that point on—be made with miniature M&M'S, an opinion I was pushing as if it would change the course of our lives. *I'm serious!* I kept saying. *Stop agreeing with me as if you aren't taking this seriously! Someone needs to write this down!* The video was mortifying. I'd watched thirty seconds of it and then retreated to my room, where I decided to never come out, and to stop drinking.

My self-imposed isolation had lasted for a few hours at best—and within a couple of weeks, I resumed my regular schedule of wine and cocktails. But I'd avoided getting too drunk. At least, until last night. And blacking out—well. That was a first for me.

As Sam's SUV hummed down the road, I refreshed my email, hoping to see a "haha, I'm just kidding" email from Fran. Instead, I got an error message, stating that my email login credentials were wrong.

Already, I was out in the cold.

———

Sam pulled into our front drive and parked in front of the Tudor-style garage doors. He handed me his copy of our house key, and I let myself in, then ran the spare back to him. Jacob was at school, so I stripped in the laundry room, then jogged up the carpeted stairs and straight into our master bathroom. Using extra apple-scented shampoo, I washed my hair, conditioned, and rinsed well, squeezing out the excess water before I wrapped myself in a fluffy yellow towel and stepped out.

As I dried off, I reassessed and solidified my decision to keep my job loss from Mike. I worked from home already, so he wouldn't miss me heading into an office, and I could fill the time normally spent in interviews and obituary creation in other ways—like figuring out what to do with the rest of my life.

Thumbing through the hangers, I pulled out a lilac pantsuit normally reserved for weddings and the occasional church event. This seemed like a worthy occasion to dress up for; I just wished I knew if there was something I was going to be apologizing for.

I put on a pair of pearl earrings and pulled my wet hair into a low bun. Maybe I should write a novel. Something about a scorned wife who hunted down her husband's mistress. Research would be required, of course. I grinned in the mirror, then watched my smile crumble as a wave of emotion hit me. God, what *was* I going to do for work? Newspapers and magazines were laying off writers right and left as internet blogs took over, subscribers opting to read their news for free and online. Paper newspapers were, as one millennial had told me (while sipping from a paper cup), like . . . the most wasteful thing ever. She predicted they would be outlawed within five years, and I wasn't entirely sure she was wrong.

I considered heels but didn't want to tower over Fran, who could be a little sensitive about her height. Pulling on a pair of gold-and-tan flats, I headed downstairs. The spare key to my Fiat was in the kitchen drawer, next to ones for Mike's and Jacob's cars. I pocketed it and flipped through the rest of the drawer, seeing what other replacements I could pilfer. There wasn't anything else of use, so I shut the drawer and then scheduled a ride pickup. *Four minutes away.*

Going out front, I brushed the dust off one of the rocking chairs on our shallow front porch. Pulling it to a spot in the sun, I opened my Twitter account and stared at the @themysteryofdeath account.

There was a riddle still outstanding. A mother, her son, and her husband were all at home on a quiet night, and one of them had died. In last night's eventful evening, I had neglected to leave a clue, and the thread had exploded with theories and opinions. I should give them something, some subtle hint that the mother is the one who dies, but it seemed too fitting, with my termination email fresh in mind, to give the hint I had originally planned, which was that the wife had recently been fired.

Still, my creative energy was too low for deviation, so I typed out the clue, then posted it.

Maybe it was time for @themysteryofdeath to die. I couldn't see continuing it, without my job, which sparked the ideas and gave me access to the *Times* database of obituaries and news. And after all, keeping it up would be like clinging to my old career in that way, which was a little pathetic, right?

Maybe. I watched the car service pull up to the curb.

I wasn't sure I was ready to kill that part of me also.

CHAPTER 20

LILLIAN

My large and crowded key ring sat in the middle of Fran's neatly organized desk. I stared at it in shock, momentarily forgetting why I was there.

"Surprised at something?" she asked dryly, her New York accent perking its head.

"Those are my keys." I pointed at one of the attachments, an outdated plastic photo of Jacob when he was starting kindergarten.

"Oh good," she said warmly, in a sort of cat-who-ate-the-canary way. "So you admit it."

Admit it? That didn't sound like something that I wanted to do. "Admit what?"

"That you keyed my car last night."

A protest both rose and fell on my lips, the result some sort of garbled scoff. I clasped my hands together. "I did *not* key your car." Was it a lie? I wasn't sure. "I didn't."

"Well, your keys were in the street near my car, and the blade on that knife was out, with bits of my paint still clinging to it."

I looked at my keys, the pink Swiss Army knife one of the many attachments on its ring. "I don't—"

"Stop," Fran interrupted. "I told you yesterday that you needed to step up your performance. You didn't want to hear it then, and I don't want to hear your excuses now. The ice . . ." She paused for dramatic effect and planted her fingertips on the desk like spiders. "The ice has broken."

"Please, Fran—"

"*No.*" She held up her palm to stop me. "It's been a good run with you, Lillian, but it's done. I didn't call the cops last night, and I'm filing this with my insurance as an act of random vandalism. Consider that a favor and head on your way. Make this difficult, and you can forget any letter of recommendation or reference."

Wow. I reached for my keys and pulled them slowly toward myself, then stood, trying to sort through the mess. Fran leaned back in her ergonomic chair, laced her fingers together on her belly, and gave me that same smug little smile from yesterday. She was, for some reason, enjoying this.

Maybe that's why I did it. Maybe after a few drinks, and thinking of that smug little smile, I'd had a bad idea and told the taxi to take me to Ladera Heights instead of home. I could have done something worse. Keying a car wasn't that bad. If I hadn't dropped my keys, she probably wouldn't have ever suspected me.

"Goodbye, Lillian," Fran said coldly.

I didn't respond, just held my head up high and left.

CHAPTER 21

LILLIAN

My first unemployed day, I dressed in a white off-the-shoulder sundress, purchased a pair of new wedge heels that tied around my ankles, and headed back to the coffee shop in Marina del Rey. David Laurent, who had been a text-messaging machine, was in town for three days and was, quote, "dying to see me."

On the way, I rolled all the windows down and blasted Gwen Stefani, channeling my inner Taylor. Did I go by Tay-Tay? I hadn't yet decided.

Now, with my hair wilder than usual, I strolled into the café with a nonchalance that felt almost natural.

"Taylor." David raised a hand from a two-top by the windows and stood.

His hat was gone, and his hair was a mess of sun-kissed waves, his glasses now perched on his head and keeping them in check. I could see his eyes more clearly now, green, and there was a bit of peeling skin at the tip of his nose. I stared at it, fascinated, because no self-respecting Californian burned, not if they were over thirteen.

Without hesitating, he zoomed toward me, and there was a freeze-worthy moment when I thought he was going to kiss me, before I realized he was doing the French thing, a smooch on each cheek, and thank God I hadn't gasped and recoiled, or puckered up and met his lips.

"You look . . . incredible." He was cupping my shoulders, looking me up and down as if in awe of what he was seeing.

I laughed as if I hadn't spent two hours in front of the mirror, in preparation for the event. "Oh stop." *Please don't. Please continue, forever.*

He released my shoulders and gestured for the table. "Should we sit?"

I moved toward the table and he pulled out my chair, a courtly gesture that Mike hadn't performed in more than a decade. Sitting, I tried not to stare as he took the opposite seat. He looked good, and my attraction to him was interesting, because it wasn't like the rough-around-the-edges, retired-surfer look did it for me. I liked . . . What did I like? The last time I was single, I was into scrawny builds, underfed abs, and boyish smirks. In this new landscape of grown men, I was a little lost. Listening to single women talk was a pros-and-cons list on steroids.

Well, he has hair, so I can overlook the extra thirty pounds.

Sure, he's dull, but have you seen his home in Del Mar?

The sex is horrible, but at least he makes me laugh.

"How's work?"

I let out an awkward laugh, and while I knew he was asking about my imaginary calendar-buying gig, I told him the truth. "Actually, I got fired yesterday." As soon as the news left my lips, I pinched them together, surprised at the confession, which I hadn't shared with anyone, outside of Sam.

"A true firing?" He looked intrigued, and I reminded myself that, as Taylor, I could spin this any way that I wanted to.

"Oh yes." I picked up the coffee cup with my new name written on it. "Big dramatics. Quite the scandal." I took a sip and smiled coyly at him. "I'd tell you exactly what happened, but then . . . well. You know."

"You'd have to kill me," he said earnestly, his eyebrows pinching in mock concern.

"Exactly." I shrugged. "Killing you would be a pain. You look like you'd put up a pretty good fight."

He laughed out loud, his gaze sticking on me as if he couldn't get enough—and I didn't know where my witty comebacks were coming from, but this role felt right, like one I was born to play.

"Well, seeing that you're soon to be in the bread lines, I'm obligated to cook you a dinner while I'm in town. I'm also obligated to give you this present, which is probably in terrible taste, now that you have become a pariah of the calendar world." He grinned in an aw-shucks way and reached between the table and the wall, pulled out a wrapped gift.

Lillian practically fell out of her chair in excitement. Thankfully, Taylor eyed the exquisitely wrapped box with the nonchalance of a woman accustomed to such gestures.

I shouldn't accept it. It didn't matter that Mike had given me a Costco membership for my last birthday. I was a married woman, and David had just invited me to dinner, and here was where I should draw the line and remind him of the ring on my finger. "Hmm . . . ," I mused. "I'm not sure a married woman should be accepting presents from handsome strangers." I smiled to soften the point, which I'd already wrapped in a cushion with the word *handsome*.

"There are some things a husband doesn't need to know," he scoffed, and pushed the box closer to me. "It's an innocent gift. How do you say? Scout's honor."

So there. Boundaries set. I gave myself a mental pat on the back and leaned forward, trying not to smile as I pulled at the red velvet bow elaborately tied on the front of the box. It was too big for jewelry, the wrong size for a book. *There are some things a husband doesn't need to know.*

So true. I pulled back the wrapping paper and opened the lid of the box.

Inside was a fact-a-day desktop calendar, the sort where you tear off a page each morning, and I glanced up to see the teasing curve of his lips. "You got me a calendar?"

"Well, I figured you didn't have one."

I laughed. "Interesting assumption."

"You mentioned that your favorite kind were the fact-a-days. I would have brought flowers, but thought this was a safer, less assumptive gift." He grinned at me. "Both informative *and* completely devoid of romance."

"It is rather unsexy," I admitted. "I actually got this exact same one for my mailman."

It was a lie, but one he appreciated, his head dropping back in another contagious laugh, and I crumpled up the wrapping paper and tried to squash the warmth that was spreading through me every time our eyes met.

It was a ten-dollar item. It shouldn't have affected me, but it did.

———

Our to-go cups in hand, we walked down the dock, past dinghies, sailboats, and houseboats, my steps slowing occasionally to read the name printed on the back of each boat. The dock was active, people passing, dogs running, crews working on the big yachts ahead of us, an easy camaraderie on the salty air. Several people called out a hello to David as we passed, and I eyed him over the plastic lid of my cup. "Come here often?"

"I should. My second home is ahead on the right." He pointed down the dock.

"You stay on the boat?" I asked, surprised. When he'd mentioned keeping a boat here, I'd thought he meant for fishing, or skiing, or whatever sporty people did on the waters outside Los Angeles.

"I do." We moved to the side to let a group pass, and his hand made contact with my lower back, guiding me around a cleat, and then stayed there. "I try to be here two weeks of the month. The boat is my hotel of sorts, one I can take out if the urge hits me."

"So your business—you can do that from anywhere?" His business card had listed a textile company's name. A quick internet search had revealed the business to be a chain of screen-printing shops that stretched across several states.

"Yep." He pointed to a white two-level boat on the right. "That's me."

It was called *Lost Buoy*, and a portable set of steps led to the back of the boat. He offered me a hand and gestured me forward.

I paused. "Wait, we're getting on it?"

"The coffee deck is on the top. Best view in the marina."

"The coffee deck?" I asked skeptically.

"Well, it's the tequila deck, normally—but I'll make an exception for you." He grinned, and there was a dimple hidden in the scruff of his blond beard.

His hand was still extended, waiting—the courtly gesture of a livery attendant, waiting to help the damsel into the carriage. I took it, climbed the three plastic steps up, and then stepped over a gap of water and onto the teak deck of the boat.

Three steps but they felt pivotal. Inside my chest, a callus began to grow around my feelings for Mike.

CHAPTER 22

LILLIAN

I was jobless for less than forty-eight hours because David had a solution. The position wasn't prestigious, challenging, or with the trappings of things like benefits, but it was available and it paid under the table, in cash. I was now a marina concierge, which was a dignified title for running errands for the yacht owners. I joined a crew of three that included a pimple-faced teenager Jacob's age (Kyle), an old drunk (Shawn), and a bubble gum–popping lesbian (Jenn). There were no assigned hours, no hourly wage, and I clocked in by picking up a walkie-talkie from the harbormaster and clipping it to my shorts.

It was perfect.

The marina was divided into classes by the size of the slips. The farther out you went, the bigger the slips, with the yachts and megayachts on the far end. Concierge service was for the sixty-footers and up, which was around eighty boats, only half of which were being used. I was boat-dumb and couldn't pick a catamaran out of a lineup, much less tell the bow from the stern. But the job didn't need any sort of marine know-how. Our tasks were simple—the radio would crackle, a boat owner would request something, and one of us would jump into action.

Literally, jump. Even Shawn hustled down the dock, his liver-spotted arms pumping, breath wheezing. I asked Kyle what the rush was for, and he said that tips were always better the faster you were. He was right. Twenties became fifties when I delivered bags of ice within two minutes, and a box of tampons from the nearest convenience store within five. The only time meandering was beneficial was during dog walks—we had twelve pups on-site—or when the owners wanted to chat.

The evening of my first day, David delivered on his promise and cooked me fresh-caught lobster on his upper deck. I stretched out on his lounger, sipped ice-cold champagne, and listened to the faint sounds of steel drum music, playing from the adjacent hotel pool. We hadn't kissed—we hadn't done anything that violated the terms of my marriage—but there was an electric wire between us, one that held a flame under the thin string of my self-control. The break was coming, and the anticipation of it was vibrating through my chest.

When I got home, Jacob was in his bedroom and Mike was in his recliner, a baseball game on. "Hey." He muted the television, a courtesy that I wouldn't have received a month ago. "Thought you'd be home for dinner."

"I had a late appointment, so grabbed something on the way back." I dropped my purse on the dining room table and started up the stairs. "I'm going to shower and head to bed."

I was sore—an unfamiliar sensation that I liked. It had been the most physically active day that I'd had in years, and I peeled off my clothes and stepped under the hot spray of the shower, almost moaning at the sting of heat.

When I stepped out, Mike was in bed, his shirt off, face hopeful, and I had a WhatsApp from David. I grabbed a blue plaid pair of flannel pajamas and returned to the bathroom, closing the door as I opened the message.

Good night, beautiful.

Oy. Three simple words that caused a bloom of joy to burst in my chest. I stared at the sentence for a solid minute, then closed the message and pulled on a clean pair of underwear and the pants, a smile curling the edges of my mouth.

I should have messaged back and reminded David that I was married. Drawn a firmer line in the sand of our friendship. I should have told Mike about my job or, better yet, gotten a normal one and focused on putting my marriage back together.

I should
I should
I should . . .

But the problem was that I didn't want to.

———

"So how's work?" Mike lifted a slice of mushroom pizza and took a bite. This was the third day this week that I hadn't cooked dinner, and apparently no one minded. He should have had an affair years ago. The benefits were starting to outweigh the pain of it all.

"It's good." I had walked the Trembles' poodles for an hour and gotten a hundred-dollar tip. Midmorning, I'd eaten an ice cream sandwich while swinging my bare feet off the dock and watching three crew members lift Jet Skis off a megayacht with a crane. One of the liveaboards had given me a bag of swordfish, and David had made tacos with them for our lunch, which I had enjoyed with two beers and our first kiss. The kiss had occurred in the tight kitchen of his boat, my back against the cabinets, his beard brushing against my cheek as he had nuzzled my collarbone, then my forehead, the tip of my nose, and then finally, while I strained and mentally begged for it, my lips.

He'd tasted like salt and mangoes, and had apologized as soon as he had done it. *I'm sorry, mon chaton. I just cannot control myself around you.* I had blushed and beamed like a schoolgirl for the rest of the afternoon.

Tomorrow we were going to take the boat to Catalina Island for the day, just the two of us. Beneath the table, my foot jittered against the chair leg, and I set my slice down after taking only one bite. Mike was still looking at me, expecting more, so I tried harder with my lie. "An older couple died in a car accident, so I have a double obit to do. I spent most of the day with their kids and grandchildren."

Funny that I used to think of my job as cool. Now it seemed so morbid and dreary. And for what? The bottom rung of journalism salaries? I was making more money in jean shorts and flip-flops than I had at the *Times*, and with no Fran to answer to, no traffic to battle, no deadlines continually hanging over my head.

I lifted my glass of ice water and took a sip. "What about you?"

Mike always loved the spotlight, and he took the mic without hesitation, launching into a long and confusing narrative about Bitcoin and a potential financing solution that involved converting funds into blah blah blah—I tuned him out and eyed our son, who was on his phone and his third slice of pizza. Jacob was worrying me. If he sensed the turmoil in our household, he didn't show it. His emotional detachment was convenient, but becoming more pronounced with time.

"But that's the issue, isn't it? If the market turns, then we're fucked. So it's this game between buying now, when opportunity and risk is high, or waiting until the price rises with stability." Mike got so excited about this shit. Was *she* into this? Was she matching him, line for line, and diving into the economies of foreign entities over late-night drinks and expensive steaks? Was that the missing piece, the opening she had used to worm into his life?

"You didn't tell me that you won Employee of the Month." I had meant to sit on the info but couldn't stop the accusation from coming out.

"Oh." He deflated slightly with the awareness that I didn't give a damn about his current path of conversation. "Yeah. Last month. And the one before."

The note of pride that crept into his voice on the added sentence only fueled my anger more. Two months he had gotten the bonus? What had he done with those? Two bonuses would have covered six months of severance from the *Times*. "So?" I folded my hands neatly on the table, one over the other, my elbows jutting out to either side. "Where is that money?"

"What money?" He glanced at Jacob, and it was a clear Let's Talk About This Later sign, one that I ignored.

"The *bonus* money, Mike. What did you do with it?"

His eyes darted to the saltshaker, then to his beer, then back to me. "Credit cards. Just paid them off."

"Hmm." I contained so much in that one word.

The question of what had been on all those credit cards.

The note that Mike had never held a balance on his credit cards, not in twenty years of marriage.

It was a point of pride for him, a notch on some invisible scorecard that made him better than other men, that made us better than other couples, and one he felt the need to point out at any loan appointment or financial-planning session. *And, just so you're aware, we don't have any credit card debt.* He had never had debt, so I had never had debt, because my husband knew best.

Mike wanted to say something, wanted to defend himself against my one snarky, passive-aggressive response, but he didn't. I let him hang there while I carried my paper plate to the kitchen and dropped my half-eaten slice into the trash. I washed my hands, opened the fridge, grabbed one of his beers, and carried it upstairs.

I locked our bathroom door and ran the tub until it was full, stepping in with a moan as I sipped the ice-cold beer. I should drink more beer. Wine was so pretentious, the elaborate sniff-and-swirl event of it all. Ice-cold beer—with a lime; I should buy some—that was more in line with my live-like-Taylor approach. I sank into the hot water, submerging up to my chin, and set the bottle on the side of the tub as I let the heat cook my tired muscles. I'd never walked or jogged so much in my life. After just a week of working there, I was stepping across wide gaps from docks to boats with ease, carrying twenty-pound bags of ice instead of tens, and could almost run from the ship store to the farthest dockage without pausing to catch my breath.

I drifted my hands under the water, running them across the stiff peaks of my nipples and then lower, my legs opening up, eager for the contact. I closed my eyes and focused on Mike, then a sexy soap opera star, before finally, reluctantly, I gave in and let myself think of David.

That confident smile.

The way his eyes lingered on me.

His fingers, drifting up along my bare thigh.

The brush of his facial hair along my neck.

The soft press of his lips.

How would they feel along the curves of my breasts?

How would he feel between my legs?

I closed my eyes, and mentally, I surrendered.

ONE MONTH
BEFORE THE DEATH

CHAPTER 23

LILLIAN

@themysteryofdeath: I am taking a hiatus from social media. Maybe I'll come back, maybe I won't. Ciao for now . . .

David's gift sat on our desk in the study, beside the landline phone. Each morning, I would check my email, read some news, and pull off the prior day's page to unveil a new fact. The gift was a bit cumbersome, due to a speaker on the front that announced the day's date if you pushed a button. It was an unnecessary feature that, if I had been a calendar buyer, I would have shaken my head over. But critical review aside, I didn't mind the heft and enjoyed the interesting facts.

Today's was interesting, if not slightly morbid. *A sea slug's head, if severed, can grow itself a new body.* Peeling a tangerine, I scrolled through my email. All junk. Closing the browser, I sat back in the ergonomic chair and popped a wedge of the tart fruit in my mouth. Stretching out my legs, I admired the cut of muscle along the top of my thigh. It was liberating, the changes I was starting to feel and see in my body. And the freedom of setting my own schedule was heaven.

I had assumed it would be a shoulder job—something to give me some cash while I figured out what my next move would be—but I was having fun.

Every day at the docks was different. I walked dogs—small, medium, and large—and sometimes Arch Billow's parrot. This week, I'd bought groceries for a dinner party and driven to Sonoma to pick up a case of custom wine. On Tuesday, I'd met a semitruck in the parking lot and watched as they'd slowly backed an off-white Ferrari down the truck's ramp and over to a freight boat. Last week, I'd called someone's teenage daughter, pretending to be the airline, and told her that her upcoming flight was canceled. I did whatever was asked, without question, and enjoyed every minute of it.

The extra pounds that I'd carried around since Jacob's birth were starting to melt off as I went from a sedentary life to one of activity. On my wrist was a new watch, one that counted steps and calories, and I rejoiced over my daily averages, ones high enough that I could eat anything I wanted.

The money was good, and the boat owners were a wealthy chocolate box of variety. *The Greedy Girl* owners had crawfish boils for two hundred guests and brought out their fiddles and sang Cajun songs at sunset. The tattooed gentleman of *Santa's Baby* played chess with me and slipped me beef jerky with his fifty-dollar tips. A lesbian couple had visited for four days aboard a superyacht—one a famous actress, the other a tech exec—and given me a box of Cuban cigars that I had passed on to David.

I was learning terms like *afterdeck* and *hatch*, and spent an entire day waxing the front of a Benetti. Afterward, I'd collapsed onto David's couch sore but happy. And when he pulled at the strings of my bathing suit top and lowered his body on top of mine . . . I didn't think of my husband and son. I'd met his kiss and felt like the entirely different woman I was growing into.

It was like I was a sail, coming free of its mast and whipping wildly into the wind.

Untethered.

Unpredictable.

Happy.

I popped another orange wedge into my mouth and smiled.

CHAPTER 24

MIKE

Every once in a while, I followed my wife. I'd been told that this wasn't normal, that most husbands didn't have GPS trackers attached to their spouse's car, that most husbands didn't sit in a parking lot, a pair of binoculars in hand, and study their wife's movements as she downward dogged in the local yoga studio.

But most husbands weren't me. They didn't perform risk analysis for a living. They didn't understand the minute actions and decisions that could lead to catastrophic and life-altering consequences. If someone dissected every aspect of my life, they'd find two weak links. Thanks to Lillian's snooping, I had removed one.

Now it was just her, and with whatever sort of hiatus Lillian had taken from her job, I was curious at how my increasingly detached wife was spending her days. So, for the first time in more than a year, I'd logged in to the GPS app and began to track her activity.

I had Heather block off my entire day so I could follow her. It was a good thing I did, because apparently I was now married to a common wharf rat, one who scurried around boats in cutoff shorts and T-shirts and hauled bags of ice and groceries for strangers.

The mother of my child had dropped to the lowest social class. Someone handed her a tip, and she stuffed it into the back pocket of her shorts as if she were a busboy. For lunch, she walked down to the gas station at the corner and bought a hot dog and a soda, and ate both on a bench next to a fish-cleaning station.

It was embarrassing, what she was doing. What she thought she was getting away with. Sam was right, with his concerns about her. The woman she used to be—successful and admired—had gotten lost in the last few years. She'd been reduced to this . . . and this *wasn't* the woman I agreed to spend the rest of my life with.

I'd let her have her fun for a little while, let her work out whatever midlife crisis she was exercising, but then I'd pull the plug, if she didn't fall back into line on her own.

She wouldn't understand or appreciate it, but then again, she never did.

CHAPTER 25

LILLIAN

David was away for the week, back in Fresno, and the docks felt empty without him. I worked less and stayed home more, putting in my dues and catching up, guiltily, on what Jacob was doing. With my new lack of career, there was no reason I wasn't more involved in his life, yet I'd been MIA most weekends and evenings, ever since I started working at the dock.

"Mom."

I jumped at the sound of my son's voice and turned to see him standing in the doorway, his backpack over one shoulder. "Yes?"

"I'm going over to Shawn's. I'll eat dinner over there."

"Oh." I tried to think of an excuse to keep him home. I looked down at the oven, which had twenty minutes left on the timer. "I made eggplant parmesan."

He made a face. "Yeah, I think we're going to do pizza or something. You need me to pick up anything on the way home?"

He was so thoughtful. Mike always said that we spoiled him, but we had done something right, because he never spoke back or raised his voice, even with all the teenage hormones supposedly turning kids his age into rage machines. "No, I don't need anything. Thanks."

"Okay, love you."

I repeated the sentiment. He turned to leave, and his bag bumped along the wall and knocked the picture of the three of us at the Hoover Dam slightly askew. I considered it, then left it alone.

By the time the eggplant was done, I was two glasses into a bottle of white zinfandel. Maybe it was the wine, maybe it was the awareness that David would be gone for a week, but when Mike came into the kitchen, I didn't stiffen with distaste. He deposited two grocery bags onto the counter and kissed me on the cheek. I let it happen and glanced at the bags. "What's that?"

"Jacob said you were fixing eggplant. I stopped at Houston's and got the cheesy bread you like and a few pieces of pie."

I tried not to smile but was touched by the thoughtfulness of a gesture that he used to do with regularity. "Thanks."

He retrieved one more item from the bag. "And . . . for you."

It was a bundle of books. Three new hardcover releases. One of them I'd already read, the novel tucked beside a pair of boat shoes in my trunk, but he didn't have a way of knowing that.

"I've noticed that you're reading more." He tapped the top one. "The guy at the bookstore said this one is going to be a TV show." He met my gaze and he was so confident, so at ease. It was annoying, but also attractive. That confidence was what had first pulled me to him. *Same with David.* Maybe I had a type, though David was a thousand times more chill than Mike, and at least twice as fun.

"Thank you." I smiled, reluctantly, at him, appreciative of the gesture and ready to call a temporary truce. "Want a glass of wine?"

———

We ate in silence, but it was a comfortable one, my nerves mellowed from the wine, the glow of Mike rose-colored in nature. He had lost some weight, looked exhausted, and I would have felt sorry for him if he hadn't brought all this on himself.

"I heard that the *Times* did a round of layoffs." He broke a piece of the bread in half. "Any of your friends lose their job?"

It was a kind statement, but I'd never had any friends in that building and he knew it. My personality was not one that collected relationships, especially since I had always, even before everything went virtual, worked from home. "No, no one I'm close with." I took a sip. This would be a great segue to mention my own firing. The opportunity was right there—all I had to do was take it. But that conversation would lead to others about job hunts, interviews, and options.

I wasn't ready to lie about all that, and I wasn't ready—might never be ready—to tell him about the marina.

"Any chance you'll do Maurice Grepp?"

I looked at Mike blankly, and tried to understand what he was asking about the Beverly Hills tycoon. "What do you mean?"

"He was a client of my firm, in case you needed an in with the obituary. Unless he's considered a celebrity and, you know." He cleared his throat. "Off limits."

Maurice Grepp must have died. Wow. I wondered how long ago it had happened. Today? Yesterday? How far out of touch was I? A wave of nostalgia hit me, and it must have been the wine.

"Oh." I swirled the pink liquid in the glass. "No, I won't be the one doing it. But thanks for the offer."

His eyes met mine and I sensed the storm in the air before it hit. "Lill, you probably don't know this—well, I know you don't know this—but in the mornings, I stop for a bagel and a coffee at this little diner around the corner from my office. It's in this shopping center they just put in, the one with the dry cleaner that lost my wool pants . . ."

He was rambling, and maybe this was the confession, the moment that he would share everything about his mistress. Did she work there? I didn't want to hear this. I didn't want to know, didn't want to picture the two of them growing closer over bad coffee and greasy bacon. "Mike," I said faintly.

"Right. Anyway. I go there because they always have the *Times*. And I read your obits with breakfast each morning. It's stupid." He shrugged. "But it makes me feel connected to you, like I'm not as big of a dunce about your job as I am."

Oh no. A gesture that would have touched me months ago had now incriminated me.

"And you're really talented. I can always pick out yours, even before I get to the byline. I cut out the favorites and keep them in a drawer in my desk." The corners of his mouth lifted in a proud smile. "That one about the lacrosse player—that was my favorite. It made me think of Jacob."

The lacrosse player was one of my favorites too. He hadn't been a superstar athlete—he'd played only a year of the sport before he had been cut—but I had made him shine as best I could. His mother had visited me after the obit had printed, her eyes filled with tears, her hug fierce and long.

"You haven't written anything since you found out about the affair." He swallowed and I realized what the tension in his face was—not anger or suspicion. Guilt.

He was wrong with the timing. My firing had come a week or two after the affair blowup, but I saw where his mindset was. A typical man, thinking that he was the cause of everything, that my psyche was so destroyed that I couldn't pick up a pen and write. It took only a heartbeat to decide to let him keep the guilt, and to move further down a path of deception. "I'm actually on a sabbatical. I'm still writing, just not obits. I'm working on a novel."

He perked up at this, and I should have picked something less exciting. "Oh really? You'd be great at that, Lill. Really, really great at that."

A naive and stupid statement. Mike had no idea whether I'd be good at fiction writing, and the chances were high that I wouldn't be. A novel was a complex fit of scenes, characters, and plot. A month ago,

I'd thought about tackling the task. Now I just wanted to get drunk and have sex with David.

I shouldn't be thinking that, especially not here in our dining room, where Jacob lost his first tooth and I'd shared the news of my third miscarriage over fish sticks and tater tots. But I was. I was thinking about how each experience with David seemed to unlock something new in me, and maybe sex would break the links that I still felt with Mike, the emotions that I couldn't seem to shake, even with constant reminders of his affair.

I was on an emotional seesaw. Up from a *missing you* text from David. Down from the puppy-dog looks Mike was giving me, like this one right here.

I tilted back my glass and finished it off. If this was the road to hell, I was traveling down it at a steady pace. "I should get the dishes in the sink. I'm meeting Sam for drinks."

"Oh. You guys have been hanging out? I haven't seen him here lately."

I started to gather my plate and silverware and paused to let out a sharp laugh that sounded convincing. "Of course we've been hanging out." After all, who else would I be filling my days with?

Mike would never suspect the truth, not from his boring plod of a wife. I was the woman who'd spent one summer reorganizing our spice cabinet alphabetically and with custom labels printed on our discount label maker.

I watched as my dear cheating husband straightened his clean knife in line next to his dirty spoon. "Tell him I said hi."

I nodded as if it would be done, but I'd made the "going to meet Sam for drinks" line up on the spot. In truth, I hadn't seen Sam in weeks. Despite his daily calls and texts, I'd made excuses every time he wanted to hang out.

"I'll do the dishes." Mike carried his plate into the kitchen. I followed suit, and when our paths crossed in the kitchen, he had that look in his eyes, one with romantic intent. When he went in for a kiss, I stepped to one side.

He let out an irritated huff. "It's been over a month, Lill."

"Exactly." I continued for the door. "It's not my fault you've suddenly decided to start paying attention to your wife."

He said nothing and I grabbed my purse and lifted my keys from the hook. My back was stiff, my words firm, but inside . . . I'd been close to kissing him. I'd wanted to sink into his touch and feel the familiar meet of our mouths. I'd wanted him to hold me and need me and still love me.

And I wasn't ready for that. Not yet.

CHAPTER 26

LILLIAN

I escaped from the house and drove north, through downtown, to the PCH, and past Venice and Santa Monica. Near the Getty, I decided to follow up on my story and called Sam, who agreed to meet me in Paradise Cove. I found a frozen yogurt stand and was halfway through a cone of blueberry when Sam's Range Rover pulled into the lot.

He gave me a kiss and a hug, then stepped back and did a once-over. "Wow, look at you."

I looked down at my workout shorts and T-shirt. "Yeah, look at me."

"No, I'm serious. You look good. Have you lost weight?"

"I think it's just the tan." But I had lost weight. Eight pounds. Between me and our bathroom mirror, I looked fantastic.

"Well," he said graciously, "it looks good on you."

"Thanks." I pointed to the yogurt window. "Want some?"

"Of course."

———

Over his bowl of piña colada yogurt with white chocolate chips, I confessed everything that had happened with David. Sam paid close attention, his forehead pinching together as he absorbed the information. He had always been a fierce fan of Mike's, and I steeled myself for a lecture on promiscuity. Instead, he stuck his red plastic spoon into the concoction and tented his fingers in front of his mouth, thinking.

"Lillian," he finally said.

"Yes?" I tucked my hands between my knees and waited for my punishment.

"I think . . . ," he said slowly. "I think that you need to be very careful and use this time to decide what you are going to do with the rest of your life."

He placed his hand on my shoulder, and it felt a little like I was being knighted. He stared deep into my eyes, and I fought the urge not to roll them. Sam was a man who planned and thought things through to the nth degree. He also listened to a slew of podcasts when he was in the car, which gave him hours of relationship, motivational, and business opinions each day. The end result was a *GQ*-attired walking encyclopedia of wisdom—most of which was complete garbage.

I didn't *want* to decide what to do with the rest of my life. I wanted to be selfish for once, and do something for me. Maybe I'd get over the pain of Mike's affair and forgive him. Maybe I wouldn't and we'd get a divorce.

A fly buzzed by, close to my ear, and I swatted at it. "I'm figuring things out."

He gave me an exasperated look.

"What?" I plucked a white chocolate chip from the top of the yogurt. "I'm figuring things out. I know you want me to just sit in a room and decide whether to stay with Mike or leave him, but that's a big decision, Sam. He's my husband. We have twenty years together."

"And he cheated on you. And you hate him."

"I hate him right now. I'm not sure how long that will last."

He sighed, then pushed the frozen yogurt toward me. "Am I preaching? I sense that I'm preaching." He swung one leg over the concrete picnic bench. "You know that it's my protective instinct at work. Plus,

I just know so much more than everyone else. It's hard to keep all of this brilliance to myself."

I acknowledged his talents with a nod. "Your self-control is admirable."

"Have you told Mike that you lost your job?"

I made a face. "Kind of. He knows I'm not working right now."

"Well, I'll keep my mouth shut, except to say that you look happier and healthier than I've ever seen you. So, whoever this guy is, I think you should give him a chance. And the same with you. Give yourself and your happiness a chance." He stood and offered his hand, helping me to my feet. Pulling me into him, he kissed me on the top of the head and I smiled against the silk of his shirt.

Give myself *and my happiness a chance*. I liked that idea. Maybe amid all his hooey, there was some gold.

CHAPTER 27

LILLIAN

Two weeks into the calendar—*polar bears' skin is black, and their fur is clear, not white!*—I settled in at my desk, reached for the day's fact, and stopped—surprised to find the clunky box missing. I stared at the blank spot in between the desk phone and a mango-pineapple candle that had been a Christmas gift from Mike's mother.

I checked the floor, on the chance that someone had knocked it off, but the Spanish tile was clear, and nothing else on the desk was askew. Rising, I circled the edge of the furniture and looked closer. Nothing. I checked the desk's drawers, then wandered out into the hall. "Mike?"

He wasn't in the living or dining room, and I spotted movement outside the kitchen window. Walking over to the sink, I peered through the glass and saw him fiddling with the lock on the backyard shed. Heading toward the back door, I stole a handful of red grapes from a bowl on the counter, then paused by the trash can. There, crooked atop coffee grounds and a crumpled Pepsi can, was the calendar. I carefully pulled it out, confused. Setting it on the counter, I opened the back door and yelled for Mike.

It took him a few minutes, in which time I decided the calendar was ruined. It had black, sticky grounds along the back and in the battery compartment, which had been opened. Cooking oil had soaked the edge of the pages, and I was pissed by the time he brushed his shoes off on the mat and opened the door. "Yeah?"

"Did you throw this away?" I gestured to the calendar.

"That's yours?"

"Yeah, it's mine. Who else's would it be?"

"Where'd you get it?"

This was something I was unprepared for, and I stumbled on the response. "It was a gift."

"A gift?" He stepped closer, his eyes dark, and I tried to understand where his tension was coming from. Had I been gazing at the calendar with doe eyes, my chin cupped in my hands? Did I absentmindedly draw hearts in the border? Or was this just his intuition, in the same way that I had gut-felt that he was being unfaithful? "A gift from who?"

"Just a barista at a coffee shop." It was the first lie I arrived on, and hopefully one with enough truth to pass his bullshit detector.

"A barista gave you a calendar and you didn't find that odd?"

"It was, like, a hundredth-customer-of-the-day kind of prize," I defended, and that was good, very believable. My patting on the back was interrupted by his next question.

"Which coffee shop?"

"What?" I let out a strangled laugh. "Why do you care? It's a calendar. Since when did you become so interested in my coffee habits?"

"Which. Coffee. Shop?" He leaned closer, and I could smell the sour tinge of orange juice on his breath.

A Starbucks seemed unbelievable, so I grabbed the first local one I could think of. "The one over by the mall, near the shoe repair shop."

Great. With my luck, he'd stop by and drill them about the giveaway. What a stupid lie. Why was he even asking about this? I should have just said that I bought it. Was it too late to change my story?

I crossed my arms over my chest and tried to change the direction of the conversation back to the fact that he'd thrown away my calendar. "I don't understand why you put it in the trash."

He started, then stopped, like my car when we were trying to teach Jacob how to drive a stick. I watched, fascinated, while he struggled to find a response. This was jealousy, surely. Was it possible that he knew, or suspected, something about David?

A warm calm settled over me, like a blanket had been wrapped around me. He did care. Me, stepping out, would or did affect my husband in some way.

I'd really begun to question that, over the last few years. The confirmation of it, even if it existed in the form of a ruined fact-a-day desk calendar . . . was comforting. I bit the inside of my lip to keep from smiling and watched as he reached back and twisted the knob of the back door.

"Well?" I pressed.

"A coffee shop just gave it to you. When? How long ago?"

"I don't know," I grumbled—though I did know, because I had pulled off the already-past days and started on the day he gave it to me: October 3. It was exactly two weeks ago. "Two weeks? Three? Maybe four?" I added the extra time in case he went to the coffee shop and started asking questions, which my normal husband would never do, but this new Mike—attentive, always-around Mike—I was beginning to fear he actually would.

"Four weeks?" He seemed aghast at the news. "You've had this calendar for four weeks?"

I let out an awkward laugh. "Maybe? Why are you freaking out about this?"

He let out an irritated breath and swung the back door open. "Just start clearing things with me, Lill. Jesus Christ." Storming out the door, he let it slam shut behind him with a bang that reverberated the tile underneath my bare feet. I turned my head and watched through the kitchen window as he returned to the shed.

Oh my word. I looked at the sad state of the calendar, then carefully dropped it back into the trash can.

I should have felt guilty, bringing a gift from David into my home, especially since our friendship had taken a definite and authoritative leap into the territory of an affair. But I didn't. I felt reckless and brave, like a woman who went after what she wanted and said *the hell with* any repercussions.

I felt like Taylor.

CHAPTER 28

LILLIAN

"We should go on a trip together." David floated beside me, his back flat on a paddleboard, his fingers loosely intertwined with mine. "What's your favorite place in the world?"

"My favorite place?" I closed my eyes. "Hmm. I don't know. I haven't been to many places."

"Where do you normally go as a family?"

I laughed. "Boring places. My husband would make a horrible travel agent. And he's afraid of flying, so we always end up in the car for days."

Mike's flight phobia was a long-standing joke, one that was extremely inconvenient, especially when he wanted to go to the Corn Palace in South Dakota or the Sierra Blanca Peak in New Mexico. We'd tried to make the best of it, renting giant RVs and spreading the trips out over two weeks, as we visited every small town and college friend along the way, but I was green with envy over social media friends who just jumped on a plane and were (ta-da!) in Florida that afternoon.

"Boring?" David asked. "Like what?"

"You don't want to know." I dangled one leg in the water and wondered if a passing shark might bite it off. We had taken his boat four miles out, to a sandbar dotted with a single palm tree. I pulled my leg back onto the board. "It's embarrassingly basic." *Basic*, a term I'd heard one of Jacob's friends use, was apparently cool and Taylor-worthy.

"I want to know." He squeezed my hand and turned his head toward mine, arresting me with his moss-colored eyes. "I want to know everything about you."

It was true. He listened without getting distracted or changing the subject to himself. And he absorbed everything he heard. While I couldn't get Mike to remember our anniversary each year, David remembered that I like sunflower seeds on my salad and that I had a dentist appointment Tuesday at three.

So I told him. I told him about the annual trips we took to Winnemucca, Nevada. I told him about the time the car broke down and we stayed on an Indian reservation, and the time that Jacob got food poisoning during an overnight hike up Mexican Hat plateau, and even about how Mike sings folk songs as he drives. He laughed, and asked all the right questions, and I loved that he respected my marriage and acknowledged Mike's presence and history in my life.

In between the true stories, I tried to inject Taylor-likely events, but surprisingly enough, David was always more interested and responsive to the normal parts of my marriage and life. Maybe, I—as Lillian—was more interesting than I knew.

Sharing the true stories made our affair feel less dirty, but maybe it shouldn't have. I closed my eyes and tried to picture Mike, floating out in the ocean and talking about me to a younger, fitter woman, one who probably laughed at the story of when I got diarrhea while we were in Cabo, or when I embarrassed him and Jacob with a drunk karaoke rendition of "Hips Don't Lie" by Shakira.

Dammit. The truth of the matter was, I hated the idea of Mike talking about me to her. I preferred the idea of her being clueless, with no idea that he had a child and wife. I pinned my lips together and vowed not to mention him again to David.

My chest cramped with guilt, and I rolled onto my stomach on the warm fiberglass. "Want to paddle over to the island?" I nodded toward the single palm tree, which David had already vowed to climb bare-handed.

"Let's do it." He shook his head and water droplets flew outward. Pulling my board toward him, he leaned over and pressed a kiss on my shoulder before pushing off toward the sandbar. I dipped my hands into the water to paddle, and I didn't love him but I'd be lying if I said I didn't love this new version of my life.

TWO WEEKS
BEFORE THE DEATH

CHAPTER 29

MIKE

Either my wife was lying or someone else was.

I wasted three days at that damn coffee shop, stopping in at various intervals and shifts until I spoke to all of the management and barista staff. All denied knowledge of any sort of giveaway, and I got skeptical looks at the mention of a calendar. I considered bringing the actual item in, but I already looked senile. Holding a plastic bag with a partially disassembled desk calendar wouldn't have helped.

It's possible that the employee in question didn't work there anymore or—and more likely—that the calendar came from somewhere else. I needed to follow Lillian more, find out if she had any new "friends," but this was not a time when I could slack on work—not right now, not when the major players were in town and my ass was on the grill.

So I took other steps, starting with bugs in her car, at her desk, and in our bedroom. Each morning, on my way to work, I listened to the prior day's recordings. Each evening, I looked over her phone records. So far, it was a lot of shuffling sounds and boring conversations.

Whatever it was, whoever it was, I'd find out. I always did.

CHAPTER 30
LILLIAN

David gave me a necklace with a pendant of a small golden fish. I fastened it around my neck and mentally swore to never take it off. My tan turned golden and I stopped dyeing my gray hairs, letting the sun bleach the surrounding strands.

Unlike the calendar, the necklace didn't catch Mike's attention. His contrite behavior continued, though there were moments when I could sense his growing annoyance with my newfound independence.

Good. I was glad he was frustrated. I'd spent the last year clinging to him while he went on "business trips" and secretly dated someone else. Just because he had been caught and supposedly ended it, that didn't mean I had to instantly forgive him.

I liked his new pursuit and courtship of me. Was it wrong for me to allow it? Sam thought so. There were times I agreed with him and times I didn't care. So what if I was also guilty? Unlike him, I had never spent the night with David, or spent money on him, or lied for months on end. I'd had only six weeks with David. Six weeks and sex twice.

The sex wasn't satisfying. That was the only missing piece of our equation. It was awkward, being naked with a new person. Mike knew my body, each button and how I liked it pressed. We'd learned those buttons together, over years and countless experiences. David had a very rough, caveman style that was filled with vocal declarations, sweat, and his version of passion—which was very different from Mike's. The night David gave me the fish necklace, I pulled Mike to me in bed, and he moved on top without hesitation, my underwear dragged down, our bodies meeting in quiet harmony. His hands had rested on either side of my head as he thrust, and then I'd rolled over and he lay on top of me, his breath huffing in my ear. There had been another minute of thrusts, and then he was done.

Not a word between us.

I'd rolled back to my side of the bed, and he'd returned to his, and it had been exactly what I'd needed. Not an Olympic event, not even longer than six or seven minutes. Perfect.

Now I sat on the grass, next to Lenny. We were on the north hill of the cemetery, the angle such that it almost felt like you were upright. Above us, the sun hid behind a solid line of clouds, putting a cool and eerie shadow over the field of graves.

There was a gentle nudge on my right side and I looked down to see him offering his flask. "Want a sip?"

"No." I gave a contented exhale. "My luck, I'd get pulled over on the way home."

"You don't have to chug it. You can just sip. It's peanut butter whiskey. Actually tastes pretty good."

"Well, then. It's a good thing I declined. Peanut allergy." I closed my eyes, enjoying the breeze on my cheeks. "I love the smell of grass, right after they cut it."

"So if you're fired, what are you doing all day?" He eyed me, and even drunk, it felt like he could see me more clearly than most.

"I don't know. I'm working down at the docks in Marina del Rey right now, running errands for boat owners."

He squinted at me. "Doesn't sound like you."

"Yeah, well." I kicked off a fly that had landed on my shin. "I'm trying to figure out who 'me' is."

"Do you miss writing?"

"Do you miss arresting people?" I shot back, immediately regretting the dig. Like me, he hadn't had much of a choice. You show up at work drunk as a cop, you tend to lose your job pretty quickly.

"Yeah," he said quietly. "I do. Not the arresting bit, but the investigations. The hunt. The clues." He sat fully upright. "I was a good detective, Lill. And you're a good writer. The best I've ever seen."

"Yeah, well." I tugged at a blade of grass. "I'm not missing it so far."

He pulled at the collar of his cemetery uniform and changed the subject. "You already visited Marcella?"

"Nah. I parked on the other side, so I haven't made it that far yet."

He climbed to his feet, his knees popping as he stood, and held out his hand to help me up. "I'll go with you. I just planted a new monkey flower bush beside her."

I took his hand, my feet almost leaving the ground as he pulled me to standing. I steadied myself, then brushed off the back of my jean shorts and my shirt. "Thanks."

The appreciation went unnoticed. He was already walking down the hill and toward Marcella's grave.

ONE WEEK BEFORE
THE DEATH

CHAPTER 31

LILLIAN

Normally, I left the docks by five thirty, but I was starting to get slack. On days when David was in town, I lingered. I liked the way his eyes stuck to me. If I bent over and picked something up, he'd watch in appreciation. I liked the weight of his lust, how it hung in the air, even if the sex wasn't great.

On Tuesday, Mike was in San Francisco on "business," and I accepted David's invitation for dinner. He bought me a dress, a knee-length, gold, slinky number that clung to my breasts and hips and swirled out when I spun. It was wrapped in tissue paper and in a box from an expensive store in Beverly Hills, a lacy bra-and-panty set also enclosed.

I showered in the small bathroom on his boat and bumped my elbow against the wall as I dried my hair. There wasn't great light, but I still managed with the extra makeup I kept in the glove box of my car. I slid the dress over my head, then stood in front of the full-length mirror and stared at a sexy, vibrant woman who looked nothing like Lillian Smith.

"Wow." David came up behind me and put his hands on my shoulders and lowered his mouth to my neck, kissing along the slope of skin. I smiled. Tonight would be another night of sex. I was mentally prepared for it, even needed it. Not the pleasure, but the hunger, the attention, the look, and touch of a man who desired me. "You're going to break the heart of every man in the restaurant."

Even if it was ridiculous, I preened at the idea, and when we walked down the dock and I saw the limo at the curb, I felt like Cinderella, being whisked off to the ball.

At a restaurant with tuxedo-clad waiters and a personal sommelier, I ordered from a menu without prices, and thought only briefly of Mike's damning receipt, crumpled in the pocket of his pants. I sipped a grapefruit martini and cut into a lobster-topped filet mignon, laughed at David's story about a red-eye flight to Cincinnati, then told my own Taylor-inspired falsehood about a girls' trip to Vegas.

When we got back to the boat, we went to the upper deck, where he smoked a cigar and we opened a bottle of champagne. From the opposite dock, the *Greedy Girl*'s owners had their fiddles out, and the music floated past on the crisp salt air. After our second glass, David stood and started to move in rhythm with the beat, swiveling his hips and undulating his arms through the air. I started to laugh. "Stop. We're too old to dance."

He beckoned at me with a smile.

I shook my head.

He took the champagne flute from my hand and pulled me to my feet. I reluctantly rocked my hips, my cheeks burning with self-consciousness.

"Yes, you gorgeous minx." He spun, his bare feet quiet on the deck, and I grew bolder as the song tempo moved into a rhythm I recognized.

I hadn't danced in a decade and I laughed aloud as we grew closer, his hands roaming over my bare arms, my exposed back, then up the short skirt of the dress. When he unzipped the back of it, I let him. When he pulled me onto the front cushioned lounge, I followed, and he tasted like cigar and bubbles, and I kissed him deeply and let every worry in my body float up to the clouds.

I didn't notice the dark figure a few boats over. I didn't see the night-vision camera or feel the weight of observation.

I was 100 percent focused on David, and on my own pleasure, and it was that selfish focus that caused everything that happened next.

CHAPTER 32

LILLIAN

Come home asap.

The text was sent by Mike and accompanied by three missed calls, none of which I saw because I was swimming in the Ritz-Carlton's pool, my access granted by a pool attendant I'd met in the marina's general store. I finished my twentieth lap and treaded water in the deep end, then practiced holding my breath. I made it thirty seconds, then forty. Forty-two, forty-three . . . My lungs ached as I burst to the surface and gasped for air. I treaded for another minute, then ducked underwater again.

It was a good day to swim. The marina-adjacent hotel was in the quiet transition time between checkouts and check-ins, and the only other person in the pool was a dark-skinned teenager floating in an inner tube, her head back on the cushion, mouth relaxed, clearly asleep.

I made it to forty-six seconds, then resurfaced, swimming to the side of the pool and pulling myself out. I grabbed the folded yellow towel and dried my ears as I returned to my chair, which was under a double umbrella, my piña colada turning soupy in the heat. Patting my face dry, I slid my sunglasses back on and reclined in the chair, humming along to a familiar reggae song being played by the steel drum band.

This was the life. I used to spend weekdays in traffic, dictating obituary lines while cursing out fellow motorists. Now I had a few chapters left to read in my new book, nothing to do the rest of today, and a wallet crammed with tip money. While my new life wasn't intellectually stimulating, the break was nice. I could grow my creative impulses in other ways. Maybe I could join a Mensa club or do crossword puzzles. Plus, I reminded myself, I could always write that damn novel.

My phone pinged and I decided to ignore it. Mike was at work, Jacob was at school, and I was tired of Sam and his judgmental opinions. I lowered the back of the chaise longue and closed my eyes.

Ping.

Dammit. I groped at the side table—oh shoot, that was my drink—and found my phone and brought it to my face. Shielding the screen from the sun, I peered at the display, then sat up when I saw the missed-call activity and the texts—now three—from Mike.

Come home asap.

Jacob is here now.

Did you know about this?

My phone rang and I hesitated, afraid to answer it. Did I know about *what*? What was Jacob involved with? What had happened?

I took a deep breath and answered the call, wincing at the realization that "Three Little Birds" would be audible in the background. "Hello?"

"Lillian."

In just my name, Mike's tone, and the pause after it, I knew that this was going to be bad.

CHAPTER 33

LILLIAN

The platform of choice was TikTok, and the video was just bad enough to be crude, while not being so adult as to be blocked from the family-friendly platform.

I sat at our dining room table, Mike's phone in front of me, and watched the video with horror. It was on a loop, the music and video restarting as soon as it ended, like a bad dream that you can't run away from.

"The number under the heart is how many people liked it," Mike said quietly. "The other figure is the number of comments."

There were 72 likes and 104 comments. I clicked on the comments, and everything instantly turned worse. If a video was worth a thousand words, here they all were.

"Jacob has seen this?" I asked quietly.

"He's the one who showed it to me."

"Who posted this? Whose account is this on?" I tried to figure out where to click, how to get off this loop of torture.

"It's a new account. This is the only video on it. But at the bottom . . ."

"I see it." At the bottom of the description, it said *More to come*. "Is this legal?" I asked. "Isn't this, like, revenge porn or something?"

"I don't know. We can call an attorney or the police."

"Shit." I pushed the phone away from me and tried not to vomit. The thought of reporting this to the police—they'd laugh. They'd send us away, their time needing to be focused on real crimes, on something more important than sixty seconds that showed me dancing in my bra and underwear—God, I needed to lose more weight—on the front of David's boat. Us kissing, my hand gripping his crotch through his pants. My head back, laughing as he knelt between my knees and lowered his mouth to my cleavage. Through all the video clips, there was a song playing, one labeled as "MILF," the lyrics describing in crude detail how much the singer wanted to bang his friend's mother. The video's creator had dubbed in Jacob's name in frequent fashion, so every reference was to wanting to "part Jacob's mama's legs" and so forth. It was a masterful and complete atom bomb of embarrassment—and the worst part was that it wasn't just embarrassing to me. Jacob, who had once refused to go to school for three days because he had cut his cheek while shaving, would be mortified. Anyone, after reading the comments section, would be mortified for him.

"We have to get this down," I said desperately. "I don't know how, but this can't . . . How long has this been up?"

"Four hours. It posted right before lunch. Apparently, it was all anyone was watching in the cafeteria. Jacob checked out as soon as he saw it."

Shit. He'd never forgive me for this. Ever. "Where is he?"

"He just left. He said he was going for a drive."

I rested my head in my hands. "It's about to be rush hour. You know how he gets." Patience was a trait that Jacob had not yet found, and he'd already been in one fender bender due to his aggressive driving. Add heightened emotions to a heavy foot, and the results could be disastrous. Deadly. Teenagers were dying all the time in car accidents. Between that, suicides, and overdoses, it was amazing that any of them lived to see graduation.

"I need this guy's information. How long have you been seeing him?"

His voice was calm and matter-of-fact, and had this been a quiz show, I would have correctly guessed this reaction.

"A few weeks," I hedged. "I met him the weekend Maurice Grepp died." It was a lie, but a believable one, with just enough false detail to stick. My husband wasn't the only one well versed in the art of deception.

"What's his name?" His pen was poised over the page as he waited expectantly, and this item I couldn't lie about. A lie here he would unfurl in minutes.

"David Laurent." I had to clear my throat, the words getting stuck on their way out. "He's nobody, Mike. I don't—I don't care about him. It was just a fling." Shit, I sounded just like him.

He didn't respond. I chanced a look at him, but he was pushing to his feet and walking out of the room.

CHAPTER 34

LILLIAN

In our bedroom, I changed out of my damp bathing suit and cover-up, the guilt radiating through me as I pulled on sweatpants and a T-shirt. From its place on the dresser, my phone vibrated.

It was David. My anxiety deepened at the realization that his face was on that video too. What happened if the next one tagged him or if someone in his life saw it? What if this was just the start of the repercussions?

I pulled my hair into a ponytail and steeled myself for what was downstairs—Mike's risk-and-solutions assessment, which was already pages long and spread out on our dining table.

The aftermath of this would not be messy, but it would be harsh. Mike was not emotional, but he was cold and vindictive. When the neighbors reported our trash cans for sitting too long on the curb, Mike audited ten years of archived satellite images of their home and then sent a two-inch-thick package of documentation to code enforcement, detailing the unauthorized improvements made, along with a list of current citations. He also sent a letter to their homeowner's insurance, alerting them to their pit bull, Snuggles, who could barely move off the couch and played with butterflies in her spare time.

I didn't think my affair would break Mike's heart, but it would insult his ego, and there would be punishment as soon as he properly handled the situation.

Would he go after David, drunk and furious, his fists swinging to protect the woman he loved?

No. The thought was almost humorous, if not heartbreaking.

I checked my text messages to see if I had anything from Jacob. My last text, sent twenty minutes ago, was still missing the "Read" indicator.

I took the steps downstairs, dreading what was ahead. "Jacob isn't reading my text messages."

"He probably has his phone off." Mike was back at the table and looked up from the notepad in front of him. "Give him a chance to cool off. You know how he is with caring about what other people think. He's mad."

Jacob, for a teenager, had a very staunch moral code. If I'd sat him down and confessed that I was having an affair, he would have been distraught. If he was ever embarrassed in front of his friends, he would withdraw in mortification and anxiety. This was a combination of both, and I was sick to my stomach with a cocktail of guilt and intense rage for whoever had filmed and posted this.

"Okay, I see this as several problems. First, we have the reputations of you, me, and this David Laurent. What do you know about him?" Mike looked up at me, his pen poised ready for action.

"Look." I sat across from him. "About that. I'm sorry. I was just so hurt from—"

"Let's focus on the problem," Mike snapped. "What do you know of him? Is he married?"

"No." I knotted my arms over my chest. "He's single. He, um. He has a chain of screen-printing T-shirt shops."

"Have you told him about this?"

I shook my head.

"Well, we have to assume he'll find out. It might affect his job, his clients, his reputation. Let's talk about yours. Will the *Times* care about this?"

The paper. Mike still thought that I was on a temporary leave of absence from the paper. I considered using this video as my excuse but dismissed that thought. We had enough lies between us already. "I was fired, before this happened. The paper isn't taking me back."

He took it well, drawing a thin line through the words *Lillian's job* in the aftereffects column. He moved to the next item, and for once, I was grateful he was so devoid of human emotion. "On my front, it's personally embarrassing, but I don't think any of my clients or coworkers will care. Other than a weakening of my perceived masculine attributes, there should not be any financial repercussions, assuming that this video doesn't go viral and isn't followed up by more—"

"Mike, can we not do this?" I interrupted, holding up my hand. "We don't even know where our son is. I can't deal with a spreadsheet of action items right now."

I should have just let him do it, should have understood that he was working through his emotions in the best way that he knew how—but I couldn't. I couldn't dissect and analyze all the ways that my actions were going to affect my family. I couldn't listen to the fallout before it came.

I didn't wait for a response. Just as he had done earlier, I stood up and walked out.

CHAPTER 35

MIKE

I had two issues in front of me, and an internet video of my wife whoring it up wasn't my biggest concern. That would get taken down. Jacob would man up and get over it. Lillian would behave, thanks to this punishment.

David Laurent, on the other hand, needed to be handled. Delicately handled, without Lillian's awareness or any red flags.

Did he have to die? That was the first question on my list, and still had a blank beside it.

I hoped not. The aftermath of death was always a bitch of loose ends.

CHAPTER 36
LILLIAN

I woke up with a sense of doom. Kicking off my covers, I stared up at the ceiling fan of the guest room, which needed to be replaced. There was a sticker of a heart on one fan blade, a carryover from when the room had been a young girl's bedroom.

I hadn't slept in the guest room in years, not since I had the flu and quarantined myself in an attempt to keep the others from getting sick. Now I'd quarantined myself due to the scorn. Mike and Jacob might be silent, but I could still feel their disdain, thickening the air and clogging my chest to a point where it felt impossible to breathe.

At two o'clock, Mike and I had an appointment with Amy Kluckman, an attorney who specialized in internet defamation. Legal representation was an item on Mike's list, and I was dreading the event and all the questions the lawyer would have for me.

At least Jacob had come home last night. At almost one in the morning, his car had pulled into the drive and he had slunk from the Volkswagen into the house, his sweatshirt hood up, hands in the pockets, a clear sign that he didn't want to talk. I'd watched him from the living room window, and when he entered the side door, I stayed in the corner as he practically sprinted up the stairs and to his bedroom.

I could have slept in our room. After I had confronted him about his affair, Mike continued to sleep in our bed, his back to me, a wall of pillows between us. I could have taken my normal place and stared at my bedside table, with the chip in the corner of the wood and the tissue box that blocks the glare of the clock. I had considered it and hesitated at the bedroom door, my hand on the knob. I'd jerked away, hating the thought of lying in bed and feeling the weight of his judgment.

All night long, I had struggled for sleep, the hours stretching by slowly as my mind had tried to sort through the complicated layers of guilt and the mystery of who, why, and how this had happened.

I kept getting stuck on how we would move forward, past this. Mike and I were both guilty in this marriage. Maybe he had been the initial unfaithful one, but I dove into the sinful waters with him, and now Jacob was being punished for my crime.

I crushed the pillow to my face and screamed, a long howl of frustration, because while I could confess my sins to Jacob and apologize, I couldn't—shouldn't—tell him what his father had done. While it might make me feel better for Jacob to hate us both, it wasn't about my feelings or justifications for my actions. It was about our son and trying to make this easier for him, and that sort of self-sacrifice . . . tasted like rotten cheese in my mouth.

I groaned and tossed the pillow to one side. Unplugging my phone from the charger, I refreshed the TikTok link that Mike had texted me last night.

The video was still up and now had 239 likes and almost 300 comments. I was staring at the screen, my heart sinking past the cramp in my stomach, when I heard Sam call out a hello from downstairs.

———

I bolted from the bed and toward the stairs. Scrambling down the flight, I rounded the final step and flung myself into his arms. Gripping him tightly, I started to cry.

"Hey, hey," he shushed as he carried me into the living room and lowered me onto the love seat. I sank into the leather and clung to his side.

"Did Mike call you?" I sniffed.

"A friend of mine sent me the link." He winced. "Lill—"

"I know. It's bad."

Sam carefully untangled himself from my grip. "Stay," he commanded, as if I were a dog. "I'm going to get you a Xanax."

I didn't argue, grateful for a friend with pharmaceutical connections. From the kitchen, I heard the ice maker, then the crinkle of a water bottle. He returned, with a glass and a small yellow pill. "Here. Take this and take a deep breath. You're shaking."

I needed something stronger than water. Vodka or, better yet, tequila. He nudged the glass toward me, and I took it. "Jacob'll never forgive me." I placed the pill on my tongue, then drank half the glass.

Sam was still standing there, and my gratitude to him dipped slightly at the judgmental look on his face. "This is where you tell me that I'm wrong, and he'll get over this within a week."

"He's a teenager. He doesn't—and won't—understand adult relationships, not for a while. He's going to be pissed, Lill. That's just how this is going to go. He's going to be mad and embarrassed, and it's going to last awhile."

He was right, which only made me more despondent. I moved to the couch and collapsed on the dark leather.

"Any words of wisdom?" I asked as I waited for the antianxiety medication to kick in. I should have called him and gotten one of these last night. I had stared up at the guest room ceiling for hours, my mind racing through how big a disaster this was.

There was, after all, the giant bomb that it had delivered to my marriage. But there was also, pathetically, the side effect to my secret life. It wouldn't survive this. There was no way that I could return to the docks, to David, after this. I would be spitting on my family every single time I made that choice, instead of staying home and focusing on my marriage and our son.

And the horrible, horrible thing of it was that loss of David, of my life as Taylor—that hurt as much as my guilt over Jacob's pain. The level of my selfishness, of my self-absorbed focus, was disgusting. I hated myself, even as I continued to mourn the loss.

"How's Mike handling this? Has he threatened to leave?"

I waved away the thought. "You know Mike. He's making a list. Attacking the problem."

The Xanax was starting to work, and I let out a soft, contented sigh.

Sam eyed me with concern and held out a tissue. "Have you been taking your medication?"

"Yes," I snapped—even though I hadn't taken my antidepressant or my mood stabilizer yet this morning, or yesterday. In the last few weeks, I'd taken it less frequently, my time with David bringing me a happy high that I hadn't experienced in years. The buzz of a new relationship was a drug in itself, and probably helped out by the vitamin D and endorphins of my new job.

Right now, what I needed was a drink. Something to distract me from all this. I used the tissue and then let it fall to the floor. Sam's eyes followed the drop. He tried to stay in his seat, but his neat-freak habits couldn't resist—and he dipped to pick it up. He was so much like Mike. Why, in my past, had I gravitated toward such precise men? Was that why I liked David? Was it his charming ease and disarray?

There was a quote about that. Something about beauty in chaos. My life had had no chaos. Maybe I'd intentionally created my own, with the vandalism to Fran's car and my affair.

Affair. Such a dirty word. It hadn't felt like an affair. Taylor had felt like a role I was playing, one that wasn't real and would eventually end, but that didn't have actual consequences or lasting effects.

Obviously, that had been wishful thinking on my part. "The video's been up for almost a day. Do you know someone who can get it taken down?"

"Do I know someone at TikTok?" Sam carried the tissue to the kitchen trash can and repeated the question slowly, as if it were a dumb one. "No, I don't."

"I thought you do ads or something for your houses on there."

"I do, but that doesn't mean that I have a personal connection there. The ads are self-serve."

Whatever that meant.

"Did you report the video?" He started to run the water at the sink, and I knew without watching that he was obsessively soaping up every knuckle and palm, plus on and under each nail. He was a man who wore driving gloves for no other reason than to protect his palms and steering wheel from unnecessary damage. I felt a sudden surge of anger over the water, which was still running—had my tissue been that germy?

He reappeared in the doorway and dried off each finger with a red hand towel. "So? Did you report it?"

"I don't know. Mike or Jacob probably did." I was still in the clothes I'd slept in, and I discreetly sniffed my shirt. I needed a shower. Maybe I'd grab a smoke first. A smoke and a drink. I straightened in the seat, embracing the idea.

"Well, I reported it as nudity, but I'm not sure if that will stick. Whoever edited the video was smart. There's a lot of innuendo there, but not anything more than PG-rated content." Sam folded the hand towel into thirds, then in half.

I pulled myself upright and stood, ready to move Sam along. "Jacob's full name is in the description; isn't that illegal? He's still a minor." I took the hand towel from him, carried it into the kitchen, and returned it back to its hook.

"Jacob Smith is a common name. Any of his friends would recognize you, and he's tagged in the comments, but . . . it's a video of two adults kissing and some really bad drunk dancing. No one would care about it, other than someone with a personal connection to you or the guy."

Someone with a personal connection to me or the guy.

"His name is David," I said faintly. I needed to figure out who had posted the video. Had that been an item on Mike's list? It should have been.

"Sure—David." Sam was watching me like I was an exposed wire that should be capped off. I glared at him and he looked away. "You should see an attorney."

"Yeah, we're meeting one at two."

"You and Mike?" Sam shook his head. "I can't believe he's *not* freaking out about you cheating."

I tried not to bristle at the *C* word. "Like I said, he has a plan. You know Mike. We're going to 'get through this together'!" I made air quotes around Mike's words.

Despite my bitter tone, I would follow whatever solution Mike proposed. When it came to making plans and controlling risks, Mike was always rational and levelheaded. And . . . I, at this point, was one well-placed poke away from losing my sanity. Other than regularly refreshing the video—which was still up—I wasn't contributing anything helpful to this disaster, and I knew that. I didn't mind pushing all my problems onto Mike's side of the table and letting him reorganize the issues into neat and compartmentalized boxes. Maybe we'd have to move. Enroll Jacob in a new school. Cut and dye my hair.

"Well . . ." Sam glanced at his watch and then planted a kiss on my forehead. "It seems like you have everything under control."

Thank goodness. He was leaving. I gave him my best attempt at a grateful smile and waved. "I'll call you later," I promised.

When he pulled the door shut, I went to the cabinet beside the microwave and pulled out the orange bottles that held my meds. Then I opened the fridge and considered my opinions. Bottled spring water. Milk. Sodas. Beers. I forced myself to grab a water.

Twisting open the first cap, I eyed the medication. I was feeling off, but the urge for a smoke and drink was outweighing the swing of emotion that the pill would bring.

From upstairs, my phone rang, its WhatsApp ringtone so faint that I almost missed it. Leaving the water on the counter, I ran up the stairs but got to it a minute too late, missing David's call.

I stared at my cell but didn't return the call.

Maybe he'd had us filmed. Maybe, in this fairy tale, he was the wolf in the sheep's clothing and I . . .

I yawned, then blinked rapidly, jumping in place a little to wake myself back up. Too mellow. I'd have to do something about that.

CHAPTER 37

LILLIAN

I fell victim to the cigarettes first—hunting down and finding a pack of Virginia Slims in the laundry room, hidden behind a box of dryer sheets. I withdrew two and smoked them in the backyard, behind the tree that still had a swing rope hanging from its largest branch. I'd pushed Jacob on that swing. I'd shown him how to spin, how to tuck his legs to increase the speed. That was back when we were close, before he hit his teenage years and became too cool for his mother, too interested in things that I had no knowledge or understanding of.

I hid the cigarette stubs in a rotten knot in the tree and replaced the box in the laundry room. I was chewing a piece of gum and washing my hands when Jacob came in the back door and stopped, startled to see me. "Hey."

"Hey."

"Your car isn't out front," he accused.

"Oh, your dad probably took it. I blocked him in when I got home last night." In my hurry, I had parked at an angle that would have made it impossible for Mike to get his Volvo out of the garage. I glanced at the key hooks by the garage door and confirmed that my keys were missing.

Jacob edged toward the stairs. "Well, I was just getting something from my room. I'm staying at Dijon's tonight."

"Wait." I caught his wrist and gripped it. If he had to drag me up the stairs, we were going to have this conversation. "I need to talk to you."

"I really don't want to talk to you."

"Well, you have to talk to me." I dug my nails into the soft skin of his wrist and he winced.

"Ow," he said pointedly. "That hurts."

"Look, I screwed up. Okay? I'm sorry. Your father and I are working to get the video down. We'll do everything we can to fix this."

He grabbed my fingers and pried them off his wrist, bending them backward until I was forced to let go or risk a broken finger. "Yeah, how are you going to do that, Mom? You don't even understand social media. You going to go to school and fight the assholes for me too? This can't be fixed, and no one's ever going to forget it. Ever."

He climbed the first few steps and then paused, looking down at me. "Oh, and Mom?" He spat out my name like it was the most despicable thing in the world.

"Yeah?" I asked weakly.

"Screw you for cheating on Dad."

He stomped up the stairs and I just stood there, my fingers throbbing from his rough handling. All those words inside me, and I had nothing.

CHAPTER 38

LILLIAN

I spun a pill on the table, then placed it on my tongue, then leaned forward and spit it out. I could feel myself slipping, and I needed Mike to be home, needed him to pin me in place and yell at me to take my damn pill and stop feeling sorry for myself.

I called his cell and hung up when I got his voice mail. I took a shower, then checked the video—still up—and headed for the good liquor, which Mike kept locked in a hidden and climate-controlled cabinet in the pantry. The key was hidden in a fake can of pumpkin filling that Jacob wouldn't touch if he were on a deserted island. I made sure that his car was gone, then popped out the false bottom and stood on a case of bottled water to open the cabinet. I was reaching for a bottle of tequila when I saw the wooden box at the back, tucked behind a row of whiskeys. *The twentieth-anniversary bottle of Benromach.* Mike had bought the special-edition bourbon when we were on a weekend trip to San Francisco, and we were waiting to open it on our own twentieth anniversary, which was still two years away.

I grabbed the wooden box and pulled it out, staring at the label and remembering how in love with him I'd been on that trip. It had been three weeks after the miscarriage, and he'd been especially accommodating and loving. I remembered him cradling me in bed and telling me that he'd protect me from anything, that he'd love me forever, and I had clung to both promises with pathetic and needy claws. Now I ran the edge of my nail along the box's seal, then folded back the top.

Well, it was open now. I might as well pull out the bottle and take a sip. Mike would be hurt. Furious. I warmed to the idea, to the middle finger that it would give to our marriage. While I should have chugged it the night I confronted him—that would have been more poignant— it wasn't too late to do it now. I pulled out the bottle, twisted off the lid, and took one small, vindictive sip. Mike was the reason we were in this situation, I reminded myself. *Him.* David and I, while wrong, were a side effect of his cheating, his dismissal of me, of a hundred nights when I was ignored and he was with her, or them, or however many women there had been.

I took my pill with another sip, returned the bottle to the box and placed it inside my purse, then locked the cabinet and rehid the key. There was a cemetery five blocks down, one with big trees and wooden benches. It would be the perfect place to toast the end of my marriage.

Screw you for cheating on Dad. No, Jacob. Screw him for cheating on us.

Halfway to the cemetery, I grew thirsty, my mouth dry, a side effect of taking my medication without food. Waiting at a crosswalk, I opened a granola bar and crunched it as I walked, my steps increasing in speed as I saw the arched gates of the cemetery lot. This was an older one, moss covering many of the stones, the plots abandoned by families and forgotten by most. Unlike Lenny's, this lot didn't have a full-time caretaker, though I occasionally saw a city worker making the rounds with a grass trimmer in hand. It was a place I often came when I wanted some solace. I climbed a small hill to my favorite bench and took a seat. Pulling out the box of Benromach, I called David through the app.

"Hi, love." He sounded like he was smiling, and I could picture him walking down the dock, one hand in his pocket, that easy smile on his face, his sunglasses on against the bright sun.

"Someone filmed a video of us and posted it on social media." I flipped open the box and slid the bottle out. Placing the box on the ground, I twisted off the lid and took a swig. *Was it you?* I wanted to shout, but accusing David was stupid. Why would David do that, unless . . . unless he was trying to break up my marriage. It was a valid possibility, and I pinched my eyes shut and tried to forensically analyze his tone.

"What kind of video?" Wary. Concerned. Guilty? Maybe.

I cleared my throat. "It's from the night we went to dinner. It's of us dancing on the boat deck. We're kissing and there's some petting. They set it to music and referenced my son in the comments. His friends are having a field day."

"Are you or I tagged in it?" If I'd expected him to be concerned about Jacob—and I had expected that—I was wrong. David's focus had flipped right past my son's emotional and social standing and landed on himself. Himself and, I guess, me. The video had Jacob's full name on it, I reminded myself. David had never asked my last name, and I wasn't sure whether I'd ever referred to Jacob as anything other than "my son."

"Are you or I tagged in it?" he repeated.

"No." I pushed my sunglasses up on the bridge of my nose. "So Mike and I will, ah . . . handle it from here. We're meeting with an attorney today to see what our options are. It's already been reported, so hopefully it'll be down soon." No need to mention the *More to come* description on the video.

"Do you know who filmed and posted it?"

My suspicions that he was involved waned at his innocent—yes, most definitely innocent—tone. Tilting the liquor back, I took a long sip before answering. "No, we don't know."

"But you don't need me to do anything? Can you send me the link?"

Talk about embarrassing, for him as well as me. "Yeah." I grimaced. "It's bad. At least it is for me. You probably won't care." Maybe he'd even enjoy it. Proof of his playboy lifestyle.

"What did Mike ask about me? Did you tell him who I was?" In the background of his call, I heard the familiar beep of the ship forklift and felt a sudden pang of nostalgia. Already, I missed it. Already, it was gone.

I pushed the emotion aside. "I told him your basic details. His focus is on Jacob and getting the video down. But I won't be coming back to the marina for a while. I have to see how this plays out."

"Of course." He sounded relieved, and I took another sip from the bottle to distract me from the way that made me feel. That was the problem with my medication. It could swing me gushy or emotionally vacant, with no predictable path. "Absolutely." He sounded almost cheerful, and the tone made me want to crawl through the phone and slice off his tongue.

"Okay. Bye." I hung up before he had a chance to respond, because I was terrified that he wouldn't respond—that he would just hit "End," and that would be the last word on our affair.

We'd been together over six weeks, and it felt like he'd just tossed me aside like a bad one-night stand. I took another sip and placed the bottle on the bench, then opened his contact on my phone. I scrolled down to the "Block" button and clicked it.

I should have blocked him on my own, and not out of the fear that he wouldn't call and wouldn't text. Regardless of my motivation, blocking him relieved me of the knowledge of any future slight—and any temptation to answer his calls.

Reaching for the bottle, I held it out and toasted the empty cemetery. "To assholes," I said quietly, then gripped the bottle with both hands and brought the mouth to my lips and took the longest sip I could manage.

I rolled my neck, my throat burning from the bourbon. It felt accurate, like a brand. *Welcome to hell; we've been expecting you.*

Hello, I thought dreamily, and relaxed back against the bench. *Don't mind me. I'll make myself at home.*

NOW

CHAPTER 39

MIKE

This affair is a problem, and one that may require an interesting and painful solution. My actions have a direct correlation to hers, because unique ideas are not in Lillian's wheelhouse. I lied, so she lied. I cheated, so she cheated.

This is why I keep secrets from my wife. She's too easily knocked off course, susceptible to vices, and emotionally drawn to problems, like a fly to a sticky yellow tape of death.

It was for her own good that my lies first began. Had she known how close we came to losing the house, she would have panicked. Had she known how unhappy I was with our sex life, she would have obsessed.

Had she known, had she known, had she known . . . she surely would have killed herself by now.

So I lie, like all good husbands do. I lie, and I protect her, and I protect Jacob, and I make contingency plans, and I keep all the pieces of our perfect little life ticking along, because that's my job. My job is to provide for and protect my family, by any means necessary.

I'm fucking great at my job.

When I enter the house, forty-five minutes before our appointment at the attorney's, there is ample time for us to drive the two-point-one miles to the office. In my briefcase, I have a printout on everything I know about the video, which, admittedly, isn't much. I went ahead and included a list of our liability policies, in case we are at risk of being sued by David Laurent. I also included a list of our assets, at least the ones that Lillian is aware of, in the event they are also at risk.

The things I don't know—the marina's security protocols and liability exposure, what she has told David Laurent about our life—I will find out. I will relisten to her recordings, do a proper calendar audit and analysis of her movements in the last month, based on her car's GPS activity and phone records. I'll ask Lillian more questions, feeding them to her slowly, so her suspicion isn't aroused. Also on today's agenda, a call to her doctor, as I'm fairly certain that my wife has not been taking her medication.

I call her name from the kitchen, my voice carrying easily through the small house. It is one of the benefits and negatives of the size. We could have bought one ten times bigger, but that would have raised questions should a federal employee come sniffing, plus there is Lillian's intellect, which does pick inconvenient times to raise its head. Though my wife is flaky, she can be very, very smart. It's one of the reasons I fell in love with her. The other was her mothering potential, and I judged that well. She is a fantastic mother, save this hiccup with Jacob.

This fling is certainly a black mark on her, but not entirely unexpected. I should have seen this coming, should have done an effects analysis and then blocked the possibility—but in addition to intellect and her parenting skills, Lillian has also been staunchly loyal. That unwavering loyalty lulled me into stupid placidity, and I'd been distracted with the aftermath of ending my other relationship. What was supposed to be easy and clean had ended up being very messy and highly emotional, a situation I had not quite solved, in large part because of Lillian.

There is no response and I take the stairs two at a time, checking my watch as I climb. She should be dressed and ready. I had to call in a favor to get this last-minute appointment, and tardiness will be unacceptable.

The bedroom is empty, as is the guest room. I look in on Jacob's bedroom—empty—and stand at the bathroom window, looking down on the backyard. No sign of Lillian's increasingly slim figure. I frown.

Taking the stairs back down, I check my watch again, my frustration rising as another minute clicks by. I open the garage and stare at my car, which is still sitting in its spot, its keys on the hook. After she blocked me in last night, I took her car, but there's no reason why if she went somewhere, she wouldn't have taken mine.

I try her cell and it goes straight to voice mail.

Where is she?

CHAPTER 40

MIKE

I park her car in the garage and swap the keys on the hooks, then take mine and leave the house at twenty minutes before two, without Lillian. I text her the address without much hope. Is she with him? She's with someone, unless she went for a run—and Lillian hasn't been a runner since her bout with anorexia almost twelve years ago. A walk also seems unlikely, unless it is to the liquor store or the gas station, and I drive by both on my way to the attorney's office but don't see her.

Her purse, upon further recollection, wasn't in the kitchen or living room, so she probably has it with her. This is why we should have a family app, the sort that tracks locations and speed of travel. Unfortunately, it was hard to require that of my family without me also opting in, and there is no way that I will ever be voluntarily tracked.

I pull into the attorney's office and park on the far side of the lot, not so close to the street as to be potentially hit by traffic but not so close to the building as to risk a door ding. The Volvo is alone on both sides and parked nose out, in case the need for a quick exit arises—not that there has ever been a need for a quick exit, but you have to prepare for any circumstances, on every day, at all times.

Lillian would have parked crooked in the closest spot to the front door and forgotten to lock the doors. My wife is not a preparer, and maybe that's why I fell in love with her. The beast and the beauty. Organization and chaos. Dark and light.

I check in with a receptionist three minutes before the appointment time and try not to let the last-minute arrival bother me. It is overshadowed by the fact that Lillian is not here, and I try her cell again, but get only voice mail.

———

The attorney has a flat chest and acne scars pitting her cheeks and jowls, the sort of woman who has become mean just to survive the cruel reception of life. She watches the video twice, then returns the phone to me. "Where is your wife, Mr. Smith?"

"I'm not sure. She was going to meet me here, but is probably running late." I smile to overcome Lill's rudeness. "But we can proceed without her. I have our list of questions."

It's really only my list of questions. Lillian doesn't want to hear about the steps necessary to make this go away. She prefers to theoretically clamp her hands over her ears and spout loud gibberish to drown out the reality of her situations. This isn't the first time she has screwed up. She doesn't realize the extents I've gone to, to pull her out of harm and financial strife. She thinks that life just turns and unfolds in easy ways, ways where problems magically disappear and people give up on arguments, and frowns eventually turn upside down.

"Before you start on your list, let me ask a few quick questions." The attorney swivels her chair left, then right, and laces her fingers over her concave stomach. "The woman on the video is your wife?"

"Yes."

"The man is who?"

"David Laurent. He has a company that screen-prints T-shirts. He lives in Nevada but visits LA on a regular basis, according to Lillian." No need to mention the other things I've dug up on David Charles Laurent, whose paper trail was clear and easy to follow. A Fresno business head-quarters and personal address, no tax liens or bankruptcies. Unmarried. No kids. No social media, which I didn't like. While I would have hated my wife screwing a selfie-posting asshole, social media was a trail that I could follow and analyze.

"He knows about the video?"

"I don't know."

"This has been an ongoing affair, or is this a one-night-stand sort of thing?" She snaps out the questions in quick succession, unconcerned with tact, and I appreciate that.

"Ongoing affair. One month in."

"And the Jacob Smith that's mentioned in the video and in the video's description, that's your son?"

"Yes."

"Biological child to both of you?"

"Yes."

"Any chance he's not your son?"

"No."

She purses her orange-red painted lips and nods, and I can tell that she isn't convinced of the fact. I don't care. I had a DNA test done as soon as he was born—not because I was worried about Lillian cheating but because surprises cause problems, and you should know all potential problems before they arise.

I flatten my list out on the table. "May I begin my questions?"

CHAPTER 41

MIKE

On the way back to the house, Sam calls. Irritated, I send him to voice mail. Lillian will surely be at home, fixing dinner with a blank look and a thin excuse for why she missed the attorney meeting. No matter— I found out what I needed to know. Our liability is nil, as are our chances of catching the asshole who did this. I wrote a hefty check for a retainer, and Amy will file a motion today demanding that the video be taken down and that any information on the uploader be given to law enforcement.

I don't have high hopes for them getting info on the uploader. Possibly an IP address, but that could be easily manipulated or shielded. In the attorney's office, I had huffed and puffed about the ridiculousness of personal protections, but in truth, I'm grateful for them. As inconvenient as they are in this particular situation, they are enormously helpful in my day-to-day life.

Right now, I need to compartmentalize my thoughts on the tasks ahead of me because there are many of them. I've presented to Lillian a hefty list of potential side effects, but I have a secondary list that I'm keeping from her. On that list, I've outlined how this could possibly affect my business.

I call Jacob, and he picks up on the second ring, his anger not extending to me. "Hey."

"Have you talked to your mother?"

"Like, this morning."

"What time?"

"I don't know." The sound of an automatic weapon sounds in the background. "Maybe like ten thirty?"

"Okay. Are you at home?"

"No, I'm at Dijon's. We're playing *Call of Duty.*"

"Why don't you eat dinner with him? I'll see you when you get home."

"Yeah, sure."

I hang up. So they spoke this morning. That's one step in the right direction. Lillian can update me on the temperature of the conversation. I try her cell again and growl in frustration when it goes to voice mail. Okay. That's fine. A short hiccup of time. Nothing to get upset over. This is Lillian, after all. Unreliability is her norm.

A voice mail from Sam arrives, and I play it.

"It's me. I haven't been able to reach Lill. I spoke to her earlier today and she seemed a little . . . undone. I think she's off her meds. Let me know if you've talked to her, and if she's all right."

I tighten my grip on the steering wheel. Sam knows better than to call me about something like this. Lillian, we had agreed, would be my responsibility, though Sam never seems to stay in his lane where she is concerned.

And that's the problem with people. They don't stay where you put them, not unless they are dead.

I eye the dash clock and take the exit for my office. I have time to do a little bit of business before dinner.

CHAPTER 42

LILLIAN

I wake up on the cemetery bench, and it's dark outside. *Shit.* How did I fall asleep out here? I was drinking the anniversary bourbon and then . . . I pinch my eyes closed and try to remember anything past that point. I creak up to a sitting position and look for my purse, my anxiety spiking when I realize that it isn't on the bench, or on the ground, or anywhere in the vicinity. Which is expected, because it's Los Angeles, and I'm lucky I'm wearing all my clothes and still alive.

I groan at the thought of what was in my purse: the bourbon—who cares; my pills—meh, take 'em; my wallet—crap. My keys . . . I brighten at the fact that Mike has my keys since he took my car today. Perfect. My cell phone is another wince-worthy loss, but my photos were backed up to the cloud, and Mike has insurance on it. We are nothing if not well insured.

I glance around, suddenly concerned that my purse thief is nearby, wanting more. There are black pockets of shadow around the trees, the gravestones casting black fingers under the moonlight; there's a chill in the air; and—for the first time in ages—the empty graveyard creeps me out.

I stand and brush off my pants, then quickly start the walk home.

I'm passing the Martins' two-story home when I realize that I missed the attorney's appointment. Cursing, I check my watch, but the numbers swim in my vision. Hopefully it's only six or seven. Mike must have gone to the attorney without me, and he'll be pissed. I'll get that look, the exasperated one where he doesn't understand what's wrong with me, then the cold shoulder where he tabulates a list of my transgressions for later analysis.

He used to not be so . . . stiff. When we met, he was almost meek. The quiet nerd who was staring at me in the bookstore. He brought me flowers on our first date. Blushed after our first kiss. Carefully applied a Band-Aid with military precision when I tripped getting out of his car and skinned my knee.

The transition was steep, after graduation, and has plateaued and spiked, as major events passed by. Jacob's birth. The purchase of this home. His promotion at work. The start of my depression. The drinking. The medications.

Maybe he had to become this way, so parental, so overbearing, just to keep us in order. There is that, about him. Despite the increasing emotional vacancy, he is a rock that our marriage—our family—leans on, one that often pins us into place when we grow shaky.

I get to the house and he's in the office, on the phone. I wait in the doorway for him to stop talking, and when there is a pause, I speak. "I'm sorry about the attorney. I lost track of time."

He stares through me, his jaw set, eyes flat. I hesitate. "Have you eaten?"

"Yes," he snaps. "Of course."

I can't tell if he's talking to me or to the person on the phone, and decide it doesn't matter. I head to the kitchen but feel a wave of light-headedness and decide to sit, for just a moment, on the floor.

When I wake up, all the lights are off and Mike is gone.

CHAPTER 43

FRENCHY

The sun rises above the horizon slowly, yawning over the black ocean, half-hidden by clouds, its rays tinting the dunes in pale peach. This stretch of sand is a hidden enclave of private homes, too far from public parking for any foot traffic, too flat a stretch of sand for waves. It's why Frenchy chose it. She wanted to lie on a beach without a tourist trampling by, without the shouts and profanity of surfers on the wind.

Surfers are trash. Literally, trash. They drip it everywhere they go, small vials of wax, ziplock baggies, cans of energy drinks, the pull cord of a surfboard. They drag lines through the sand, and set up boom boxes and disrupt the quiet to light bonfires and smoke weed and bang their sand bunnies.

At first, Frenchy thinks the woman is one of them. Someone who partied along the shore last night, wandered too far down, and passed out in the dunes. She sees the curve of the woman on her side, her long hair sandy, her body tucked up against the seagrass.

Frenchy pauses, her tennis shoes already caked with sand, and considers waking her and asking her to leave. Surely the woman won't argue, especially when Frenchy points out that she's on private property. Technically, that isn't true, but none of the stray surfers and tourists ever argue with her when she says that.

Calling the police is another option, but they often dismiss her. It is, after all, public property, and people can sleep on the beach, despite how it ruins Frenchy's day. Sometimes she gets lucky, and an officer is sent out. There's that one beach patrol uniform who always stares at her breasts and does anything she asks, but she hasn't seen him in ages.

She continues on, past the sleeping woman. Maybe she'll leave on her own. After all, it's almost seven. It'll be hot soon. The woman will need to move to the shade, or will grow hungry, or will have to pee, and one of those things will force her into action. Besides, Frenchy has committed to her trainer that she will walk four miles today, and that will never happen unless she focuses on the task and dedicates herself, and look, here she is getting distracted and wasting time.

She heads north with a purpose, her arms pumping, and makes it almost thirty yards before the next item, a green tote bag, catches her eye. It looks expensive, and her steps slow to give it a closer look.

She's right, it is a quality bag, though it looks like it's been out all night. She crouches, tsking at the wet and sandy condition of it. She actually has this same one, but in blue. It's almost empty, and she glances around, seeing a few items—a ChapStick, a tissue packet, a tube of sunscreen—almost buried in the sand. Gathering what she can find, she puts them back in the bag and stands. If this is the woman's, it should be returned to her. It's the perfect excuse to wake her up, and then Frenchy can continue with her exercise, and the beach will return to its quiet and empty solitude.

Decision made, she marches up the sand, her steps as quick as possible, given the heavy traction. "Hellooo!" she calls out. "Excuse me!" Nothing worse than scaring someone. And plus, you never know with these people. She could be a drug addict, or mentally unstable. Frenchy could bend over her and the woman could spring to her feet with a knife and haul her up the empty beach to Frenchy's home. She could force her inside, rob her blind, and kill her.

It happens. Two miles up the road, it happened just last year.

"Hey!" Frenchy stands a safe distance away and waves her arms, the bag swinging from her left hand. "Miss! I have your purse!" It's got to be her bag, right? What are the chances that two women both were on this beach last night?

She risks a step closer, then another. The woman doesn't move. *"Can you hear me?"* Frenchy's shouting now, and there's no way the woman can't hear her. She digs her white tennis shoes into the sand and climbs farther up the dune, at an angle where she can see the woman's face.

Oh. Frenchy stumbles in the loose sand and falls onto her knee, the one that she had surgery on three years ago. She forces herself upright and stares, her dark lips falling open as she studies the woman's slack expression, her eyes open, sandmites already milling around the glassy irises.

The woman hasn't heard Frenchy and won't care about her purse because the woman, just a hundred yards from the back of Frenchy's home, is dead.

CHAPTER 44

MIKE

When I wake up, the house is still empty and the guest room bed is undisturbed, Lillian's phone going straight to voice mail. I take a shower and then begin the old actions. First, I check her call history, which is light. One to Sam. Several to me. Any hope of syncing her affair timeline with phone calls fizzes out, as I realize that there have been no consistent strange numbers in the few weeks I've been monitoring her.

Again, my wife is smart, but the level of preemptive subterfuge in using an internet-based app to place calls—that I wouldn't have expected. Maybe they only texted. I open that window and browse through that history, but again, no red flags.

The potential options are plentiful. They could have communicated through social media. That Twitter account of Lillian's—though recently dormant—is an open portal of communication that I have never been fond of. Thankfully, she has never become one of those Facebook or Instagram moms, though again . . . maybe she has. My lack of attention to her is becoming alarmingly apparent.

I return to her call log, and the last few numbers she dialed yesterday are unfamiliar to me. I open a fresh internet browser and search them.

The first unfamiliar call is to a taxi company, which is interesting. My wife has a car app on her phone, one that alerts me to any usage.

There would have been little need for a taxi, if she'd been too drunk to drive.

I type in the second number, then double-check and enter it again. I frown. It's a hotline for a battered women's shelter, which doesn't make sense. Did Lillian meet someone and decide to help them out? That would explain the taxi and this call, though the first thing she should have done, in this circumstance, was to call me. Lillian isn't equipped to help herself out of holes, much less others.

I scroll down to the next phone number, and something taps on the side of my skull. Intuition, rapping hard and fast, a tap-tap-tap that something is about to turn south.

I pause my wifely research and check my phone, then my email. There is a new message from the attorney, who reports that the video is now taken down, and the user account is blocked from posting anything else. I text the update to Jacob, then turn to the dark web and check my other accounts. All monies are still in place. My message portal is empty. Nothing to raise an alarm, yet I have the distinct feeling that I have forgotten something, somewhere—a loose thread I didn't sew shut, a pothole I didn't fill, a lie I didn't sniff out and uncover.

I sit there for a moment, staring into nothing, and carefully retrace my steps over the last twenty-four hours, but there are no missteps there. I have been flawless in my execution, as I almost always am.

To be safe, I do a second mental examination, but get the same result. Forcing the worry out of my mind, I do an internet search on the third phone number.

It is for the *Times*, and I digest that information slowly, ticking my chair minutely from left to right as I try to work through who and why Lillian would call her former employer. Plenty of reasons. Paycheck had an error. To check on her benefits. Reach a coworker. Renew our subscription. No reason for that to raise a red flag.

Still, in the back of my head, my paranoia knocks even louder.

CHAPTER 45

LILLIAN

God, it's a beautiful day. Everything seems brighter and happier, though fuzzy around the edges, and I applaud myself for jumping back into my medication. Why did I ever stop it? I break from my admiration of the fall leaves, which are starting to flutter from our backyard tree with slow and patient sweeps, when I hear Mike's voice from the office. He hasn't heard me come in, and I almost call out, but his voice is low and urgent and I tiptoe closer to the office door, curious who he is talking to. At the sound of his concerned tone, my stomach twists, like a vampire recoiling from the sun.

This has to be *her*. I'm gone for a day and he calls her first, like a sheepdog checking on his charges and making sure one hasn't scampered too far from the herd.

I step over the creaky board where the kitchen flooded a year ago, the board that was supposed to be replaced when we redid the floors, but that project was held off until our next chunk of money came in. Money that could have been his bonuses (*two* employee-of-the-month bonuses!), yet he spent it on something else. I clench my fists and try to push the anger aside long enough to catch his next lie.

I hear the words *call log* and *departments* and frown, confused. Maybe this isn't her. He's using the stiff and formal tone he uses when interacting with strangers. My anger deflates a little, and to be honest, it's a little disappointing to not have a little dirt to help me retake the upper moral ground.

Someone raps sharply on the front door, and it's the sort of authoritative knock that matches the feel of an IRS letter in the mailbox. Mike's chair squeaks as he stands, and I quickly backtrack a few steps so my eavesdropping won't be noticeable. I'm back in the kitchen by the time he hurries out of the office and toward the front door.

"Oh hey," I say breezily, but he doesn't hear me and is beelining for the front door. I follow him and catch a glimpse of the street through the front window and freeze, a half dozen steps behind him. "Mike," I say faintly. "It's the police."

It's a waste of breath because he's already opening the door, and my fears spike when I see the tight looks on the two officers' faces.

"Mr. Smith?"

Oh my God. *Jacob.* My beautiful, perfect child. They wouldn't come here if he was in the hospital. They would come here only if it was worse. I told Mike; I told Mike this was a risk.

I try to grip Mike's arm but can't. I try to swing the door open farther, to push beside him so that I can hear, but I can't.

"I'm sorry to tell you this, but your wife, Lillian Smith, was found this morning in north Malibu . . ."

"What?" I try to understand what they are saying about me, and then it clicks, and in one sharp moment, I realize why everything feels so strange.

I'm dead.

CHAPTER 46

MIKE

There will be a time for mourning, but this is not it. I take the news with a curt nod, then shut the door and return to the office. Starting a fresh list, I consider the arrangements that need to be made. Jacob is the first item to be handled. I need to locate him, get him home, and handle the fallout. Unfortunately, this is the area that Lillian always excelled in. I don't know how to handle grief, and my parenting limits have already been stretched with his embarrassment from the video.

I consider Lillian's mother for the task, then groan at the realization that I will need to alert her as well. Same with my parents and her friends, what few she had.

Sam could be the one to handle all that. *Yes.* The idea grows legs. A grief-stricken husband wouldn't be expected to deal with all that. And once Sam finishes sobbing over Lillian, he'll probably enjoy it. He's the one who always prides himself on his insight into and manipulation of human behavior.

The next task is burial and funeral plans. I open the top file drawer and move down the alphabetic tabs to *D—Death*. There is one folder for Lillian, and one for me. Lillian has never reviewed mine, has always left those details to me. If she ever had grabbed my folder, she would have been surprised at how thin it is. Inside, there is just a business card for Frank, my attorney. Frank, who would accept a call from Lillian only if I were dead. At that point, my dear wife would have found out the truth about everything.

Could she have handled it? Now we'll never know.

Inside Lillian's death folder is information about her plot and her casket, all prepurchased. She actually has two plots. The first I purchased more than a dozen years ago, in a very respectable cemetery that has low maintenance fees and guaranteed upkeep. I've never told her about that plot, and was irritated when, six years ago, she announced that she would be buried in Angelus Rosedale Cemetery and had already put down a deposit on two plots—hers and mine—in the upper section.

I had been gracious and accommodating—*oh sure, honey, you know best*—but set a quarterly reminder to check on her payments and see when she lost interest in the purchase. Shockingly enough, she never did, and the plots were paid off within three years.

The next pages are her life insurance policies. There are three, two whole-life and one term policy, which total $6 million. Suicide is a disqualifier for one of the policies, and I set that one aside and mentally cross those $2 million off my mental tally.

Four million dollars will be nice. It's documentable, taxable income that will allow Jacob and me to move into a substantial home, without raising pesky questions about source and documentation.

I line the pages up in a neat, orderly row, then relax back in the chair and put my hands behind my head and stretch out my shoulders.

For a moment, I feel the pain of loss, the dawning understanding that I will never hold her, see her smile, listen to her laugh.

I push past it.

CHAPTER 47

LENNY

I'm sitting in the landscaping hut, at the cramped desk they keep there, when the walkie-talkie on the desk crackles and Abigal's voice comes through. I'm not asleep, but I do have my eyes closed and I've lost track of my thoughts, so it takes me a minute and I miss the first thing that she says.

"Repeat that." I rub both eyes and try to focus on the face of my watch. My sight is going, and it's fuzzy, unless I hold it farther away than my arm is long.

"We need a plot prepped. Number 102."

"Ten-four." I ease to my feet and grab the place card I'll put on the stake used to mark the grave for the funeral home. "Name?"

"Got a pen?" Abigal is an annoying mix of helpful and overhelpful, the result of a retired kindergarten teacher not understanding that grown adults can, in fact, do things on their own.

"Yes. Name?"

"Lillian Smith. That's with an *L*. L-i-l-l-i-a-n. Smith."

My pen freezes and I raise my gaze to the cemetery map pinned to the wall above the shelf of pesticides. At that distance, my eyes can see just fine, and I confirm what my gut already tells me to be true—that

102 is a plot on Marcella's side of the lot. Not the most desirable area, which is why Lillian was able to easily get a twin set.

"Are you sure you want to be over here?" I squinted at her in the harsh California sun. "There's two nice plots on the other side, right under the palms."

She lay on the grass and spread her arms and legs wide, then sighed contentedly. "Yep. This is good."

We didn't discuss Marcella, thirty plots over, with an empty grave beside her, waiting for me. I just nodded. "I'll have the office do the paperwork."

It had been a nice gesture, one that I had never thought I would see in action. One that I never should have seen in action. I am, after all, just waiting for a chance to die. I'm hoping my liver goes out, but each doctor's visit delivers the same grim news—healthy. *Healthy as a horse!* the last doctor cackled, as if that were something to celebrate.

"You got that, Lenny? Lillian Smith, plot 102."

"Yeah." I set down the pen because I can't write her name down. Not without a stiff drink. I pull the bottom drawer of the desk and withdraw the bottle of Hendrick's, still in the liquor store bag. Twisting off the lid, I forgo normal efforts and bring the bottle directly to my lips and take a long, needed drink.

CHAPTER 48

LILLIAN

I'm starting to understand my limitations. I can't move things. No one can hear me. I can move in and out of places and to and from locations by just thinking of them. I realize now that Mike never saw or heard me when I went home from the cemetery.

I seem to be stuck, with no memory of how I died, and with nothing to do but watch the never-ending channels of real life. The colors are duller now than they were earlier, the sounds softer. Everything is starting to fade, which makes me think that soon, I will disappear entirely.

While I am contemplating this, Jacob walks in and drops his backpack on the table. Hitching his pants higher, he starts up the stairs, his head bobbing to some music on his headphones.

Oh no. I follow him as he checks something on his phone. He doesn't know, and I'm tempted to fade away, to shield myself from this.

Mike calls his name and Jacob groans at the top of the stairs. "What?" he shouts down.

"Come here."

No, Mike. You should go up to his room, should deliver the news somewhere other than the dining room. Then again, is there ever a good place to tell your son that his mother is dead?

Jacob takes his time, changing his shirt first and pulling off one shoe, then the other. My anxiety rises as he plugs his phone into the charger, his face insolent as he intentionally drags out the trip downstairs. He's pushing Mike's buttons, but this isn't the time, and I cling close to him, inhaling the scent of him, unsure how long I will be able to experience it.

By the time he makes his way slowly down the stairs, one foot thudding before the other, I am crying, as much for myself as for him. Our last conversation was a fight. That video . . . Will that be the last imprint of me on his mind?

I won't be at his wedding.

Won't hold his child.

I won't be able to give him advice on life, or love, or college, or anything, ever again.

I didn't know. I didn't realize that that conversation would be our last. If I had, I wouldn't have let him go. I would have begged him for forgiveness. I would have forced him to listen to me, and then I would have given him every piece of wisdom that I had.

Now Mike delivers the news with slow, carefully chosen words. He probably practiced them in the office before Jacob got home, emphasizing different words in different combinations to see how they delivered. The winner still hits sour on my ears. *Your mom was found on the beach. It looks like an overdose. We're waiting on more information.*

I'm shaking my head because an overdose can't be right, but I will have to deal with that later. Right now my focus is on Jacob, who has sat down at the dining room table, in the chair I normally use, and his hands are in his lap, and he's not looking at Mike. He's looking at the table, and I can see a shell shuttering around him, like a beach house boarded up before a storm.

"Are they sure it's her?" He's not crying, and that's the Mike in him. The complete swallow of emotion, the energy focused on the diagnosis and next steps. "A lot of people look like her. People are always saying that she looks like that actress. The one from *Weeds*. Maybe it's that woman."

I try to touch his shoulder and I can't.

"I'm going to the station to identify her body, so I'll make sure— but the police are certain. She's wearing the clothes that your mom was last seen in."

The clothes I was last seen in. I close my eyes and try to remember the last thing I was wearing, but I can't even remember what I did yesterday.

Then Jacob lets out a sound, a stiff gasp, and as I watch helplessly, his flat features seize, then crack, and my stoic boy, my boy who never cries at anything, begins to loudly sob, and watching it is the single worst moment of my life.

CHAPTER 49

MIKE

My assistant is bent over her desk, her perky ass offered to the room, sharpening a pencil. I walk through the reception area without saying anything and quietly shut the door to my office. I'm taking a seat behind the large walnut desk when she rings my line.

"Yes?"

"I was just making sure you were here. I didn't see you go by." Her voice has a chipmunk lilt that makes me want to dissect her throat with my pen, but the male clients seem to enjoy it, which is one of the reasons I haven't let her go, despite a dozen reasons why that action is justified.

"I'm here."

"Okay. You have two messages from Mr. Thompson."

I pinch the bridge of my nose. "You're supposed to call my cell if he calls."

"Oh, I did. I left you a voice mail."

I pull out my cell to check her story, and dammit, she did. I don't know how I missed her call, but the discovery of my dead wife is not the sort of excuse that Ned will accept. "Next time, power call me until I answer. Do you understand?"

"Uh, yeah," she snaps, and all it would take is me to blame the missed message on her and Ned would have her killed before tomorrow morning. I hang up the phone and return his call from the cell I keep in my desk.

"It's been three hours," Ned says by way of greeting.

"I'm sorry. It's been an odd day."

"We heard about your wife."

I press my lips together but don't say anything. His statement could mean a number of things, from a reference to her video to a confession of murder.

"I want to make sure this doesn't negatively affect my business."

"It won't."

"An investigation into your life isn't something we're interested in, so do what you need to do to make sure that doesn't happen."

Because avoidance of a police investigation won't raise suspicion, at all. "Of course."

"To be safe, we'd like to move Colorado back to our care."

I let out a hiss of air. "Sir, Colorado has been with me for—"

"A long time, I know. We just want to hold on to it for a little bit, just until this wrinkle gets smoothed out."

There are a dozen reasons Colorado should stay with me, but a person doesn't argue with Ned, not if they want to live another day. Moving Colorado, even for a short period of time, will mean a significant loss of value, at least a year's worth of appreciation, if not more. Not to mention that any move always risks the chance of catching someone's attention.

But again, you don't argue with Ned. You say yes, and your lungs continue to flex with breath. A fair trade.

"Yes, sir. I'll start tonight and move it over the next two days."

"Wonderful. Call me when it's done."

The call ends and I start up my computer and check the balance in Colorado.

Just over $432 million. The main savings account for the Los Colima cartel.

I start prepping the transfer.

CHAPTER 50

LENNY

I cap the gin and put it back in the drawer, then go into the bathroom and take a long look in the mirror above the sink. I splash water on my face, then bend over the toilet and push my finger deep down my throat. The liquor comes up, as does the strawberry Pop-Tart I ate on the way in. I wince at the taste, then use my hand to scoop water from the faucet and rinse out my mouth. Pulling my Dodgers hat from the hook by the door, I grab a can of marking spray and the keys to the cart.

Lillian's plot is in the sun at this time of day, and I park a bit away and approach slowly, gathering my emotions as I spray the outline of the plot. I used to be a man of few tears, but Marcella's death broke that dam. Now I tear up at the sight of an abandoned kitten, or at a teenager helping an old man across the road. As I draw a thick orange line down the green grass of her grave, the tears begin.

"It's natural to cry." The writer from the paper stood on the hospice front stoop in a black sweatshirt and jeans, her hair in pigtails that were too young for her. "If you have to, just go into the bathroom and let it all out."

"I'm fine," I said curtly. "Don't worry about me." Maybe this was a mistake. A stranger, meeting Marcella? How important was an obituary after all?

Marcella had shrieked from her bed, the noise shrill and long, and I sighed, my patience long gone. "Just follow the noise."

Lillian Smith passed through the door. Her head barely reached my chest. That was the first thing I noticed, how small she was. The second thing was the pitch of her scream. Rushing into the room, I found the writer standing at the foot of Marcella's bed, screaming back at my daughter with one long and angry yell.

I stared at her, confused.

Marcella did the same.

When Lillian finally stopped—and damn, that woman had lungs on her—Marcella cleared her throat and spoke in the dignified manner she reserved for poor fashion choices and cooties. "Um, what was that for?"

"It made me feel better. What was yours for?"

Marcella regarded her blankly. "Attention, I guess. I'm dying, in case you weren't aware."

"Oh, let me be sure to write this down." Lillian made a big production of pulling out a pen and uncapping it, then rustling through different notebook pages until she got to a blank one. "Michella Thompson—"

"It's Marcella," my daughter interrupted, then gave me a look as if to ask what discount store I got this woman from. "M-A-R—"

"Yeah, yeah, yeah. I got it," Lillian said mildly. "Marcella Thompson, who passed on xyz date, was a screamer. It was a shrill scream, one similar to a chimpanzee dying." She looked up and raised her brows for approval. "Good?"

"I don't think I sound like a chimpanzee," Marcella said indignantly, and I smiled for the first time in almost a week.

"Well, accuracy is important." Lillian fished a phone out of her bag. "Let's look up animal screams and find a good fit."

I stepped back into the hall and watched as Lillian sat on the edge of the bed and showed her phone to Marcella. She tapped the screen, and a wail of some sort erupted from the device. Marcella giggled. "Not that one."

Lillian was there two hours that first day, and when she left, Marcella made her promise to come back the following morning, which she did, and every morning after, for the next thirteen days.

And then, on day fourteen, Marcella was gone.

The area is relatively level, which means the backhoe could do most of the heavy lifting, but I still grab a shovel out of the shed and start the slow and laborious process of digging her grave. It's early—this task would normally be done the morning of the funeral—but I don't mind refreshing it, if needed. I need the hard physical labor and the time to process the fact that she is gone.

As the grave deepens, sweat pools on the fat of my lower back and runs down the sides of my arms. I pause a few times to stretch my back and catch my breath. The ache and strain of muscles feel right, like I'm paying a penance to her.

Not knowing the cause is hard for me to swallow. I need to know more, need to be able to put it in a logical bucket before I set it on the shelf. Once I get back to the shed, I'll turn on the ancient computer and do an internet search on her name.

I pause again and wipe the sweat off my forehead, then pull the baseball cap tighter. I could have waited until dusk. It would have been cooler then, but I like the work, and need to move the toxins out of my body. When I get back to the office, a gallon of water will be in order. Already brain cells that haven't functioned in years are starting to fire, and the fog that typically hangs over my emotions is beginning to clear. Some of that is good; some of it isn't. Stabbing the shovel into the dirt, I trudge up the hill and into the shade of a palm tree. Breathing hard, I pull the phone out of my pocket and scroll down to a number I haven't dialed in years.

"Lenny, you sonofabitch," Rancin answers, the familiar sounds of the police bullpen in the background.

"Hey, Rancin."

"We were just talking about you the other week. Lapet says you're the reason we lost the fancy coffeepot with the pods."

I have to smile at that. "It was that stripper, the one with the dentures."

"Oh shit, you're right. So sorta your fault."

"I'll take the blame if you can give me some info on a recent death." A squirrel runs by, pauses to look at me, then skitters up the tree. Lillian always threw them bits of her crust, but I have only loose change and a few peppermints in my pocket.

"Gimme the name."

"Lillian Smith." I make it over to the cart and pull out a small notepad. Withdrawing a pen from my front pocket, I flip over the top cardboard of the pad and stare at the empty notebook page. I carried a pad like this for seventeen years, and now it feels foreign. I click the pen into action.

"Let me see who has it." There is a clatter of keys. Computers, which were my Achilles' heel from the start, have probably taken over by now. "Okay, looks like Detective Gersh. Just from looking . . . looks like she OD'd, but . . . suspicious." More clicks and clatters. "I can't open the file, but I can get Gersh to call you. He's, uh, you know. He's a baby."

Meaning he doesn't understand or respect the old way. The "take his keys and drive a fellow officer home if they've been drinking" way. The "using fists and force has its time and place, especially when kids or women are involved" way. And most applicably: "Once a badge, always a badge." Gersh probably won't share shit with me.

"Well, just get me what you can. You said an overdose?"

"That's what it says. Autopsy isn't complete yet—the ME is backed up like the 405. The vic was having an affair, so the husband and boyfriend are being looked at."

An affair. That's interesting. I write the word down and add a question mark to the end. I wouldn't have pegged Lillian for that.

"Okay, thanks. How are Rose and the kids?"

"Rose's on a different husband now. Got tired of the job."

Yes, the job. The job that pulled me away from Marcella on hundreds of nights when I could have been reading her bedtime stories, or fixing her ice cream, or watching her play and cataloging memories to keep for the rest of my life.

"But the kids are good. You know teenagers. They care more about their phones than us."

No, I don't know. Marcella should be twelve, but she isn't. I let his careless comment slide. "Thanks for the info. Call me if you hear anything?"

"Yeah, definitely. I'll do some snooping."

"Appreciate it." I hang up the phone and think, my gaze settling on the empty, half-dug grave.

CHAPTER 51

LILLIAN

I'm in a white room and can smell bleach and another chemical that I can't place, but it makes me dizzy. A dark-skinned man with a shaved head and a lab coat is standing beside a body and talking to Mike.

The body is covered in a white sheet, and I know—without them pulling back the cover—that it's me. I move to stand beside Mike, and I can feel his discomfort at being here, at having to listen to the instructions from the coroner. He asks Mike if he's ready, then folds the sheet back to reveal my face.

I lean forward, shocked. I've never seen my eyes closed before. It's an odd thing to realize, that you don't know what you look like, dead—but here I am, face slack, eyes closed, my mouth slightly open. I gotta say, it's not my best look.

"That's her."

My husband doesn't budge from his spot at the head of the table, his voice calm and, as always, in perfect control. I glance at him, annoyed that he can't manage to shed a single tear, for appearance's sake, at least.

I return my focus to my body. My hair has clumps of sand in it, and it's all over my skin, as if I were rolled in it before being carried here.

As if sensing my critique, the doctor speaks. "Her body will be washed prior to the autopsy. We're still collecting evidence from it."

Evidence. That's interesting. I move to the other side of the table and crouch, wanting to see my profile.

"Are you suspecting foul play?" Mike seems to be following my thoughts.

"I'll have to let the detectives answer that question. You're speaking to them, correct?"

"Yes, later today." Mike's phone rings, and he reaches for his front shirt pocket and withdraws his cell and checks it. "Do you need me for anything else? I need to take this call."

"No, that's it." The doctor's tone is mild, but I can feel the judgment toward Mike. I'm right there with him. His wife is dead, and he has to interrupt the viewing of her body for a phone call?

Strike one, Mike.

Empowered by my new ability and unfettered access, I follow him out the door to see who he's so anxious to talk to.

Is it *her*? Is she already swooping in to take my husband?

CHAPTER 52

MIKE

It's Sam, and I move quickly through the halls of the medical examiner's office, not sure who might be listening. "Yes?"

"I got your message about your friend's vacation home." Our code is fairly simple—*Colorado* equals *vacation home*—though Sam isn't great with using it properly. "Are you sure they're ready to sell it now? The market isn't great."

"They don't care."

"Okay." Sam falls silent for a beat. "Will you be home later? I'd like to come by."

"No," I say curtly, and if he doesn't understand why it's not a good time to come to the house, he's an idiot.

"Someone will need to pick out Lillian's outfit for the funeral. I know her style better than anyone."

"I don't want anyone at the house right now. Jacob isn't taking this well."

"Well, his mom died," Sam points out. "What the hell do you expect?"

I didn't say that there was anything wrong with Jacob mourning. Sam is misassigning my emotions, which he does often. I decide to ignore the statement, because arguing with Sam is like racing on a hamster wheel. Even when you've won, you're stuck in circles.

I take a different path. "Have the police called you?"

"No."

"They probably will," I caution.

"I hope they do."

I know it isn't meant to be threatening, but it feels like there's a bit of malice in the words. I see Detective Gersh striding down the hall toward me and hang up on Sam without responding.

CHAPTER 53

MIKE

It's critically important that I answer the detectives in a way that removes all suspicion both from me and from Lillian's death. With that acknowledgment in place, I'm aware that I'm royally fucking this up.

They have introduced themselves as Alec and Emily, and Alec Gersh was the one who questioned Lillian about Brexley Axe at the time of the restraining order, a year ago. They aren't the officers who informed me about Lillian's body being found, and that's probably a good thing, because I'm not certain I reacted to that in the most compassionate way.

I'm trying to do better here. I've made sure that my voice cracks at times. I continually pinch my features. Pause at times, as if I'm too overcome with emotion to continue. I've rambled, intentionally. Been praiseful of my wife, but not too much so.

All the right things, but still, I can feel the suspicion in the air. It chokes me, the weight of it sitting on my lungs, and it doesn't help that we're in the police station, a place I've spent my entire adult life plotting to avoid.

Of course Lillian would put me here. Even in death, she is a weakness in my armor.

"We've pulled Lillian's phone records and credit card activity from the day she died." The woman pushes a few pages toward me and I lean forward, pretending I'm seeing them for the first time.

"Let's talk about the phone records first. Do you recognize any of these numbers?" The man taps on the left column of the printout.

They have assured me that I am not a suspect, that they are not even sure whether there is a suspect, that this is probably an accidental death and they just need to do some pesky paperwork to make sure that all the i's are dotted on the death, but I am the husband, and the husband is always a suspect, especially in a case where the wife is unfaithful. Have they found my own affair yet? They shouldn't. They shouldn't suspect anything, yet cops always do.

I look at the lines of numbers with care, the way any diligent widower would because maybe—hopefully—the killer's information is right here, right in front of us.

"Ah, I think this might be Sam's number. That's her best friend. He's a Realtor. It might be. If you let me look at my phone, I could make sure."

They nod—*yes, of course you can look at your phone, please type in these other numbers, just to see if they match any in your address book.* They give me an encouraging look and the man leans back in his chair and stretches, then drums his fingers on the belly of his uniform, as if they don't know who these numbers are, and as if they haven't already pulled my phone records also.

I go through the motions of typing in the numbers, nodding in mock confirmation when I verify that—yes!—I am correct, and this first number is for Sam, her best friend. The other phone numbers don't match anything in my phone, and I push the list back to them. "Can't you look up these numbers? Maybe call them? They might know something." I'm just a poor dumb husband, but gee whillikers, guys—this might help.

"We've done that," the girl says gently, and I let her tone slide because I need her to think that I'm as idiotic as she's assuming I am.

"The first is to a taxi service. We've contacted them and found out that Lillian scheduled a pickup from your house, going to this address." The man pushes a page forward. It's a printout of an internet map search, showing the marina's address.

I'm not sure I'm supposed to recognize it, so I keep a blank look on my face. "What's there?"

They do this big hem-haw routine, where there's a lot of shrugging and head-scratching. I let it slide, and hope that someone is notating the fact that I'm ignorant about the marina.

"What's interesting is that, when the taxi showed up at your house, Lillian wasn't there." The man sits back in his cheap chair and folds his arms over his chest.

"So she caught another ride?"

"Maybe, but if I caught another ride, I would call the taxi and cancel it." The woman glances at the man. "Would you?"

"I would." The man nods like a marionette. "Would you, Mike?"

Do they think she was killed at the house? I think of my office, of the shed in the backyard, of the locked liquor cabinet, and of the guest bedroom closet. I try to think of something to say to reassure and distract them from my home.

"Yes, I would cancel the taxi, but Lillian is . . ." I sigh and look up at the ceiling, trying to decide how to word this. "She's scatterbrained." There. That was a nice way to say it. "We went to the Grand Canyon once and she forgot her suitcase. When we got to the hotel and were unloading our bags, she realized that she never packed one. Just . . . forgot." After that, I started to go around behind her, with every school trip of Jacob's, with every family excursion, and any home project, just to make sure that she had properly completed the task. "So yeah. I wouldn't be worried or think twice of her forgetting to call and cancel a car."

"Okay." Detective Gersh nods slowly, like he's testing the flavor of the idea on his tongue. "So let's look at the second call, which was to a domestic-abuse hotline."

As practiced, I perform a minor lift of my eyebrows and widen my eyes. They are watching me as closely as possible, and this is where the interview starts going downhill. I swallow. "Why did Lillian call a hotline?"

"Excellent question!" the woman says, slapping the tabletop as if she's struck gold. "We had the same question, which is why we called them. Lillian asked to speak to one of the abuse counselors. We've requested the recording of that call, if it exists."

It doesn't take high intelligence to connect the dots they are laying out. Lillian was being abused, planned to run away, and I killed her. I clear my throat. "I didn't abuse Lillian. In almost two decades, I've never laid a finger on her." And God knows, it was hard at times. "I *loved* her." My voice clogs on that sentence, the truth sticking to the vowels and keeping them in my throat. I did love Lillian. I may be a lot of things—a liar and a cheat—but I did love my wife. I loved every broken, cracked piece of her.

"They'll check for damage during the autopsy," the woman reassures me with a snippy little smile, as if she knows exactly who I am and everything I've done.

Great, I want to retort. I hope they do. Because they won't find anything. They won't find a single bruise or scratch on that skin.

"Okay, let's move to the last call." Detective Gersh scratches the side of his face. "I got to say, Mike. This one is odd."

"In what way?"

"Well, she called the *Los Angeles Times*, which, as you know, had recently fired her. They faxed over the paperwork, along with a copy of her severance package." He flips open the folder and thumbs through the pages, then withdraws a few and tosses them across the table. "We thought perhaps she was calling about that, but that's where things get odd."

I try to keep up, but I'm distracted by an item on the termination paperwork. "This says that the reason for the termination is vandalism?" I look up. "What'd she do?"

"She keyed her boss's car, apparently over a negative employee review." Detective Gersh watches me closely, and I struggle over how to react.

I can't believe I didn't know about this. I'm as annoyed by that as I am at Lillian's reckless behavior. Vandalism of personal property is a misdemeanor, a felony if the damage is over $400. She knew better than this.

My irritation mounts and I force my features to remain calm and concerned. If Lillian had told me, I could have arranged for repairs and handled any insurance claims. Add to that the fact that Lillian shouldn't have signed any termination paperwork without me reviewing and negotiating on her behalf. She was with the *Times* for two decades—that had weight and power. They couldn't just turn her out without some real compensation.

My hands are starting to tremble, and I pull them off the table and put them in my lap, where they will be hidden. "You said things got odd. So why did she call the *Times*? She wanted her job back?" This all makes no sense. She called a taxi, but she wasn't there when it arrived. She made an appointment at a women's shelter, one that she didn't keep because she was dead. And she called a company that she no longer worked for.

"Oh no, something much more interesting than that." Detective Gersh pauses for dramatic effect, and I swear I'm going to rip out his tongue if he doesn't start using it. "Lillian placed an order for an obituary."

I don't have to fake surprise for that one. I stare at him, then at her, verifying that it is true. The female detective nods.

"An obituary?" I frown, trying to follow Lillian's thought process. "For who?"

"Well, for herself." The detective grins like a Cheshire cat. "What do ya think about that?"

CHAPTER 54

MIKE

I prep nineteen accounts for Colorado's transfer. They're all accounts I've used before, with varying amounts of activity, enough to give them age and legitimacy. Each account is an island, with no ties to me, to the organization, or to anything that sniffs of illegality.

I promised to move it within two days, and my clock is ticking. I should move it now. Everything is ready—I am just tense at the thought of initiating the send. The transfer is where the catch typically occurs. All it takes is one sharp-eyed banker or federal agent, one established trigger parameter that I haven't anticipated, and—boom. Game over.

Of course, it won't happen that quickly. Oh no, they'll be smart. They'll leave the funds alone while the hyenas circle and sniff and gently pull one thread, then another, and approach my assistant and neighbors with bribes and threats, and tap phones and go through every financial transaction that I've ever made, and start earmarking assets for seizure. My car. Our home. My 401(k). Our time-share. Jacob's college fund. Lillian's life insurance.

I close my eyes and tilt back in my chair, inhaling deeply, holding the breath for three seconds, then exhaling, trying to reset my heart, which is galloping like a racehorse who has grabbed the bit in his mouth.

If Lillian had just waited to die for one year. One fucking year. Or if she had keeled over during a routine surgery or a car accident. No, she had to die on the damn beach at Malibu, after making a series of ridiculous calls, and right after making a fool of me and our marriage. She had to die, which freaked out the organization and prompted this move, which just might sink everything.

My phone dings and I groan and pick it up. It's a text and I want to throw the device in the garbage disposal as soon as I read it.

Have you started the transfer yet? Ticktock.

I've stalled long enough. I need to just bite the bullet and do it. I push away from the desk and go to the pantry, the faux pumpkin can right up front, the key to the liquor cabinet popped out and in my hand in a second.

Lillian always thought I locked up our liquor because of Jacob, but I could give a damn if he steals a few sips. There're not many bottles of value there, and only one worth more than a few bills. I reach up and fit the key into the fireproof locker and open the case. I reach in for the twentieth-anniversary box of Benromach, but it isn't there. I sweep a hand over the inside of the cabinet, my panic mounting as I look for the distinct wooden box, the box that is *always* there, the box that has been in this case for nine years, the box that contains a slip of paper, tucked underneath the velvet lining, with the sixty-four-digit Bitcoin encryption key written on it. The encryption key that I need to access Colorado.

The box isn't there.

CHAPTER 55

LENNY

Detective Gersh agrees to meet and suggests some preppy breakfast joint, way up in Hollywood. There's no parking within five blocks, and I'm sweating and pissed by the time I shoulder past four hipsters and into the cramped front entryway. The interior is cool, and I squint, finding a uniform sitting in one of the booths halfway back, a damn mimosa in front of him. I pause beside him and nod, indicating for him to switch seats.

"What?" He looks up at me.

"Let me have that seat."

"Shut the fuck up. Take that one."

"I don't like my back to the door." I move to the side to give him room to get out.

"Yeah, neither do I." The man stays in place, and if he is intimidated by my six-foot-four build and massive beer gut, he doesn't show it.

"Fine. Scoot over." I grip the table and begin to slide in next to him, using my ample ass to push him toward the wall.

Gersh moves just enough to accommodate, then gives me a look that could peel plaster. "You're a pain in the ass."

"That's what they say." I push his mimosa toward him with a finger that's still grubby from digging out graves.

"Aw, screw this." He shoves at my arm. "I'll move to the other side. You have shoulders like a damn bison."

I oblige, and within a minute everything is as it should be and I grunt with contentment and pick up the menu. There is chocolate chip cookie–crusted french toast, which sounds interesting, and I order that, along with a cup of black coffee.

I nod to his mimosa flute. "Drinking on the job?"

"I just got off the night shift. I'd take an Irish coffee, but I plan on hitting the bed as soon as we finish up here."

An Irish coffee. I try not to stare at the drink card that is stuck in between the salt and pepper shakers. I'd kill for some Jameson right now. Or better yet, a Bloody Mary with an extra shot. I grimace at a pain that rips through my stomach. "Well, I won't keep you long."

A woman walks by in shorts that expose half her butt cheeks and legs that go up to her ears. I try not to look and fail. Gersh grins at me, and I scowl back. So this is the new generation of cops. Champagne-drinking preppies. The man has clean fingernails, for shit's sake. Probably enjoys the paperwork.

"What?" Gersh leaned forward. "What are you thinking?"

"I had a guy like you in my academy. Name was Loresner."

"Loresner . . ." This guy tilts his head, trying to place the name.

"He's not there anymore. Had a nervous breakdown the first time he shot his weapon in the line of duty. Now he sells lawn mowers at Sears." I grab the mug from the waitress and bring it to my lips.

"Nice." The kid adjusts his belt. "So Rancin says that you knew Lillian Smith."

"I did."

"How well?"

This is show-and-tell time, which I don't mind, as long as he does his part. "I've known her six years. She visits me at work. We shoot the shit. She did the obituary for my daughter."

Gersh nods, and if he already knew about Marcella, he doesn't mention or show it. I'm glad. I've had enough apologies to fill a Greyhound bus. "When's the last time you saw her?"

"Ten, eleven days ago. She brought me lunch. We ate. She left."

"How'd she seem?"

I sit on the response as the waiter sets a mountain of potato skins, ham, eggs, and hollandaise sauce in front of Gersh. Okay, so maybe this place isn't so bad.

My plate is as large as his, and is a recipe for clogged arteries and diabetes. I nod at Gersh with approval, but he is already tucking a napkin into the collar of his shirt and picking up a fork and knife.

"So?" he prods. "How'd she seem?"

"Fine. She actually seemed better than she had in the past. Healthier. She normally has this sort of dark gloom about her—it's just her personality. She's a quirky, weird type, like—"

"Yeah, I met her," Gersh interrupts. "Questioned her about the Axe sister investigation. She'd been a bit obsessive with that family."

That's interesting news, though I'm not entirely surprised. Lillian had an addictive personality. During the early days after Marcella, before I left the force, before I started working at the cemetery, Lillian used to come by my house with a handle of whiskey, or vodka, or gin. We'd lie in Marcella's bed and pass the bottle between us, and she wouldn't say anything; she'd just lie there and give me liquor and company if I needed to tell a story, or be an asshole, or bend over the toilet and vomit. We became alcoholics together, though I suspected that Lillian had already been pretty far down that path. She was better at hiding it, and may have gotten a handle on it. I hadn't seen her drunk in a few years.

"You ever met the husband?" Gersh pierces a stack of potato and ham.

"Yeah, once. He showed up to pick up Lillian. We were high—she had bought a roach from someone, and we were in a shitty apartment that I moved into after my house was repossessed. She was on the couch and I was on my bed, and we were laughing about something about giraffes, and he walked in the front door. Didn't knock or anything. He just walked in, told her to stand up, and he pointed to the door, the way you'd do to a dog. 'Out,' he said. 'Out.'"

I shrug. "And she just stood up and stumbled out. Didn't look at me, didn't say shit to me. And I didn't see her again for two or three weeks."

"Really?" He sets down his fork and gives me his full attention. "Did you get the sense that she was abused by him?"

I consider the idea. "No. If I had, I would have stepped in. I mean, I would have tried, given the state I was in." I struggle for a way to describe what that dynamic had been like. "I viewed it more like she was a kid—and he was a parent. Controlling, yes. But it was with care and love. At least, that's how I saw it. You have to realize, I only met him that one time. She rarely mentioned him after that." I straighten, irritated with myself for just now remembering the last time Lillian had mentioned her husband. "She thought he was having an affair. Was worried about it."

The detective doesn't react, his jowls moving in uninterrupted cadence as he chews. "You know with who?"

"She didn't say. I don't think she had any proof. Just a gut feeling."

I should have brought it up the last time I saw her. Should have been focused on something other than myself. I pull my plate closer and unwrap my silverware, ignoring the stab of guilt. "So what do you know about it? Was he?"

CHAPTER 56

MIKE

I do a slow and careful inventory of the liquor safe. The lock is clean, with no evidence of picking. I line up the liquor in very precise rows and check the labels of each twice. There is an expected amount of rums, vodkas, tequilas, and gins. While there might be a bottle missing here or there, or missing amounts from this one or that, that is expected, especially with Lillian's occasional spikes in drinking. But the one bottle that is always there, the one that Lillian has *never* touched, because tradition, ceremony, is one of her sticking points—it and its box are gone.

I didn't purchase the bottle to use as a hiding place. The original purchase was entirely innocent. We had taken a vacation at a time when I had been particularly in love with her, her fragility after the miscarriage triggering a protective bubble of rare emotion. Walking home from dinner, we'd passed an upscale wine and liquor boutique and walked in.

The bottle was a special edition, one that the salesperson had promised would appreciate nicely in value and taste, as long as it was kept in a climate-controlled location. And that night, tucking it away in our suitcase, we'd made plans to open it on the evening of our twentieth anniversary and toast to our future.

I'm trying not to panic, because reckless emotion doesn't help anything. I pull out a padded chair and sit, needing to think this through. The only people who know where the key to the cabinet is are Lillian and I. I certainly hadn't taken the bottle, which leaves Lillian. Normally, I would track down my wife and question her within an inch of her life, but—thanks to recent events—that's no longer possible.

So I do the next best thing and pull the camera footage.

———

For obvious reasons, I don't have cameras in my house, with two exceptions. I have a cam in the guest bedroom closet and one built into the air-conditioning vent of the pantry. The pantry cam is motion activated and angled to catch the full view of anyone who opens that cabinet. The video feed is wired, not wireless, and therefore not dependent on the reliability of an internet connection or the security risks of one. The wiring, which was put in place when we renovated our kitchen six years ago, runs along the back of the cabinet and to a small flash drive that will hold 420 hours of footage. Since the camera is only activated by motion, there is no chance of filling up the drive, but if that unlikely possibility ever occurred, it would simply overwrite the oldest file. I insert the flash drive into my computer's USB and wait for the folder to load.

It is, as predicted, not full. In fact, there are only six and a half hours of footage, across hundreds of video files. I start at the most recent, and immediately hit pay dirt.

On the video, Lillian appears, wearing the same white T-shirt and yoga pants she was found in. Her hair is in a ponytail and her movements are jerky, almost manic. As she gropes in the cabinet, she reaches for one bottle, then another. She stiffens, and this is probably when she spots the special-edition box. She stands on her tiptoes to reach the back, and pulls out the box. She examines it, and I can see the moment where she considers returning it. The war of right versus wrong. Marriage vows versus disrespect. The anger—*hell hath no fury like a woman scorned*—wins out, and she uses the edge of her fingernail to break the seal. Then she opens the lid, pulls out the bottle and twists the cap, and takes a small sip.

It's unnerving, the smile that passes over her features. A long, knowing grin, one dipped in revenge, but my wife thinks she's stomping on a planned tradition, a keepsake. She has no idea of what she really holds in the box tucked under her arm—the financial infrastructure of one of the world's most dangerous bodies of organized crime. She puts the bottle back into the box, and I want to smash my fist into that smile, to destroy the computer screen, to break her face and not stop punching until there are no more bones left to move, no more life left to open those light-brown eyes.

She opens her purse, puts the box inside, and then is locking the cabinet and returning the key. Fifteen seconds later, she's out of the pantry and the video goes dark.

I rewind the clip and watch it again. The video is time-stamped at 11:02 a.m. on the day of her disappearance and death.

My cell phone rings, and it's Lillian's drunk of a mother. I silence the ringer, unable to take another round of her sobs and nonsense questions. No, I do not know why Lillian did it. No, I do not know if she was alone. No, I do not need you to come here and grieve with me. No, I do not want to talk with your latest boyfriend and answer his questions. No, Jacob is not okay and doesn't want to talk to you either.

Her mother seems convinced that it's a suicide, but I'm not sold on that. Originally, I hadn't seen a motive for murder either, but maybe her holding the key was it.

I start the video again, and on this take, I focus on Lillian's facial expressions and demeanor. It looks like Sam was right, and she was off her medicine. In the video, she goes through an entire range of emotions when it comes to selecting the bottle. This was a potential risk that

I should have calculated when she got wind of the affair. Relationship heirlooms would have been at risk, and my wife has always had a fondness for being drunk, a fondness that spikes dramatically when things go south.

I thought I was being smart, putting it in a firesafe box in a pantry that a robber would never look twice at, locked by a key that no one other than us knew about. I should have put it in the guest-bedroom closet, with the other sensitive items, but I always reasoned that if something happened—if the organization, or the feds, or someone I had not anticipated came here and threatened me—I could give up the guest-bedroom stash and still have Colorado.

There is no recovery from a loss of Colorado. That loss is one with dozens of side effects, ones I have never calculated, because if Colorado is lost, I am dead, so the fallout is irrelevant.

Four years ago, when this sixty-four-digit encryption key was created, the bourbon box had actually been the backup plan—in case option one fell through. Option one was the number handwritten on the back of a framed family photo of Lillian, Jacob, and me—a photo I gave my grandmother, who added it to her mountain of frames on top of the baby grand piano in the corner of her Oklahoma City farmhouse. I'd expected that to be a safe location. Then five months ago, a tornado—a freakin' tornado—picked up the entire house and spun it into a thousand pieces. Somewhere, a relief worker probably found and bagged the picture frame, oblivious to the lottery ticket that they were throwing away.

I should have found a new location, but Sam and I were working on an apartment-complex deal, and Luis was leaning heavily on me to research and invest in lean hog futures. Pigs. That's what distracted me from what should have been my number-one priority—backup plans for backup plans. Pigs . . . and then the slow and eventual destruction of my marriage.

I call Sam, ready to hear whatever he has to say about Lillian's state of mind that morning.

"Hey." His voice is low, as if he is with clients, but that has never stopped him from answering. It is one of the nice things about Sam, if I had to make a list of the nice things. Excellent communication. Always on time, if not early. Always has me finish first, regardless of whether he does.

"You said you spoke to Lillian the morning that she died and that she seemed off her meds. I need to know everything about that morning."

"I can meet you. Just tell me where."

"The coffee shop in Brentwood, by the farmers' market. Meet me in the parking lot. I'll be in the car."

"Sure. I'm . . . uh . . . twenty minutes away. Okay?"

"Yeah." I end the call, then play the video again. She put the liquor in her purse and then . . . I look at the timeline of her calls. Three and a half hours later, she calls the taxi and then the abuse hotline and then her office, then somehow ends up in Malibu, dead in the surf. Her bag was there too—I remember the detective mentioning it. I hadn't cared because I hadn't been aware of the missing bottle at that time. Now it could be the most important thing in my life. Was the bottle still in the purse, in the evidence locker?

I replace the drive and tuck the cords back in, returning the cabinet to its normal operation and the key to the can, though there is no longer anything of value inside. You still need to put things back in their place; otherwise your home, your marriage, your life is just one continually crumbling edifice.

I take my key from the hook and call up the stairs to Jacob, who is playing music at a level that is unhealthy for his ears. I wait, then head to the garage. I have thirteen minutes to make it to the coffee shop parking lot to meet Sam.

On the way, I call the detective to ask about the purse, but he doesn't answer. I leave a message and make sure that I sound broken and weak, a man in mourning. The stress is easy to inject into my voice. The grief . . . I'm still working on the grief. For now, all I feel for her is hatred, and this new development has poured kerosene on that fire.

CHAPTER 57

LILLIAN

I'm in a strange house and standing in the middle of a skinny hall, trying to place my surroundings. At the end of the hall is a mirror, and it's odd to look at it and not see my own reflection. The walls are a pale blue, and the other end of the hall opens to a living room with mid-century-modern, white furniture and a large dalmatian, who launches off the couch and begins barking at me. I watch him with interest, and when I crouch and hold out my hand, he trots over and sniffs it, then barks again. *Interesting.*

A woman yells at him to shut up and I straighten and turn toward the sound, following the hall to an open doorway. Pausing on the threshold, I look in to see a small office, one with stacks of books and papers on every surface. Behind the L-shaped desk is a woman I don't know. I move closer, watching her with interest. She has almost translucent white skin and black hair, which is pulled into a low braid and contained with a thin red headband, which gives her a young look, though she is probably five or six years older than me. She's wearing round tortoiseshell glasses and a pair of jean overalls with a red tank top, her shoulders hunched forward as she types away at a keyboard, her attention on the computer screen before her.

The dog has followed me in and is still barking at me, and the woman yells at him again. I point to the door, and surprisingly, he obeys, walking into the hall and sitting and staring at me as if waiting for his next command.

I do a slow spin of the room, wondering why I am here. I've never been in a strange place before, at least not as a dead woman. The woman sighs in frustration, and I circle the desk to see what she's working on. It is an email, something about code enforcement and a backyard deck. I perk up at the same time that she does, both of us hearing the slam of a door and a male voice calling out a name. *Caroline.*

"I'm in here," she calls.

I step back from the computer, conscious of how it will look, then remind myself that I don't exist, at least not to these people. Then he appears in the doorway and I forget, for a moment, that I am dead.

David.

He looks different. The scruff is shaved and he is in a golf shirt and jeans, his hair shorter and neater. He's wearing glasses, ones that match hers, and they look like the sort of couple that goes to organic swap meets on the weekends and open-mic poetry readings. When I look at her, she's smiling and he's coming around the desk and kissing her on the lips, and a sharp knife of jealousy hits.

So he's not single. This is his house. That is his dog. This is his . . . I look at her hand and see the ring. This is his wife. He is also now wearing a ring, a thin silver band that glints as he caresses the back of her neck, and I think of him on top of me, grunting. A drop of sweat had come off his forehead and splattered on my cleavage. A wave of revulsion hits, and I turn away from them.

"I thought you were going to be gone this week," she says.

"That project's over." And . . . wow. No French accent.

"Oh." She is surprised. "Everything work out?"

"Not exactly." He sits on the edge of the desk. He turns away from her and leans down to pet the dog, the action shielding her from the view of his features, which twist in pain, then are forced smooth. I watch, fascinated. "She, ah. She didn't make it."

"What?" She sits back in her chair. "What do you mean? She caught you?"

"No, no." He takes off his glasses and wipes his eyes with the pads of his fingers. "Overdose."

"Was it you?"

Was it you? I frown at the question. *Is she asking if he killed me?*

He sighs, as if disappointed in the question. "Caroline."

"What?" She shrugs. "I can ask. You don't have to answer." She doesn't seem concerned about my death, and I decide that I don't like her.

David puts his glasses back on, but there is a tear he has missed, a dot of moisture that hangs on his right cheekbone. *Ha!* I want to shout. *See! He liked me. He really liked me.* "I'm going to get a shower."

"Are you in trouble?" She spins in the desk chair as he heads for the door, passing me so closely that I can smell his cologne, and even it is different from the one he wore with me.

"They're not happy, but I'm fine. Things happen. We'll find another way to get the rest of what we need." His true voice has a hint of a New York accent, and I'm fascinated by the differences between this man and the one I knew. *The rest of what we need?* What is he talking about?

I'm trying to piece together the meaning of that sentence when he scratches the dog on the back and heads out of the room.

"Welcome home," she says quietly, and I bare my teeth at her and growl for absolutely no good reason.

CHAPTER 58

LENNY

I pay the bill with three twenties that have seen better days. Gersh eyes the limp cash but doesn't say anything. I made it through breakfast without ordering a drink, so other than having a raging headache, I'm doing pretty good. I will need something soon; otherwise I'll start detoxing, and that won't help Lillian at all. So my reward, once this pretty boy coughs up the rest of his intel, is a pool hall I walked past on the way here. Low lights, assholes in the doorway, a collection of cigarette stubs on the windowsill—it looks perfect, and I'm trying not to think about it as I follow him to his car.

The last time I sat in a black-and-white, it was a traveling garbage can, one I shared with whatever rookie was unfortunate enough to be stuck with me for the week. They always gave me the rookies, in part because I was too big an asshole to have a partner but also because I had a way of dealing with the public that the brass liked. Just enough velvet and steel, as they said—though the truth was, I just knew how to defuse a situation. Grow up with an alcoholic father, and you learn that skill quickly. Add in a frigid mother, and you have empathy for just about every type of person you come across. The only people I didn't do well with were the entitled, which was why they pulled me off Beverly Hills and the other rich zip codes real quick. As much as I shone in the ghettos, I tarnished in the sun. Gersh, on the other hand, seems like he'd be a yuppie's best fucking friend.

He takes the driver's seat and I sit on a passenger seat that shines with fresh Armor All. I eye the air freshener coil in the cup holder. "You offer the perps hand sanitizer and a breath mint when they come in?"

"That's funny." He opens a laptop that is set into a stand beside the gear box and starts typing, his fingers flying across the keyboard at a speed that irritates the shit out of me. I hate this, the constant reminders of why I would have been forced out of the job, even if I hadn't lost Marcella. Guys like me were dinosaurs, upstaged by young idiots like this guy who, dammit to hell, seems capable of more than just flossing his teeth.

How does Rancin handle it? Does he sign out at the end of each day and just wonder, for a moment, about quitting? He's hit retirement age. He could join the likes of me, and drink and do crossword puzzles and sleep until ten and lament the good old days while hating his new lot in life. *Come on, man. Retirement is great. Please, join me in my misery so I don't look so fucking pathetic.*

"So I told you about the calls, right?" Gersh glances at me, but his fingers keep moving somehow, and it's unnerving.

"Yeah. Three calls. Taxi, women's center, the paper."

"The taxi company doesn't keep recordings; neither does the paper. But the women's center does, so we got this." He hits a key and a woman's voice comes through the speaker of the computer.

"Domestic help line, is this an emergency?"

"Uh, no. Not really. Not yet?"

"May I have your name?"

"Lillian Smith."

I scoot forward and close my eyes, concentrating on the voice.

"How can I help you, Lillian?"

"I need to talk to someone about my husband. He's angry at me. I'm worried . . . I just want to talk to someone. I just don't see a way out of this."

203

"*Lillian, where are you now? Do we need to get you someplace safe?*"

"*I'll have to call you back. I have to go. Maybe this was a mistake. I think . . .*" She pauses. "*I think it'd be easier on everyone if I just went away.*"

"*Lillian, listen to me. Let's make an appointment for you to talk to someone. There are options—*"

The recording ends and Gersh hits a key. "That's it. Anything strike you as odd about the call?"

"Yeah." I look at him and can tell that he already suspects what I'm about to say. "That's not Lillian's voice."

"How certain are you?"

"One thousand fucking percent."

CHAPTER 59
LILLIAN

Mike is alarmed, but I don't know why. I also don't know why he has a hidden camera in our kitchen pantry, but he watched footage of me taking our anniversary bourbon a half dozen times, then knocked over a lamp in anger. Maybe he cares for me more deeply than I thought, but my female intuition tells me that it's something else.

He left the house an hour ago, after calling up to Jacob and being ignored. I waited for him to go upstairs, to try to talk to our son, but instead he headed for the garage and drove away.

Now I move upstairs and into Jacob's room. He's on his back in the middle of his mattress, music pounding through his speakers. It's that horrible music, the kind where someone screams unintelligible words into a microphone while cymbals slam together. His eyes are closed and he is mumbling something. I put my ear very close to his mouth and realize he's singing the words of the song—there are actually words to this.

I want to sit with him, to be with him, but I couldn't stand this music when I was living and can't take it when I'm dead, so I pass into the hall and start down the stairs. I'll go into the backyard and lie in the hammock. I can't make it move, but I can still smell the jasmine blooms and feel the sunshine and the breeze. It might be one of the last moments that I get to enjoy outside, before I fade away forever.

I'm smiling at the thought, my movements quicker, but then I round the hard right turn in the staircase and stop because there are two strangers in my house, and they are coming up the stairs toward me.

I stare at them, confused. My mother would describe them as swarthy—with thick muscles that are too big for their heights, their shoulders almost brushing the sides of our stairwell. One wears an Aerosmith T-shirt, the other a tank top, and they are creeping up the stairs in a silent fashion that scares the hell out of me.

These are not home repairmen, not with the stealthy way they move. And they're missing the stiff haircuts and constipated expressions that mark Mike's acquaintances. They're also too old to be friends of Jacob's. I stumble back, higher on the steps, and spot the gun in Aerosmith's hand.

A gun. If I had a heart, it would freeze. All I can think of is Jacob. I claw at the framed pictures on the wall, but nothing happens. I run up the stairs and into my son's room and scream at him, but he doesn't move; he just lies there, his eyes still closed, one finger tapping against the front of his chest.

I am trying to do something, anything, but this is not a movie. There is no cosmic power in the air, nothing is rattling or shaking, and my son is just lying there, his mouth quietly moving along with the words of the song when they open his door and quietly move to either side of his bed. Aerosmith leans forward and presses the gun to Jacob's forehead, and it is at that moment that his eyes flip open and everything in my vision fades to black.

CHAPTER 60

MIKE

Money should be moving by now. What's going on?

I'm finishing a call with the detective and pulling into the coffee shop lot when the text arrives. I need my blood pressure cuff, because I'm fairly certain that I'm moving into problematic range, and my current blend of thinners and medications doesn't seem to be doing the trick. Putting my Volvo into park, I take several deep breaths and work to calm the rapid beat of my heart.

My call with the detective didn't help. I needed to know whether the liquor was still in Lill's purse, in evidence. Asking the question had only seemed to raise Detective Gersh's dislike and suspicion of me, but there had been no way around it. Unfortunately, his answer was to the negative. There had been no liquor bottle or box recovered at the beach scene or in her purse. Before I ended the call, he asked for me to stop by the station. We have an appointment in an hour.

My clients are not patient or understanding people. The idea that I may have misplaced Colorado's encryption key is not something that will be received rationally or kindly. They will panic, immediately. I've never seen them panic—nor given them reason to—but eight years of perfect transactions mean nothing and would be forgotten in an instant if I were to lose the location of one of their minor cash accounts, much less Colorado.

Sam's midnight-blue Range Rover is parked by the curb, and he opens the driver's door and unfolds from it like a praying mantis, clothed in a Versace suit and mirrored sunglasses. He is a different person every time we meet, and today he has gone for the successful-fashionista look. The effect is dampened by the quick scurry of his steps around a bum sleeping under a palm tree. He waves at me through the window.

Always so anxious, so eager. It was that, more than anything, that caused what ended up happening. I'm not a gay man, but I'm a man of opportunity, and Sam gave me plenty of that.

"Hi." Sam opens the car door and a flood of California heat comes in.

I don't say anything, and wait for him to shut the door. Twisting the air knob to high, I watch as he shifts in his seat to face me. There is a moment of silence. The last time we saw each other, I told him no, and he said yes, and even though I had promised Lillian that it was over, we did it one last time.

I meant what I told Lillian. This, between me and him, it is just sex. There is no feeling, at least not on my part. The thought of being intimate—of holding or kissing him—makes my stomach curl. While Sam satisfies my sexual needs, I have been emotionally loyal to Lillian since the day that I married her.

He reaches for me, and I tuck deeper into my seat. "Don't. I need to ask you some questions."

His features harden, and he withdraws, like a child who has been told that he can't have another cookie. He should know how this works, especially given that my wife is being cut open, on an autopsy table, just a few miles away.

My wife. His best friend.

It's been a fucked-up situation for a long time, but one that I was handling, one that had an exit strategy in place, if my wife hadn't grown nosy and jumped onto the train early. "Tell me about when you saw Lill."

"It was yesterday morning. I came by the house, talked to her for a bit."

He isn't emotional, which I appreciate. Between Jacob's tight face and all the phone calls from Lillian's family, I can't take any more memories or crying. "What time was it?"

"Around ten thirty. Maybe eleven."

Okay, so before she went into the pantry. "Did she say what she had planned for the day?"

"Said she was going to the attorney with you. Didn't mention anything else in terms of her day. She was off her meds, though. I asked if she was going to take them and she got a little pissy at that." He rubs his forehead, thinking. "She asked me about the video, if I knew anyone who could get it taken down. I told her that I'd reported it."

Pinching my eyes closed, I try to put myself in Lillian's headspace. Her meds, which are to combat bipolarism and depression, were a crutch that she often abandoned. The withdrawal effect followed a fairly consistent pattern of mood swings and erratic behavior, followed by increased alcohol dependency, paranoia, and occasional blackouts.

The chances were high that Lillian had taken the alcohol somewhere to drink. And then what? Thrown the liquor bottle away? Given it to someone? If only she had taken her car. I could have easily followed the recorded path from the tracker. Instead she walked out of the house—and maybe that *is* a blessing, because at least I have a radius to begin with. Though between that and the taxi request and the Malibu beach where she was found . . . I lower my forehead to the steering wheel and consider, for one long moment, killing myself.

I am a man who prides himself on anticipating problems and contingency plans, and yet I was egotistical enough to put every single egg in a nostalgic basket that my wife had access to. My wife, who I had recently scorned and who was a loose cannon on a good day. I deserve to have my balls sliced off and fed to me with a spoon. That unfortunate punishment is top of mind, a threat recited with cheerful frequency every time I come close to potentially fucking up with Ned.

"What's wrong?" Sam puts his hand on my arm, then withdraws it. "I mean, I know what's wrong. I know that she's dead, but you—"

"I'm not upset that Lillian is dead." Saying those words aloud is a luxury that I never expected to have, and the fact that I am saying them now is not an indicator of success, but rather of how tilted this situation has become.

"Oh." Sam pulls off his sunglasses and folds them up, then carefully inserts them into the pocket of his jacket. "So, ah. What is the problem?"

"She had something I need. Something for Colorado."

Sam turns to me, and I am almost grateful at the look I see there. The slow understanding tinged in fear. The look I must have myself, at a level five times higher than his. "How important is it?" he asks carefully.

At this moment, there are two paths I can take: one where I tell Sam the truth, and one where I lie. Can I trust him? The probability is high but not certain, and my wife is not the only lover I lie to.

"Not crucial," I say briskly. "But it's annoying, not having it. Anything you could find out about Lillian's last day . . . let me know, first. Before you tell the cops, or anyone else."

"Sure." He grins at me, and when he reaches for my hand, I don't pull it away despite the crawl of discomfort it creates in my chest. This, us—it needs to stop. "Come to my place tonight."

"I can't. Fuck, Sam. Lill just died. I have a son. For all I know the cops are watching me."

My chest tightens and I fumble with the center console lid, anxious for my inhaler. This has been a complete waste of time, because Sam knows nothing. The Benromach box could be in a public trash can right now, a $400 million key tucked inside it, waiting to be picked up by a janitorial service.

I need to find it, and every second that passes could be the difference between my doing so or it being picked up and taken away. I need to establish a grid around the house and then walk it. Meet with David, see what he knows and whether he saw her that day. The police should be able to ping locations off her cell phone. I need to go to the station, right after this, and see if they've already done that and, if so, what they've found out.

I grip the inhaler in my right hand and suck in a deep breath, holding the medicine in for a long beat. Coughing slightly, I adjust the strap of my seat belt. "Call me if you think of anything. I've got to go to the station now, answer some of their questions."

"Are they suspicious of you? I mean . . ." He colors around his ears. "Do they think there's any chance that Lillian didn't kill herself?"

I pause, my hand on the gearshift. "They haven't said that yet, but probably. You know, husbands are always suspects in the beginning." Especially husbands with $6 million life insurance policies. "Which is another reason why you should go. Just in case they're watching."

They aren't watching, but I need to hurry, and he's slow in opening the door, one expensive shoe testing the pavement before the other, and he gives me a final, plaintive look before he ducks out into the sunlight.

"Call me if you think of anything," I remind him.

He gives me a mock salute and he's irritated, but I don't care. God, he's worse than Lillian with the drama. That's one thing I won't miss, his competition with her. One romantic dinner with her had to be topped with a more expensive one with him. One weekend away countered by two. Sam had started to get bolder and bolder, and we were unbelievably lucky that she had never caught on.

I reverse out of the parking spot and am pulling onto Santa Monica Boulevard before he is back in his SUV. I head straight for the station, but can't get past the last things that Sam said.

I know that I didn't kill Lillian, but I also expected an investigation, so I've both accepted and dismissed the police's questioning as routine.

Lillian was a fragile person, one who had suffered from depression and overindulgence for most of our marriage, so the idea that she had overdosed is plausible, and one that I briefly grieved—in my own way—and then accepted. But if she was murdered, there is a chance that the killer has the liquor bottle, and the key to Colorado.

I check my reflection at a stoplight and fix the collar of my shirt, then smooth down my hair. Lillian used to always lick her fingers and then twist my hair into place, a disgusting habit that I suddenly miss. I try to do it myself, on a wild hair that is curling across my forehead, but it doesn't behave.

Gersh did ask, in the moment just before we ended our call, whether Jacob could come with me. He has yet to be questioned, and while I don't like the idea of it, there doesn't seem to be any way to avoid it. I assured Gersh that I would bring him in tomorrow, which gives me some time to address the more pressing issues with Colorado. Legally, Jacob can't be questioned without me there, though I'm not worried about what my son will or won't say. An innocent man has no secrets—and while I'm laughably far from innocent, in the area of my wife's suicide or potential murder, I'm a saint.

I stop at the light at Crescent and try to tick through the next item on my to-do list—the funeral. Sam mentioned picking out an outfit for her to wear, and while he thinks that he knows Lillian's style best, I already know what I want her to wear. It's a powder-blue dress, with straps that tie on the tops of her shoulders and with a knee-length skirt that flares out when she turns. I bought it for her two years ago, when we were in San Francisco for the weekend, and she had spilled spaghetti sauce on her blouse an hour before an Andrea Bocelli concert that we had third-row tickets for. She'd gotten the tickets through work, and was supposed to write a review of the show. The dress was expensive and unnecessary—we could have spot cleaned the spaghetti stain—but it had been a long time since I'd bought a gift for her, and the look on her face was almost heartbreaking. She was so excited and preened over the white bag and tissue-paper-wrapped dress as if they were something huge, and not a last-minute purchase from the women's shop in the hotel lobby.

I glance in the rearview mirror and catch myself smiling at the memory. I quickly school my mouth back into a flat line that is more appropriate for a man in mourning, and put on my turn signal for the police station. The last thing I need is for Gersh to see video footage of a Cheshire cat grin as I pull into the parking lot, even if it is from a loving memory of my wife.

I take a spot along the street and call Jacob before I go inside. His cell is off, and my irritation builds. I leave him a terse voice mail and then put my cell on vibrate and step out of the car, making sure that every element of Grieving Husband is properly in place before I shuffle toward the front door of the building.

CHAPTER 61

MIKE

"I don't understand." I look at Detective Gersh's computer screen, which displays a map of Los Angeles, covered by colored dots. "What is this?"

"It's everywhere Lillian's phone has pinged in the last forty-eight hours." The detective taps a few dots. "Each dot is a satellite-tower connection. These aren't her exact locations, but general areas. Underneath each is the day and time of the ping."

I look over the dots and try to understand what I'm seeing. Half of the dots are green, some are yellow, and some are red. A legend at the bottom tells me that green is for alive, yellow is for possible time of death, and red is postdeath. "Some of these movements are after she died."

"Yep." He nods like I have won a prize. "We're thinking that it was in a taxi or some other vehicle. Whoever has it, they took it all around the city, and it stopped connecting with towers this morning. We're assuming the battery has died."

"So you don't know where she went on the day she died?" I fumble with the top button of my shirt and undo it, needing some air. Don't they normally offer you a drink? Water?

"Well, this gives us a starting point, and we're working on putting together more precise movements now." He smiles at me as if he will figure out my evil plan—just give him a little more time.

"Okay. So she was in our house that morning, made the phone calls that afternoon, and died sometime that evening?" I tried to remember if the coroner had given a time of death. "And you guys have *no* idea where she went during that block of time, or where she died? Was it definitely on the beach?" I wipe my palms on the thighs of my pants, annoyed that he is feeding me information in crumb-size bites.

He stops smiling, and maybe I was a bit harsh with my tone. "As I said, we're putting together more precise movements."

"But you can't share them with me? Don't I have the right to know where my wife was?" I press. "I don't understand. Is this some big secret?"

"We'll share information when we can. For now, we need to clear your own movements on that day."

"Fine, sure. Of course." My right foot begins to nervously tap, and I dig the heel of it into the tile.

"You had asked me about the contents of her purse." Gersh pulls a fresh piece of paper out. "I have the listed inventory of the bag, if you want to review it and see if anything seems to be missing."

"Any luck finding the liquor?" I sound too eager. I frown and pinch my forehead together. There. Concerned Husband in place.

"No. I double-checked it to be sure." He slides the list of purse contents toward me. "What's the importance of the liquor?"

"It was a unique bottle that is missing. I don't care about the cost, but it seemed worth noting." I scan the list a few times. All useless shit.

He flips over a page and stares down at some writing. I'm dying to look at it. "Okay . . . ," he says slowly. "As you can see, there was a bottle of pills in her purse. Do you know what your wife was prescribed, Mr. Smith?"

Five years ago, I would have rattled off brand names and dosages with perfect accuracy. I made sure she ate a good breakfast every day and had her medications by eight thirty, and I was in bed with her each night, a cup of water and evening pill caddy in hand. She acted like she didn't like it, but Lillian always craved the attention, even if it was for the wrong things. At what point had I stopped monitoring her medication? It hadn't been an overnight thing. It had been one missed day, then two, then a bigger account that had taken me away for a week, and then Lillian had moved down a rung, then another, on my list.

I swallow. "I don't know," I say weakly. "Seroquel, I think. And maybe olanzapine?"

Gersh writes down the two medications, then flips over a different notebook page. "Looks like she stopped both of those last year and switched to Symbyax. Does that sound right?"

Another test, failed. "She changed medicines a lot." I shift in the hard metal seat. "So maybe."

"Let's get back to what you were doing that day."

I try not to look at my watch, but I need to hurry this along so I can drive around the neighborhood and spot, within walking distance of our house, where Lillian might have gone. I need to stop by the convenience store at the corner, and the liquor store on the other side, and ask that nosy neighbor, the one who is always bitching about our garbage cans. I could also ask the dog walker, the one with four leashes tied to each hand and a fanny pack full of shit. Someone had to have seen Lill, and I realize that I never checked the Uber app to see if she had decided to take a car somewhere, despite her ordered taxi.

"Mike?"

I move my hand under the table to keep myself from checking the time on my watch. "I woke up at six fifteen. Ate breakfast. I watched the news, worked out, took a shower, and left for the office at seven forty-five. I arrived at the office at around eight fifteen, and stayed there until twelve thirty, then drove home to pick up Lill. We were supposed to go to the attorney's office, but she wasn't at the house."

"Were you alarmed?"

"No. I was annoyed. I thought that she forgot or was intentionally avoiding the appointment. She's a little—she was a little stubborn about things. She'd 'forget' to do things that she didn't want to do. I tried to call her, then finally went on to the appointment by myself. What time did she die?"

Now it is the detective's turn to shift in his seat, and I can tell that he is warring over whether to give me the information. "Between three and seven that evening."

Inside, I groan. Only Lillian would pick such an inconvenient time to die.

"What did you do after the attorney appointment?" He has a pencil out, and he's writing all this down. After this, he'll confirm what I've said. A drop of sweat runs down the middle of my back. To tell the truth or not? My mind seesaws back and forth over the two options. I had decided to do some business, and fuck Lillian for going and dying during that window of time.

I cleared my throat. "I went to the office. I was there until around six, then I came home." It was my first lie, but one that would take time to disprove.

"And you were home all night?"

"Yes."

"Anyone who can verify that?"

"Ah . . ." I pause, thinking. "My son spent the night at a friend's house, but he stopped by the house around ten-thirty to get something."

The detective is looking at me with distaste, and I can anticipate the next question before it comes. "Didn't you wonder where your wife was?"

"I'd just discovered that she was having an affair. I assumed that she was with him, if she wasn't at home. And for all I knew, she was in the guest room. That's where she'd spent the night before." I need to wrap this up. Explaining myself to this prick is going to take all day. "Look, I hate to rush this, but I didn't do anything to Lillian. You're talking about an emotionally unstable woman who had a history of self-harm and substance abuse. She—"

"We don't know that," Gersh interrupts.

"Don't know what?"

"What history does she have of self-harm?"

I sigh. "Are you serious? Don't you have her medical records? Or her police records? Last year, Lillian was hospitalized for a suicide attempt. And her behavior is self-destructive. She—"

"We have her medical records," Gersh interrupts. "And in her hospitalization last May, her stomach contents included a heavy amount of ketamine."

"So?"

"Her doctors marked it as suspicious."

"Lillian's used ketamine as an antidepressant in the past. She microdoses." This is why I should have married a normal girl. Becca Parks was ripe for the taking, junior year. She would have popped out two babies for me and never gotten so much as a parking ticket. Instead, I married a beautiful, creative train wreck, one who needed me with a desperation that Becca Parks couldn't touch.

There is a part of me that already misses her.

"Did you hear me, Mr. Smith?" He is staring at me with barely disguised contempt.

"I'm sorry?"

"Until we can verify your alibi, we have to consider you a person of interest. The sooner we can speak to Jacob, the better. You can bring him here, or we can interview him at home. Up to you."

"His mother just died. I don't want to freak him out."

"Of course. He's not a suspect. We just need to verify some information with him."

I nod, because I don't know what else to do. This is crazy. I've spent ten years shielding my family from this sort of scenario.

"So we can come over now and talk to him?" Gersh looks at his watch, and I take that as my cue to do the same.

"I'll have to see where he is. He wasn't home when I went by there earlier."

"Okay, but today. We'll come by if I don't hear from you."

"Sure." I don't like the way he said that, with an edge to the words. He can talk to Jacob whenever he wants. I'm not afraid of anything that Jacob will say. I force myself to ignore the tone. Right now, I need to be the Perfect Grieving Husband, and that means helping the police is supposed to be my number-one goal.

"Let me give you Jacob's cell. You can just coordinate directly with him. I'm assuming I have to be present during the interview, since he's a minor?" I take the pen and piece of paper that he offers and write down Jacob's cell, crossing one item off my list. Look at me, Mr. Helpful. Definitely not guilty, not in any way.

"California law allows us to interview him on his own. And like I said, he's not under suspicion. We're just trying to find out what happened to Lillian."

Oh yes. Sweet, perfect Lillian. Let's all stop everything to find out why she killed herself, or got herself killed. This is Los Angeles, for God's sake. People get killed for going the wrong way down a street, much less for being a crazy white lady walking around by herself with a bottle in hand. "Are you looking at this as a suicide or as a murder?" It's a question that I should have asked earlier, but my hands have been full, and right now, I'm just trying to not get my head cut off—literally, cut off—by the Mexican cartel.

"That's still up in the air. There are suspicious circumstances around how she was found."

"But she wasn't raped, or anything like that?" I press. "And she didn't have anything odd in her system?"

"There was no sign of sexual assault or violence," he says, confirming half of my question and standing. I don't press further because if I'm free to leave, I just need to keep myself from sprinting out the door.

He extends his hand and I shake it. "I'll be in touch."

"Great. Let me know any way that I can help."

His grip tightens, and I squeeze right back and remind myself to smile. *Helpful. Helpful Perfect Husband.*

CHAPTER 62

LILLIAN

My son has been kidnapped. I'm repeating that phrase over and over to remind myself that I should be freaking out. Instead, I'm strangely calm, and maybe it's because Jacob hasn't been taken to a dark cell or a woodshed, or anyplace I've ever seen in the movies. Instead, he's seated at a dining room table and being served steak empanadas dripping in queso. Every seat at the round table is full, with an extra folding chair to make up for his presence. He's silent, but everyone else is talking, rapid Spanish bouncing back and forth across the table as food is passed in red bowls and yellow platters.

On one side of him is Aerosmith, the tank top on the other side. Also at the table is a girl Jacob's age, then a pregnant woman, then a prepubescent boy, then a wrinkled older woman and an overweight bald man. A soccer game plays from the living room TV, and occasionally the men break into cheers or shouts, depending on what happens on the screen.

Jacob sits back in his chair, his hands in his lap, his gaze jerking nervously between the men on either side of him. He hasn't touched the food on his plate, though the pregnant woman keeps prodding him to eat.

Who are you? I ask the question but no one can hear me. *Who are you and what are you doing with my son?*

A timer goes off on the stove, and the older woman rises and moves to the skillet, using a spatula to stir the browning meat, and a mouth-watering scent of onions and ground beef fills the room. As the conversation continues at the table, she tosses comments over her shoulder, then laughs at something that has been said. Dialogue ricochets, and I wish Mike were here. With his fluency in Spanish, at least he would understand what they are saying.

I look for a weapon for Jacob to grab, something he can use to protect himself. There are knives and heavy skillets everywhere, and no one seems concerned about the potential threats. Instead of giving me comfort, I feel even more alarmed. They aren't afraid of Jacob running. Why? Why is everyone just going about their meal as if my child wasn't taken at gunpoint from his bedroom?

I circle the table and crouch beside Jacob, watching as he tentatively cuts at the crust of the empanada. It falls open and steam breaks into the air, and I'm surprised to find that hunger exists even when I am dead. He stares at the food and I mentally urge him to eat, because who knows when or if he will be fed again.

My son has been kidnapped. This makes no sense. Are these the people who killed me? What do they need Jacob for?

"You should eat." The girl two seats down is watching him. "It's good. A little spicy, but they are my favorite." She smiles shyly and the corner of his mouth crooks up. Poor Jacob. Three more sentences and he'll be in love.

"Rosa!" The pregnant woman waves her fork in the air, at the girl. *"¡Cállate la boca y ponte a comer! Él no está aquí para hablar contigo."* She glares at Jacob and points, and I don't know what she is saying, but the girl rolls her eyes and scoops up a chunk of ground beef.

"She says I can't talk to you."

"*¡Suficiente! Una palabra más y le diré a tu padre que te castigue a golpes.*" I flinch at the anger in the woman's tone, and whatever she says, the girl's attitude lessens and she slumps in her seat and doesn't look at Jacob again.

I need to get him out of here. While it may be mouthwatering smells and family time now, at some point this will turn ugly. These men had a gun, one that they pointed at Jacob's head.

I stand behind my son and wait to see what happens next.

CHAPTER 63

LENNY

The pieces of the puzzle are coming in slowly, but they are there and Gersh is not all useless for a child born in the eighties.

Lillian's stomach contents include what appear to be a pumpkin spice latte, half of a banana, some crackers, and a cocktail of medicines, including enough Xanax to kill a three-hundred-pound man. Blood tests show a blood alcohol level of .29 and GHB—the former would have had her stumbling around, and the latter she *could* have gotten her hands on. Together they make me suspect foul play.

If her cell phone's location pings are reliable, which they aren't, all they share is that her killer was smart enough to ditch it before he took her anywhere important. If anything, we should probably look at the places the cell phone didn't go, rather than those it did.

Gersh has a tail on the husband, and the traffic department is back-tracking his car movements for the last forty-eight hours, including the time of her death.

At least there was no rape. No evidence of prior abuse, despite the faked call to the domestic center. Also missing . . . any distinguish-able foreign hairs, blood, or DNA on her body. If she fought some-one off, she did it without her fingernails, and without damaging herself at all. Unfortunately, with GHB in her system, she probably was cooperative. Probably opened up her mouth for the pills, then asked for more.

Now I sit in a place I used to know well—the questioning pod—only this time I am behind the glass, beside the transcriber and some asshole from Legal, who apparently watches all questioning to make sure the suspect is given cupcakes and back massages. On the other side of the glass, Gersh sits across from Lillian's boyfriend, who looks cool as a fucking cucumber and is refusing to answer any questions, except to some badge named Pat Horkins.

"Who the fuck is Pat Horkins?" The Legal guy asks the question before I have to.

"He's in narcotics." The transcriptionist speaks from his spot at the table, and I swear, everyone in this joint is barely old enough to grow facial hair. "Works with a lot of the agencies."

Okay, so maybe rosy-cheeked youths are helpful. "Agencies?" I grunt. I examine the boyfriend as best I can through the glass. Maybe he's connected. An informant.

"Why you waiting on Horkins?" Gersh asks David Laurent, and I like that he doesn't use a pad of paper. Makes him seem like he already knows what you're about to say, and I never knew what to write down anyway. Plus, with this pencil head typing and the cameras humming, you're getting all the notes you need without having to move a finger. "You an informant? Running drugs out of your boat?"

The man smiles and says nothing, and in the good old days, now is when you would smack him in the jaw. A woman is dead and he's toying with us, withholding information that could lead to her killer. Maybe it's him. He certainly doesn't seem brokenhearted, and I'm annoyed at the commonalities I'm seeing between him and her husband. At least Mike made an effort to seem upset. This asshole is two seconds away from whistling a cheery tune.

The door to our cramped room opens, and a uniform comes in and presses the intercom button to Gersh's room. "Horkins is twenty minutes out. Says he's DEA."

In our room, everyone reacts. The attorney sighs, the kid at the table whistles, and I automatically reach for my flask, then realize it's in the car. If any news qualifies for a drink, that does. DEA. Talk about a wrinkle.

"DEA . . . ," Gersh muses, and if there were a way for David Laurent—who is probably not named David Laurent—to preen, he would be doing it. Fucking feds. Always, *always* thinking that they are better than us. "Now that's interesting."

Gersh hunches forward. "Now I realize why you aren't talking. You're scared, right? That you'll say the wrong thing, will violate one of those ten thousand rules you suits have to follow. So how about I just toss some ideas out there—just dumb local-cop ideas, you understand—and you just nod if I'm anywhere close to being right. Nothing for the transcript; in fact, I'll turn off the cameras."

Smart. Gersh is smart. I'm nodding, and almost give him a thumbs-up when he faces the window and reaches up and unplugs the camera in the upper corner of the room. I keep my thumbs to myself since he can't see me, but the sentiment is still there.

"I'm going to assume that you didn't kill Lillian. Yes?"

He pauses, and this is an easy nod for David to make, but an important one, one that will concede his willingness to play this game.

The man rolls his eyes behind a dorky pair of glasses—*What did Lillian see in this dweeb?*—and nods.

"Okay, great. Now I'm going to assume that she wasn't just a side piece of ass you picked up while suntanning on the job. Was she a part of an operation?"

This David is less reluctant to answer, and I lean closer, my breath fogging the glass. *Come on . . .* "I'll speak to Horkins, when he gets here.

Just Horkins. I'm not confirming that I was or wasn't part of any sort of operation."

I growl out a curse. Pansy-ass feds. I swear to God, they're more trouble than help.

"I just need to stop running in certain directions if they're dead ends, you understand?"

"Oh sure." David gives a shit-licker smile. "Don't worry, Detective. We're all on the same page here."

"It's a fucking nod," I yell, and the attorney flinches. "Just nod, you fucking fed!"

"Mr. Thompson"—the attorney clears his throat—"you are here as a courtesy. Please remember that. Also, they can't hear you."

"Is it her husband?" Gersh presses. "Were you trying to get to him?"

I glare at the boyfriend, but he just sits there in silence, that obnoxious little smirk stuck on his face.

CHAPTER 64

MIKE

There is a point in every problem when you must decide whether to solve the problem or run. My problem is simple—I need this damn encryption key, and it takes only three hours of looking for me to realize that I am not going to find it, not soon enough to satisfy my clients. Which is a shame, because running is going to be a huge pain in my ass. Like, colonoscopy-prep levels of gut-wrenching shitassery.

I have, of course, prepared for this. You don't work thirteen years for an organized crime syndicate without having backup plans stacked on top of backup plans. I have three cars at various lots in the city, each gassed up, their trunks full of suitcases, food, weapons, and cash. I have two alternate aliases for Lillian, Jacob, and myself, and Bitcoin balances in both US and foreign accounts that could fund us for the next three years, which is plenty of time to set up new lives and employment.

The issue is that once I step off that ledge, once I go dark for longer than a few minutes, I will be marked, and then there will be no going back, ever again. It won't matter if I find the key and move Colorado in time to save the day. It won't matter because trying to deliver Colorado will create a trail, and the minute that last digit is entered, my fingertips will be cut off and my eyelids peeled back, and I will be forced, from that position, to watch as my child is tortured because doing it improperly is not acceptable.

I am out of time and out of options because this city has swallowed up this bottle and I am the idiot who put it within arm's reach of a borderline alcoholic with some belief that nostalgia would prevail. Who gives an F if nostalgia worked for the last nine years? It was stupid, and as a result, I have to run, which means Jacob has to run.

I park in the driveway beside Jacob's car and walk up to the house, holding my breath as I check the recycling bin by the side door, on the off chance that Lill chucked it there. Nothing. The side door is unlocked, and I step inside. Another rule Jacob hasn't listened to. Always lock the doors. Always. Tick. Tick. Tick.

Mentally, I assemble a list. Grab Jacob, get a few blocks over, flag a taxi to the closest flee car—the Mazda in the Century City parking garage—and leave. I call out his name as I climb the stairs to the second floor, my mind clicking through the rest of what I should do before we leave the house. Wipe the computers. Leave the phones. I knock on the door to Jacob's room and turn the knob. I need to take the—

I stop because there's a man sitting on the edge of his bed, smiling at me. I look for Jacob, but the room is empty. I look at the bed but don't see any blood.

"Michael," Luis says warmly. "It's been a long time."

CHAPTER 65

MIKE

"What's going on, Mike?" Luis folds one ankle up on the opposite knee and looks at me. "You have not started to move Colorado. Why?"

Jacob's bathroom is just off his bedroom, a Jack-and-Jill layout that connects to the guest room, and I listen, hoping and also not hoping that he is inside. Luis follows my gaze and shakes his head. "He's not here, Mike."

I sink against the dresser in relief. "He doesn't have anything to do with—"

"Oh, Mike." Luis tsks. "The young never do. But that doesn't mean that they don't suffer the sins of their fathers, right?" He shakes his head sadly. "I mean, take your father. You suffered from his sins. Both you and your mother did."

I don't respond, and my relief at Jacob not being here is replaced by the growing fear that Luis is the reason that he isn't. "Where's Jacob?"

"He's safe, Mike. You understand, of course, why we had to take him."

I shake my head. "Luis, I've worked for you all for thirteen years, I would never run—"

"Of course you wouldn't," he says broadly. "I'm not worried about that. Because you know, Mike. You know how we would react to that.

And it's a shame, with you already losing your wife . . ." He stands and claps his hands on either side of my shoulders, and I remember when I first met him. I'd found him charming. We'd met at a Vegas craps table and then taken shots with cigars, and he'd asked me a dozen questions about diversification of portfolios, and I had come home and bragged to Lillian about the new client I had. The new client, who was bringing over a mid-six-figure account. Back then, I thought that was big. Back then, I was so impressed by Luis and his future possibilities that I bent a few securities laws. Wee ones. Unimportant ones.

I stepped over the line and it moved. Then I stepped over it again and it grew fainter. Blurrier. I took a few more steps, and now I'm here, and my son is somewhere "safe," and all I need to do to bring him back is move $400 million that I can't access.

His hands tighten on my shoulders, and he is looking up into my face and giving the same warm, encouraging smile that he gave to Wes Flockhart, right before he used a drill bit on his left collarbone. "We want to make sure you're okay, Mike. Because my partners, they are getting nervous."

As they should be. They should be shitting their pants, because if this savings account is gone—and it is gone—every one of them is ruined and dead. Including me. And including Jacob.

He smiles again, but I can see the fear in his eyes. "So let's go together, Mike. Let's go and transfer Colorado to where it belongs."

CHAPTER 66

LILLIAN

Something has changed, and Aerosmith and Tank Top are all business, and they are moving Jacob down a staircase and into the basement. Now is when my mothering instincts scream the alarm because nothing good exists in this basement. There are shackles—actual shackles—attached to the wall and hanging, waiting for someone's wrists and ankles. I don't have to see this. I could fade away, return to the morgue, where I could watch as they pin my skin back together in a way that will look natural for the funeral. Or I could go to the house and watch as my husband continues to coldly rearrange his life to accommodate one fewer person. But if Jacob has to be here, I will be here. I will feel each pain and watch and agonize because that is my duty as a mother, even if I feel like I'm fading with each hour that passes. Even now, as they say something to him, as they push him into the chair and one of the men draws his gun . . . their voices are beginning to muffle, and Jacob is blurry, then sharp. I blink rapidly and try to ground myself, try to stand in between his chair and the gun, try to say something that someone will be able to hear. I plead that we have money, that we will pay, that they do not need to kill this boy.

Now a folding table is set up beside Jacob's chair and I know what they are going to put on it. Elements of torture. Wire cutters. Shocks and knives. I am nauseated as they carry in a cardboard box, set it on the surface, and reach inside.

Then a surprise. The first item pulled out is not a knife but a laptop. Then a keyboard and mouse. A long extension cord, which is plugged in to the wall and then attached to the back of the computer.

Jacob is as confused as me and watches everything they are doing, his head jerking from side to side as he tries to take it all in.

I catch the word *padre* in something they say to him, and I'm not sure whether this is someone else's father or his, but I hope they call Mike. Mike will handle this. He will find whatever money is needed for a ransom—and I suddenly think of my life insurance money and wonder whether that is what this is about. We had two policies on me, and they totaled more than $5 million, maybe six.

People would certainly kidnap and kill someone for that money. It could pay off this house and buy five more. Cover the costs for a caregiver for the older lady. Private school and college tuition for the girl.

Repercussions. Mike loved to talk about them. Small and large, the trickle effects of our actions. Here is the trickle effect of mine. I died, and my life insurance put my son at risk.

No matter, because Mike will pay. He *has* to pay, and he won't just pay: he'll think through how to pay in a way that will ensure Jacob's safety, and he'll anticipate any dangers, and he'll examine the situation from each side and every angle, to guarantee success.

I take a deep breath and try to channel the confidence toward Jacob, who looks terrified. From behind me, the door at the top of the stairs opens. I turn and look up, and there is Mike.

My hope and confidence plummet at the look on his face.

CHAPTER 67

LENNY

I give up on David Laurent's interview when the brass and the feds show up. It isn't just Horkins; two other suits arrive, which is enough to convince me that Laurent was an undercover agent and Lillian was a target. Why is still a giant question mark, but I trust Gersh to get to the bottom of it and leave the station before anyone starts asking questions about why I am there.

I drive over to Lillian's house to take a look. As a detective, I wasn't Sherlock Holmes and didn't break any sort of department records, but I was a good cop. I noticed things that others didn't, and I had an intuition that kept a few bad characters from slipping through some cracks. So I take a moment, a long moment, as I drive by and just observe.

I've never bothered to think about what sort of house Lillian Smith would live in, but this one is painfully dull, one that has gone out of its way to be normal. It's brick, with a double garage that faces the front, two windows on the second story, and a wide front porch that holds two rocking chairs and a pot of dead geraniums. Three houses down is an identical duplicate, and across the street is the same home, flipped and minus the front porch. They have three parking pads, and there's an older sedan in one with a Nine Inch Nails window decal. I circle the block, then return and park a few houses down, in front of a ranch style with a **FOR SALE** sign in the yard.

Gersh shared with me what they knew—that the neighbor across the street saw Lillian walk out her front door and head to the left around eleven. After that, she disappeared. The closest major intersections with cameras don't have any record of her on foot, and there are no taxis or car services that enter or exit the area that haven't already been questioned and cleared. I knock on the neighbor's door and wait, eyeing Lillian's house across the street. According to Gersh, she's a bit of a busybody, but that works well for me.

I knock again, and look down the street. A truck passes, then a sedan. It's fairly busy, which should help. Someone had to have seen something, and we just have to find that person, and then the next person. She got from here all the way to Malibu, so someone, other than her killer, saw something.

I step off the porch and cross over to Lillian's house, then turn the direction that the neighbor said she walked. According to the husband, she left the house with a bottle of bourbon, a fact he was very insistent about. So she was drinking, and I can certainly put myself in that mindset. I pause at a cross section of streets. Ahead, a major road two blocks up. To the right, a cul-de-sac. I turn left.

I wander down streets and across lawns. I stop a kid on a bike and show him a picture of her. I sit on a bus stop bench and call Gersh and ask him to check the bus activity. I walk and take my own sips from a flask and think through everything that I know so far.

Women don't just disappear. If not by their own hand, they are taken by a stranger or by someone that they know.

First, the potential stranger. She's an attractive woman, though that isn't necessary to attract danger. She's alone in public, in a fairly safe area, if any part of Los Angeles can be considered safe, but she's drinking and she's off her medication, which makes her unpredictable and prone to blackouts, according to her doctor, husband, and best friend.

So maybe she blacked out or flagged down a stranger. And that stranger could have drugged her, accidentally or intentionally killed her, and dumped her body in Malibu. It's not a horrible theory except for . . .

The phone calls. Someone needed an intimate knowledge, or at minimum a working knowledge, of Lillian in order to make those phone calls. And whoever did make those phone calls was intentionally casting red herrings. So I was leaning away from a stranger's involvement.

And the phone calls also eliminate the possibility that Lillian got drunk, got herself over to Malibu, and overdosed, either intentionally or accidentally.

I trip over a crack in the sidewalk that I should have seen, but I didn't, because my attention is on what I have just found: Lillian's drinking spot. I know it because she described this spot before, in a conversation I had forgotten but now recall.

"I cheat on you, you know." She peeked at me through hooded eyes, and if I still had a heart, I probably would have fallen in love with Lillian already.

"Do you now?" I'm trying to stay upright, trying to maintain a cool air of dignity, but the tombstones are beginning to spin, and I need to just lie down and close my eyes for twenty, maybe thirty, minutes.

"I do. I have another cemetery, much cuter than this one. And it has benches." She said the word as if it were special, as if we couldn't buy benches if we wanted to—though I wasn't sure we could, since the board wouldn't approve the budget to repair the broken trash can that someone backed into last December. "Plus, it's in walking distance of my house. So . . . none of this"—she waved both hands in the air to encompass her car and the LA traffic—"driving nonsense."

"But does it have me?" I asked.

"A grouchy groundskeeper who steals my food and drinks?" she deadpanned. "No, that is an excellent point. It's clearly lacking."

I had toasted to that and then lain back on the grass to keep the world from spinning.

Before me is a small neighborhood cemetery, one surrounded by a neat iron gate. I open it and step in. There is a bench, I note. And past that, another one. I walk down a thin paved path. Maybe fifty plots, many of them disturbed by the mature roots of the trees. And it's quiet, pleasantly so. She probably sat here and got drunk. And then . . . what?

I weigh the possibilities and listen, counting the cars and people as they pass. Not many. If I slouched down, I could sleep on the bench and no one would bother me. No one would likely see me.

I return to the street and look left, then right, getting my bearings. The road is a cut-through, one that people take when jumping between the two main roads. Maybe on her way here, or on her way back, someone she knew—her husband or a friend—saw her walking and stopped. Offered her a ride. Opened the trap door they would later push her down.

I quicken my steps, aware that the sun is starting to sink in the sky. I don't want to drive in the dark, not with my bad eyes. I make it back to her street and am passing the neighbor's house when I detour back up the front steps and try her door once more. This time, it opens immediately and I'm met by a birdlike woman with white hair and darting, suspicious eyes. "Yes?" She keeps the door half-closed, so I can see only the edge of her face. Behind her, there are stacks of boxes and papers, and the faint odor of cat urine hits my nose.

"I'm Leonard Thompson, formerly of the LAPD." I take off my hat, which Marcella used to say makes me look nicer.

"Formerly?" She squeaks when she speaks.

"I'm retired, but I was a close friend of your neighbor's, Mrs. Smith."

"Are you here about my call?" She edges the door a hair wider and pops her head out, craning her neck to look around me and at the street. "Where are the others? Are they coming?"

"What call?" I step back so that she can get a better look.

"The call about the boy," she snaps and steps onto the porch and pulls the door tight behind her. She's wearing a LeBron jersey and green pajama pants, and I try not to stare at her feet, which are bare, with toenails so long they curl into ringlets at the ends. She points toward Lillian's house. "The teenager. Two men came and took him, just a few hours ago. I've called three times about this."

"Took him?" I repeat cautiously, and I'm not entirely surprised that no one has shown up yet. According to Gersh, she called 911 forty-three times last year, to report litterers, dogs off leashes, seat-belt violations, suspicious characters, and the belief that her next-door neighbors were selling drugs. They weren't. "What do you mean?"

"I mean that two guys went around to the back of the house and, five minutes later, walked out with him and put him in the back seat of their car. And he was scared. I could see from here, the way he was walking, like if he moved wrong, they were going to hurt him." She nods, her arms crossing over her chest, and I believe her.

"What can you tell me about the men? Do you remember what they were wearing?"

She smiles, and if she could have cackled, she would have. "I can do better than that. I took a picture."

———

Rosa Bertawich took six photos, and all of them are worthless, save one, which shows the vehicle that the two men and Jacob got into: a white Nissan Altima with black tinted windows. The smaller of the two men took the driver's seat, while the other got in the back seat, with the teenager. Rosa was right to be concerned. Even in the still frames of a photo, you can see that Jacob is in trouble, his posture stiff, his face pale and afraid. I have her text the photos to me and step out on her porch to call Gersh.

CHAPTER 68

LILLIAN

They sit Mike down at the computer and point at the keyboard and mouse and wait. Silence falls and it feels like everyone is holding their breath, staring at him, waiting on him. For what?

"Make the transfer." This is not Aerosmith or Tank Top; this is a new man, dressed in a nice white golf shirt and pleated shorts. He looks like a businessman: an expensive watch on his wrist, straight white teeth, and a clean-shaven face with a fresh haircut. Subtract the extra forty pounds he's carrying, and he could be a menswear model, posed by a smiling child, someone I would trust to give me directions or accept an offer from to fix my flat tire. My judgment is off, because he appears to be in charge, and Mike is obeying him as if he were holding a gun to his head, which he isn't.

"I can't." Mike's hands are on the keyboard, but they aren't moving, and the look that he sends Jacob's way terrifies me. It's apologetic, like Mike can't get them out of this, like this is the end. But that can't be right, because Mike always has contingency plans, always. Even if we don't have the insurance money yet, surely our 401(k)s, our home equity, the balances in his whole-life policy—surely there's enough there to buy him some time, to give him a week or two to come up with more. And we know people. Sam would pitch in, and Mike has other friends, rich friends, who would loan some money if it meant saving Jacob's and Mike's lives.

"What do you mean, you can't?" The businessman leans over Mike and stares at the screen. "That's the account, right there. So move it."

"I don't know the private key. I have the address, but not the key."

The man's grip on Mike's shoulder tightens and my husband winces. "Who has the key?"

Mike closes his eyes and exhales. I've never seen him like this. My husband is always in control, always confident. It's annoying, the consistency of his self-assuredness—but now I want it back. I want his cocky, smug look, his know-it-all tone, his condescending overexplanation of concepts that are dumbed down to an elementary level. I want that Mike back and this one gone. "I'm trying to find the key now."

Aerosmith brings another chair out, and the businessman sits in front of Mike and leans his elbow on the table. "Explain this to me, Mike."

Yes, I beg. *Please, explain this to us.*

"I couldn't store the key in a digital wallet, or anything connected to the web, due to security risks or potential government seizure. The safest place to put it was old-school—pen and paper, which was a storage system that I've used for Colorado since we first moved to Bitcoin."

There is complete silence as Mike pauses, and if he expects a nod and murmur of understanding, he doesn't get it. "I also needed something portable that could be easily moved in case of emergency. Something that could be protected in an instance of fire or flooding." He glances at Jacob, who looks like he's going to be sick. "So I hid the key in a box with a bottle of liquor, and stored it in a safe in our pantry."

Oh no.

"The liquor had sentimental value, and we'd planned to open and drink it on our twentieth wedding anniversary—"

The man in the golf shirt cuts in. "Get to the point."

"I haven't figured out why, but my wife took the box on the day she died, and left the house. I was tracking her movements today but haven't found the box yet. With the police, and all of this"—he gestures to Jacob and the other men—"I've been distracted."

"Distracted from Colorado?" The man chuckles, but there is no amusement behind the sound. "How do you get distracted from Colorado?"

I don't understand what Colorado is and why it needs a key, but it appears that I may be the one to blame for Jacob being kidnapped, and for Mike bleeding sweat in front of this computer.

"Your wife has been dead for almost two days, Mike." The man slowly stands and moves the chair away from the table. "When did you discover that this key was gone?"

"This morning."

"This morning?" He doesn't like that answer, and I'm feeling faint and slightly nauseated myself. I'm not sure if it's because whatever connection I have is fading, or if I'm just ordinary-living-person nervous, but all this is bad. Really bad.

I strain to remember what I did with the box of bourbon. I walked to the cemetery and started to drink it there. I remember sitting on the hard concrete bench and watching two mockingbirds go at it and wondering whether Mike and I would be divorced by the time our twentieth anniversary rolled around. And then . . .

"This morning . . . ," the man repeats. "Before or after you met with Sam Knight?"

"Uh, before." Mike sounds unsure, as if he's testing the temperature of the water with his toe before stepping in.

"You know, Sam's an interesting cat."

"Luis . . . ," Mike pleads, putting his palms together.

"You have done many deals with him, with our money. Some good deals." The man tilts his head. "Some bad."

"Everything washes the cash," Mike says quietly. "Even the losses."

240

"Yes, but we have to wonder . . . Is Sam really the best person for this task?" The man—Luis—sits back down in the chair and it creaks, metal against metal hinges. "Which makes us wonder if you are really the best person for this task."

I'm mentally torn between my attempt to chase down the memory and the information that is unfolding before me. I glance at Jacob and he's also listening closely, the both of us trying to put together pieces of a puzzle that we didn't know existed.

I'm proud of him. I'm proud of him for keeping quiet, for not crying, for waiting and watching and staying in control of his emotions. Part of that is the Mike in him, but part of it is me. I am half of him. I raised him, more than Mike ever did. I move behind him and try to wrap my arms around him, but I don't have arms and legs anymore. I am just here, waiting for the moment I will be gone.

"You see . . ." Luis pulls at the leg of his shorts, straightening the material. "We did not know the nature of your relationship when you brought him to us. Specifically, while we knew his sexual proclivities"— he shrugs in acknowledgment—"they are fairly obvious, but we were not aware of yours."

Yours? I am lost and stare at Mike, trying to understand why he has gone even paler.

"Romance doesn't mix well with our business. Neither do secrets."

Romance? He's alluding to the idea that Sam and Mike are involved, but that can't be right. Jacob makes a soft sound, like a cat crying, and then more footsteps come down the stairs.

"Let's share all of our secrets, Mike," Luis says. "Shall we?"

My mind skitters, like a flickering film frame, and suddenly, I remember.

CHAPTER 69
LILLIAN

The day of the death

The thing about Mike and his girlfriend, thinking back on it, is that this wasn't an isolated affair. I suspected he'd been unfaithful at multiple intervals over our eighteen years of marriage. And I was happy with David. I felt different, and I liked different, and maybe . . . if Mike wasn't being faithful and I was happier with someone else, maybe this whole marriage thing had no point.

I tipped back the bourbon bottle. The flavor was beginning to grow on me, the bite less stiff as I took smaller and more frequent sips. I used to love bourbon. That drink that I used to have every Christmas . . . the cinnamon maple bourbon sour. That was it. Sam would make it, along with his famous eggnog, and serve them both with chocolate biscotti. *I should save some of this for that.*

I would definitely get Sam in a potential divorce, despite his fondness for Mike. I took another sip and smiled at the thought of going out with him and letting his matchmaker tendencies go wild. Maybe I could move in with him. He had enough room. That giant house? Granted, he was a bit of a nag about organization and neatness. He'd probably kick me out the first time I tracked in dirt, or didn't use a coaster, or left hair in the shower.

I glanced at my watch and sighed. I should head home. We had the meeting with the attorney in two hours, and I needed to change and freshen up. I could put the bourbon back in the box and in the liquor cabinet. Mike wouldn't even notice until after our divorce was filed or the anniversary occurred, and by then—if we made it that long—who would care about a few missing sips?

I eyed the bottle. Maybe I had taken more than a few sips. Had I really drunk that much? I stood, and the gravestone closest to me swayed. Okay, yeah. Maybe alcohol, on an empty stomach, with medicine, wasn't a great combo.

I pushed the bottle back into its box and returned it to my bag. Sighing, I pulled the strap of my blue Marc Jacobs purse over my shoulder. I took an unsteady step forward, then another. My right leg buckled and I grabbed the edge of the bench for support.

Okay, I had this. I glanced around, and considered inducing a vomit. No one was around. No one would see if I hurried over to the closest palm, leaned against it, and let everything fly out.

A car drove by, on just the other side of the low iron gate, and I nixed the idea. I was only four blocks from home. I could make it there and into the privacy of my bathroom. With my luck, I'd do it here and end up with chunks of last night's pizza all over the front of my shirt.

Gathering myself, I aimed for the gate and made it out and onto the sidewalk without incident. I kept my eyes on the sidewalk ahead of me and plodded, one foot in front of the other, to the stop sign at the cross section of the nearest street. My street. I just needed to hang a right and go three blocks and . . . voilà. I'd be home. Easy peasy.

Jeez, I was thirsty. My tongue felt like it was caked in dryness. An ice cube right now would be glorious.

Glorious. That was a word you didn't hear enough of. In fact, with over a thousand obituaries written, I'd never once used the word *glorious.* I could have fit it in. *She lived a glorious life as a . . .* I frowned. Maybe *glorious* wasn't a good adjective for an obit.

"Lillian?" Someone was calling my name and I straightened, realizing I was leaning against the stop sign.

It was Sam, my knight in a shiny black SUV, his window down, looking at me as if I had two heads. "Are you lost?" He chuckled and waved at me. "Come on. Get in."

I looked left, right, left, making sure that no cars were in sight, then carefully made my way over to the passenger door and climbed in. Dropping my bag by my feet, I turned to him. "Hi. Nice car."

"Hi. Thank you." He grinned at me from beneath a blue baseball cap. "You look drunk."

"I'm fairly drunk," I admitted. "I may have dipped into the liquor cabinet after you left."

"Well, here." He lifted a Starbucks cup out of the cup holder.

"Oh, I love you forever." I cupped the pumpkin spice latte reverently with both hands. "Were you bringing this to me?"

He smiled at me. "You seemed down this morning. I wanted to check back in with you, figured you could use the caffeine."

"Bless you, child." I took a deep sip, then another. I closed my eyes and set my head back on the rest. "I've got this meeting with the attorney at two."

"You got plenty of time. Don't worry." He took a right on the street before our block.

"Wait, take me home." I pointed limply toward the direction of our house.

"I will. I just need to check on a listing real quick. Just relax. You need to sober up a little before Mike sees you anyways." He tapped the screen and pressed an icon, and my seat reclined.

I groaned in appreciation and took another sip of my latte. "You should have gotten the venti."

He chuckled and made a slow turn down a residential street. "Greedy girl. Most people would just say thank you."

"Thank you. Next time get the venti." I took another long pull and then shook the cup, indicating how empty it almost was. I reached over and squeezed his arm. "I'm just kidding."

"Sort of," he countered.

"Sort of," I agreed.

"I solemnly swear to never buy you another minuscule-size pumpkin latte." He placed his hand on his heart to underline the vow.

"Thank you." Leaving my hand on his arm, I noticed the white gloves he was wearing. "What's with the gloves?"

"They're moisture gloves." He nodded toward my knees. "Want to try them? There's an extra pair in a bag by your feet."

I waved off the offer, the glove box too far away for me to reach from my reclined position. "This car is nice." I looked in the back seat. "Is it new?"

"Loaner from the dealership."

"Cool. Oh, Sam?" I yawned.

"Yeah?"

I had a question to ask him, or maybe it was a comment, but the interior of the vehicle was starting to spin and I had to close my eyes to stop the motion. Beneath me, the seat whirred and reclined farther, till I was almost flat, and he was so sweet and thoughtful. That was my last thought, before I fell asleep. How sweet Sam was.

I couldn't imagine what my life would look like without him.

CHAPTER 70

SAM

How do you justify murder? I had two reasons: jealousy and revenge.

Screw her for not appreciating him, or me, or respecting and understanding what was right underneath her nose. Screw him for tossing me aside every time she snapped her fingers, or paid him the slightest bit of attention, or screwed up in some new and unimaginative way.

I had a few options. I could have walked away from him and her, licked my wounds, built my life without them and the nonstop blender they put my heart in, but the problem was the money. Mike's business kept me fat—money always needed to be washed, and real estate flips were one of the best ways to do it. Last year, he accounted for more than 70 percent of my business and referred me more big-ticket clients than I gained through any other source. Ignoring the heartbreak, I literally couldn't afford to lose him, which was why I ditched that option for an easier one—getting rid of her.

Poor Lillian made it easy on me. Put a drink in her hands and she'd guzzle it. Swap a pill in her medicine bottle and she'd pop it. A year ago, for two months straight, I replaced all her bipolar medication with an estrogen blocker to see how she reacted. I tested GHB in her drinks at Perch, and she blacked out for a solid six hours. I could have cherry-picked a variety of options to take when she was in my car, that pumpkin latte clutched in her spindly little hands, but I had a plan, of course. As Benjamin Franklin once said, by failing to prepare, you are preparing to fail, and killing someone wasn't something I could afford to fail at. Imprisonment, along with poverty and emotional abandonment, would not be in my future, and I spent hundreds of hours envisioning the perfect way to end Lillian Smith's life.

That's why this was the perfect murder, and it's why I will never be caught. Tomorrow belongs to the people who plan for it today, and I planned for this day for years.

But before I walk into the brilliance of how and why I killed Lillian, I do want to clarify that I didn't set out to sleep with her husband, or to fall in love with him. Five years ago, I met a cute and quirky writer in a meditation class, and that was where our friendship began.

I didn't know or care that she had a husband. I liked her. She made me laugh. She was fragile and found me entertaining, and I was in between relationships and bored and warmed to the idea of a more intellectual friend, one who actually knew who Eckhart Tolle was and could debate modern philosophy and theories of life and death and the battles and journeys of each.

I didn't just like Lillian; I grew to love her. I took her son to bike meets and taught him how to play chess and set him up with my house-keeper's daughter—a beautiful girl he should have banged but didn't. And I talked business with her husband and lured him into the real estate market with a few inside deals that no one else could have gotten done. I drank beers while he grilled steaks and played the "man's game" because I'm good at that. I can butch up better than a straight guy, and when Lillian began to struggle . . . that was when things turned. She was going through emotional dips and peaks, and Mike and I played baby-sitter, taking turns watching and helping her, which put us in almost constant communication. In the late nights, when she fell asleep on the couch, we would sometimes stay up drinking, and sometimes I would stay over, because I was drunk and it was late, and everything was still innocent but there was a vibe.

God, that vibe. It was electric and reminded me of my very first boyfriend, back when I was straight as an arrow—a preacher's son, for shit's sake—and already had a girlfriend, one who wore proper things, and sang in the choir, and didn't ever push me for anything, anything more than a kiss. A girlfriend with an older brother, John. When our eyes met, my breath would hitch in my chest and my heart would race. He made the first move, and when he kissed me, I felt like it was the single most exciting and significant moment in my life.

I felt that same forbidden electricity with Mike, and maybe it was caused by Lillian, or by the fact that he tried so hard to avoid it, so hard to stay in the straight lane that he had committed to already. Whatever the reason, just a single brush of our hands felt miraculous, the air between us so charged with energy that I didn't know how she didn't feel it, how it wasn't glaring and obvious to anyone who passed within a mile.

And that vibe only heightened when the market turned and—for the first time—one of Mike's client's real estate deals went south. That was when he brought me into the fold, when we did some slightly illegal maneuvering and his trust in me grew, our bond tightened, my profit share increased, and Mike Smith turned into a verifiable badass, right before my eyes.

Intelligence is hot. Intelligence, money, and power are sexy as hell—and Lillian had no idea what her husband was packing.

So yeah, I fell for him. But he also fell for me. He could tell her that it was just sex, but that was a lie. He loves me. We are in love. He had to put us on hold to satisfy Lillian's temper tantrum, but she showed her true colors quickly with the affair, and I assumed he would run back to me once that happened.

I assumed. That was my first mistake, and one that Mike himself always hammers into me, which only made it taste more rotten when

Lillian told me that he was standing beside her, that they were fighting this together and would make it through the embarrassment and reality of the video—the video that my private investigator had filmed, the video that I myself had edited and posted for maximum damage, both to Lillian and Mike's relationship, and also to her and Jacob's.

It should have been an easy nail in their marriage's coffin—proof that their relationship was flawed past the point of repair. It should have been an easy and quick decision for Mike, but he failed in that decision, just like he had failed in how he handled Lillian finding out about his "affair."

So I had to kill her. I had to make the decision for him. It wasn't easy, but it helped that she had been so selfish, of late. It helped me to look at our friendship and realize how one-sided it was. Just like her marriage to Mike, my friendship with her was all about helping Lillian. Supporting Lillian. Picking up her pieces as she fell apart and putting her back together.

Killing her was the end of a long road, with plenty of places for her to veer off and into safety, had she just been less selfish and more considerate of others.

And now, even in death, she's being a pain. Luis wants me in Lynwood, so I'm canceling a showing and driving over to do a puppet dance for him and his thugs. I'm certain this is about Colorado, and I have all the figures with me, but pulling out of our pending deals, as I told Mike, is a mistake. Not my mistake, thank God, but no one would be freaking out if Lillian were alive and the cops weren't sniffing around Mike.

Maybe it was a mistake to make the fake calls from Lillian's phone. At the time, I'd considered it to be brilliant. No one would be looking at me, the dearest friend, not when there were two fantastic candidates for her murder—David and Mike. And if Lillian had killed herself, she would certainly have called and ordered her own obituary. It's the exact kind of off-the-wall action she was known for.

I originally moved to Los Angeles to become an actor, so mimicking Lillian's quiet rasp was a breeze, especially given that I mocked her sayings regularly to Mike. The phone-call recipients had certainly bought it. The concern in the voice of the domestic-abuse center's operator—*Do we need to get you someplace safe?*—had been a testament to my vocal skills, and I had driven an erratic trek through the city, dropped her cell in the back of a courier truck, then spent the drive back to Malibu patting myself on the back for my creativity while Lillian's body rolled around on the back seat.

Now I've followed Luis's men through a shitty ranch-style home, and we are walking down a set of unfinished stairs into a basement. There is a group waiting for us, and I duck my head to avoid hitting the ceiling and squint as my eyes adjust to the dim light.

Jacob's is the first face I recognize, and my stomach sinks at what it means if he is here. Luis turns in his chair to face me, and just past him, seated at a folding table beside Jacob, his head in his hands, is Mike.

Okay. So it's this sort of meeting.

CHAPTER 71

SAM

This basement is filthy. In prior meetings with Mike's clients, we met at steak houses and expensive hotel suites and, once, on a G5. This is the sort of exchange I'd prefer to stay out of, though the danger factor of the cartel business has always given me a sort of bad-boy factor that I have enjoyed, a secret hidden layer of my life that added dimension.

Now, seeing the looks on Mike's and Jacob's faces, I realize that I might be in over my head. My first thought is that this is about what I did to Lillian, but the cartel doesn't seem to care about personal squabbles, as long as they don't affect business, and I made sure that I always kept my affair with Mike and my friendship with Lillian clear of work.

My mistake—the voice mail to the domestic-abuse center, which undoubtably put some attention on Mike—pokes at me, but again, how would they pin that on me?

I meet Mike's eyes, and they are afraid and apologetic, and maybe I shouldn't be the one worried about my mistakes. I take in the scene. There's a stiff tension in the air, and a half dozen cartel members stand around as if ready for war. Luis is their stark counterpoint in his clean and pressed attire.

"Good evening, gentlemen." I smile warmly, and my father's belief that my acting classes were all a waste is proven wrong, once again. The greeting comes out smoothly and confidently, and when Luis looks at me, I can tell that he is gauging and confirming my innocence in this—whatever this is—from my poise and calm demeanor. "What's all this about?"

"We're trying to move Colorado," Luis says, and tilts his head to Mike. "Mike says he's lost the private key to the Bitcoin account."

"W-w-what?" I gawk despite my best efforts. "What do you mean, 'lost'?"

"I hid it with a bottle of liquor in our safe," Mike says dully. "Lillian apparently took it out on the morning she died."

A bottle of liquor. Lillian apparently took it out. The puzzle pieces click into place, and I think of the box of liquor that was with Lillian when I picked her up. I found it when I was cleaning out the SUV I had borrowed for the task, and recognized it as their anniversary token. I took it home as a perverse F-you to Lillian and toasted the end of their marriage on my back deck, overlooking the ocean. The bottle and box are in my trash compactor, safe and sound until the maid arrives in the morning. My heart beats faster at the realization of what I have. The key to the Bitcoin balance of Colorado, which has to be close to half a billion dollars. I look from Mike's stricken face to Jacob, who looks as if he is about to have an anxiety attack, to Luis, who has a few beads of sweat along his hairline. For a man who prides himself on staying cool under pressure, that is tantamount to a mental breakdown.

I'm the only one who knows where it is. The power behind this knowledge is staggering, and I slide my hands into the pockets of my shorts so that I can ball them into fists without anyone seeing.

"So." I clear my throat. "Why am I here?"

"Well, you're here for motivation." Luis smiles. "We're hoping to jog Mike's memory—plus you know Lillian. Any idea of where she might have put this bottle?" He glares at Mike with clear disgust at him putting something so valuable in such a weak hiding place.

"Because I got to tell you, Sam." Luis clicks his tongue against his teeth. "Without that key, we're going to have to start punishing everyone involved. And I'm not saying that you're involved, Sam . . . but we all know the fondness that Mike and you share."

Punishing. I've seen what that looks like. Mike once showed me a photo that Luis sent him, of a developer who had screwed us out of a real estate commission. The man's eyes had been cut out while he was still alive.

Hmm. The moral dilemma here is tough. I could share that I have the key, but then Mike would know that I saw Lillian after she took the bottle, which would lead to him figuring out that I am the one responsible for her death. Sharing the key would save his and Jacob's lives but certainly ruin any chance of us getting back together—so Mike would be officially, from this point forward, lost as a long-term relationship prospect. My heart sags at the thought because I truly did see us together. Not in my house—we'd buy a much bigger property and travel. So much travel. Mike always told Lillian that he was afraid to fly, and that was why they road-tripped everywhere, but those road trips had been to cover up items that he was transporting and side errands that he went on. In truth, Mike loves a first-class seat as much as the next man, and we've escaped on mini-trips all over the country together. I had anticipated so, so much more, once we were out from underneath her thumb.

"So let me ask you, Sam. You knew Lillian well. Can you think of anywhere she would have put this box and bottle?" Luis stands up and walks in front of me.

My dilemma comes around full circle with the amount of money involved. If my relationship with Mike is dead either way—by his death or by me confessing that I killed Lillian—then shouldn't I at least benefit from the money? That kind of money is more than life-changing. It is life-creating. It could insulate me with enough security and anonymity to ensure a long, happy, and peaceful life, one of extravagant wealth. I deserve that. I've earned that.

"No," I say weakly—and it comes out perfectly and convincingly. "I . . . I don't have any idea where it could be. But please—maybe if you give Mike some more time, he could figure it out." I put the focus back on Mike so cleanly, so perfectly, that I have to resist the urge to smile. Sometimes I do that—I give this smug smile that, as my father once said, makes someone want to "section off my lips with a bolt cutter." Luis seems like he'd be good with a bolt cutter, so I keep my lips pinned together and my eyes concerned. *Let's not forget who is to blame here. Make Mike fix this.*

"Mike seems to be struggling with the motivation to figure it out. I think we could help him along." Luis holds out his hand toward a man in a black T-shirt and a full beard. The man passes him a gun, which he swings toward me. I inhale sharply, but before I can speak, the gun is moving farther left, sweeping past Mike and stopping on Jacob.

Jacob. When I met him, he was a chubby-cheeked twelve-year-old. We bonded over a shared love of crude comedians and action movies. He once confided in me that he found alien women more attractive than real ones. He thinks that his father is a dork and his mother is a horrible cook. He is terrified of high school judgments and opinions. In some ways, he is very similar to a young me. In other ways, I don't understand a thing going through his head.

It was hard for me to post that video of Lillian. Not because of her—I could give two shits about her. But I understood exactly how Jacob, his friends, and his school would react to this. I understood how deeply it would negatively affect him, and I needed that level of embarrassment—and his reaction to it—to properly damage Lillian and Mike's marriage.

Now I watch as he swallows, staring at the nose of the gun, and a tear leaks from the corner of his left eye. He shouldn't have to die for Mike and Lillian's mistakes. Am I really about to let that happen?

I have the key. I could tell them, right now, and throw myself on the sword.

Throw myself on the sword and lose Mike.

And the money.

And maybe they'll kill all of us anyway.

I pull my gaze away from Jacob's face and concentrate on a crack on the concrete floor.

Mike sobs out a plea, and I wait for the sound of the shot.

CHAPTER 72

LILLIAN

I can't take this. I'm screaming at my husband, at Sam, at someone to do something . . . but they are all just standing there, while the businessman points a gun at my son.

Sam has the key—he knows he has the key—and he looked straight into my son's face and stayed silent. It was then that I *knew* he had killed me. That drink, or maybe something after it—whatever it was, this man I welcomed into my heart, into my home . . . What was it that Luis said? *Romance doesn't mix well with our business.*

He's a snake and a liar and a killer, and I am once again responsible for all this. I brought Sam into our lives. I trusted him. I loved him. Apparently, so did Mike, who should be strangling the truth out of him.

The businessman gives Mike one last chance to come up with an idea, and Sam is staring at the ground like a coward, waiting for my son to die. My fury erupts and I'm trembling, and why can't this be like the movies? Why can't I create a gust of wind, or knock Luis backward, or sneak into Sam's head and force the words out of him?

There's a loud bang from above, not like a gun but like the thud of collision, and we all look upstairs.

Another thud sounds, followed by shouting and heavy footsteps, and all the men in the room, save my three, start to move and shout, but there is nowhere for them to go. We are all trapped down here, and something is thrown down the stairs and suddenly everything explodes in a glare of light and sound. I try to duck out of instinct, and I'm suddenly outside the home, and there are uniforms everywhere, surrounding the house, guns drawn, and then I see something that makes my heart soar with happiness and relief.

It is Lenny, in his work uniform, a bulletproof vest over his chest, standing away from the house, his back stiff, eyes scanning the house, features tight.

Lenny. My alcoholic knight in shining cemetery garb.

CHAPTER 73

MIKE

Four days later

Maybe Lill's an angel and she called in a favor. Whatever the reason, my ass was saved in the fourth quarter with three seconds left on the clock. The task force was a combination of DEA and local cops, and they arrested everyone, even the old lady upstairs, then sorted out the pieces back at the station.

My fourth or fifth contingency plan was always to turn state's evidence, and in handcuffs, it was an easy decision to make. My house is a treasure trove of documentation, and I gave up the combination to the guest-room safe, plus the shed—both items they would have found on their own.

For the third day in a row, I'm sitting in a room with four feds and a local cop and giving the details of every single cartel member and transaction I've ever been a part of, including ones with Sam—though I insist that he never knew anything about the nature of the money being used in the transactions.

They're skeptical about this. I can see the looks that shoot between them. They aren't sure whether I'm stupid or lying, but I stick to the lie and they move on, because I have a lot of other things to share.

I want a deal. Full witness protection, for the rest of Jacob's and my lives. I want it somewhere cold, in the mountains. Near a big city but not in one. They nod—*oh yes, sure*—and are agreeing to everything, even the full immunity, which I expected but am still pleased by.

I am fine with them seizing all my assets, but I want Lillian's life-insurance policies to go to whatever new identity Jacob gets. They aren't sure about this—$6 million is a steep amount—but someone calls someone and it is approved. *Congratulations, son. You're a future millionaire.* I insisted it be put in a trust until he's thirty, which will give me enough time to teach him proper money management.

Jacob is pissed and I don't care. I almost saw his head blown off, so I'm just grateful that he's breathing—later, once everything settles, he will understand, or start to understand, why we cannot ever go back home and cannot ever speak to anyone we ever knew, ever again.

For me, it's a relief. I was sick of Sam. Tired of the constant pressure of the cartel. I'd spent the last two years dreaming of retirement—granted, I expected to be in a mansion with a view of the ocean—but I can adjust to small-town life. Work at a job where no one will kill me, no matter how badly I fuck something up. Meet another woman, maybe a man. Do a better job of raising my son.

Tomorrow we're getting on a private plane and heading to our new home. Midair, we'll get our new identities and location, which is around the time that Lillian's burial will be held. I haven't mentioned this to Jacob, and he hasn't asked about a funeral. Maybe he'll think of it in a week or so, but it's not like we will be able to ever visit her grave.

"So?" The man in front of me taps his pen on the page. "You're telling us that four hundred million dollars is just lost? Irretrievable?"

I'm always amused by how people just don't understand cryptocurrencies. They are always certain that there is a customer service line you can call, or a form you can complete, to retrieve a lost key.

"Unless someone finds the key and knows what it is, and can locate the account address to use it." I give the same answer I've given twice already.

"How would someone locate the account address?"

I shrug. "A good hacker who knows what he's looking for could find it. It's not like a key. The addresses are less secure because they don't really matter. It's like the account number, which is on the bottom of any check."

"So the money is gone?" Another suit just can't keep his mouth closed.

"Yeah." A week ago, the knowledge would have devastated me. Now I'm just ready to move the fuck on.

CHAPTER 74

LILLIAN

I think that everything is about to end for me. I can barely hold on to Jacob. I follow him as he goes through white hallways and talks to counselors and has his photo and fingerprints taken and put on new identification, but I'm disappearing and then reappearing, blocks of time gone, and I find that I don't really care what I missed.

My emotions are diluted, my care and concern stretched thin as I watch my husband sign contracts and deliver the secrets and details on what appears to be a criminal organization. How long did he work for them? I don't care. Did he really have an affair with Sam? I don't care.

It's freeing, the loss of human emotions and concerns. Maybe Jacob and Mike will be found and killed—that's okay. Death is fleeting. I don't even remember dying. I drank a drug-laced latte and I slept. According to what the police are telling Mike, Sam is likely the one who killed me, and isn't that amusing? I'm not sure if it was that latte, or if the pills came a little later, but all I remember is the delicious taste of cinnamon and pumpkin . . . and sleeping. Like I said, not a bad way to go.

I do think . . .

I faded for a moment, and now Jacob is on a plane and I'm looking down on Los Angeles and wondering whether my funeral has already occurred. Is it now? Soon? Funny, I put so much thought and importance into obituaries for so long, and I couldn't care less what mine says. Still, maybe, I should write one last one, for me.

Or maybe I will just go. I'll just close my eyes and float away . . .

CHAPTER 75

LENNY

The funeral was canceled. I guess the husband organized all sorts of things, but then he disappeared and the funeral home was left with their thumbs up their asses.

I made sure that she got a nice casket—he had prepaid for that—and she was brought here to Angelus Rosedale for her burial. We lower her into the ground using the same crane that was used on Marcella's small casket, and as the glossy mahogany box hits the dirt, I bawl, just like I did at Marcella's burial—only this time, Lillian isn't here to stand beside me. This time, I am alone, and I have to find a reason to keep living because standing at her grave, I was ready to give up.

There is a possibility on the horizon, in the unlikely form of Gersh. He's called me every day since the raid, and is trying to talk me into coming back on the force. Not as a detective, just a desk job, but it'll give me a reason to get out of bed, and not drink, and say goodbye to this place and its daily reminder of Marcella's death.

I do miss the camaraderie. The good fight against the bad. The games of finding clues and sniffing out lies. Even just being on the sidelines of that—it would be nice, and give me health benefits. I could get this damn molar fixed.

I posted the details of the burial online, but only a handful of people showed up. There was Rosa from across the street. Fran from Lillian's work. David Laurent, or whatever his name was, showed up, which was an interesting surprise. Her mother, and five or six others, but I don't know who they were.

Most notably absent: Sam Knight and Mike and Jacob Smith. I know where Mike and Jacob are—en route to their new home, with new identities and all the other benefits that witness protection affords. On the edges of the cemetery are plainclothes officers, curious to see if Sam will risk showing up, but I know better. He's hiding somewhere. Maybe here in the city, maybe not, but there's a warrant out for his arrest, so he won't show, not even for her burial.

Sam Knight is, if I look back at the criminals I have encountered, one of the smarter ones. Her body didn't have any clues or an ounce of discernible DNA evidence; neither did the crime scene. While his presence in the basement hinted at his involvement with the Los Colima cartel, there wasn't enough evidence to hold him for longer than twenty-four hours. Mike Smith, who had pointed fingers and given the names of at least a dozen key cartel members, had insisted the real estate broker was oblivious to the illegal source of the funds and was there under duress, same as Jacob Smith, so he'd been released.

The path to his warrant had been a cumbersome one, which had rewarded good old police work. A home-security cam from a beach house a quarter mile down the Pacific coast road had recorded 442 vehicles that had passed between the hours of 11:00 p.m. and 4:00 a.m.—which were the body drop times, according to lividity and the tide patterns on the beach. Of those 442 cars, only fourteen made a return trip within an hour of their passing. The camera was angled down the road, which gave a clear view of the tag numbers. Fourteen vehicle owners were researched, none with any direct connection to Lillian or Mike Smith or a motive, but one owner of a black Chevrolet

Tahoe—a Tricia D'nario—had purchased her home with Sam Knight. When Gersh reached out to her, she was in France, at her second home, and professed to have not driven that vehicle, which was parked in her LA garage, in three months. When asked if anyone had access to her home, she provided three names, one of which was Sam Knight.

Now, it still wasn't a slam dunk. The bastard had gone out of his way to avoid any traffic-cam intersections near Lillian Smith's house, and they still hadn't tracked down the Starbucks where he'd purchased the latte she drank, but he'd certainly paid cash for it. Forensics had gone over the Tahoe with a fine-tooth comb and hadn't found a hair or fingerprint from him. Same for Tricia D'nario's home.

Lillian's DNA had been all over the passenger side and back seat of the car. No blood, but plenty of hair and prints. That and the camera footage had been enough for a warrant against Sam, though the evidence probably was too circumstantial to hold up in court.

His guilt was cemented, at least in my mind, when he ran. Just disappeared from his multimillion-dollar mansion and his expensive car. Left artwork and furniture, even his pet eels.

Eels. That should have been Lillian's first sign that the guy was a psychopath.

Everyone left quickly after the grave was filled, but I take my time in laying the sod over the plot and arranging the sprays of flowers. I plant a small rosebush beside the stone, then sit on the hill and watch the first sunset over her grave.

LILLIAN SMITH
MOTHER. DAUGHTER. WIFE.
MAY YOUR LAUGHTER AND SMILE CARRY YOU INTO HEAVEN.

The last line was my suggestion, and Lillian's own words, which we had also used on Marcella's stone. It fit Marcella a lot better than Lillian, but I thought that she would like that link. Maybe she wouldn't, but we make the best decisions we can with what we have.

Once the sun is fully hidden, and the mosquitoes are out, I grab my shovel and bucket and make my way back to the caretaker's shed.

Now, alone in the shed, I sit down, turn on the lamp, and do my best with her obituary.

CHAPTER 76

SAM

Here's the thing about $400 million: it lets you do whatever the fuck you want to do. And oh, it stretches. The interest on my new nest egg is fifteen mil a year. That's forty-two grand per day. I've been shelling out money right and left, purchasing anything I see and want, and the balance doesn't change. Yesterday I bought a vintage Patek Philippe. Today I gave the pool attendant five grand as a tip. Everyone at this resort knows who I am, the type of drink I want, and the car I drive—which, by the way, is a 1957 Pininfarina.

I roll onto my stomach and adjust the face cradle, letting out a long and controlled breath as the masseuse's strong fingers strum along the tight muscles of my neck. The ocean wind rustles the silky sheet against the sides of my arms, and I focus on the soft sounds of the waves crashing into the rocks, then subsiding. Crash, withdraw.

Crash, withdraw.

A bird softly caws, and from the pool, there is the strum of a ukulele.

Next week my identification and passport will come in, and I'll officially be a new man. Nicholas Delph. I've been working on my backstory and researching the ideal place to live. I'll have several homes, of course, but I figure I'll try out one country at a time. Right now, I'm in Venezuela, but with my passport, I'm thinking a château in France or a mountain range outside Mont-Tremblant.

I'm still healing over Mike. It was a bitter cocktail of love and hate, and I think I was addicted to the roller coaster. I feed on drama, I know that. The danger of his job, his secrets, the mental games I played with Lillian—there's a hole in my heart that all that used to fill. I'll find some rugged backpacker or a sandy beach god to distract my heart, but in the meantime, I have four hundred million reasons to be appreciative of Mike, and of his lies to the police—lies that allowed me to walk free after that basement fiasco.

"Mr. Knight?" I turn my head to one side and see a man in dark jeans and a sweater.

I start to respond, start to turn my body for a better look, but then there is a gun pressed against the back of my head, and I realize that this vacation, this new life . . . is already over.

ACKNOWLEDGMENTS

It's not really fair, this authoring business. As the author, I'll get the lion's share of the reception for this book, when I am just a piece of the puzzle that puts it together and gets it into a reader's hand.

Sometimes, that reception is fantastic—glowing emails from readers or gorgeous Instagram flat-lays with five stars in big, bold font. Other times, it is more critical, but just as well appreciated. The behind-the-scenes team almost never sees or hears the good stuff, and will always be woefully underacknowledged for the large part they play in its production.

This section of the book is my one opportunity to try to shine some light on their contributions, so let me try to do my best.

First, my favorite person in publishing: Maura Kye-Casella. Way back when, when I was just a wee sprout of an author, with one risqué novel to my name, Maura took me under her agent wing, introduced me to prosecco (I told you, I was helpless!), and then went to war for me. She's brilliant, fearless, encouraging, but also insightful—and I am continually grateful for her efforts and feedback, and for pitching me to Thomas & Mercer.

Second, the Thomas & Mercer family, starting with Megha Parekh. My relationship with Megha started with *Every Last Secret*, deepened with *The Good Lie*, and now brings you this book. I hope many more are ahead. Megha is my first step with a big-picture idea and outlines, and she helps me solidify and improve the idea before my pen hits the page. She is also incredibly patient, since my pen often hits the page and then goes in a horrifically unknown direction, one that she has rolled with on many occasions. I vow to one day cause her less headaches and stress, and be a properly behaved author; I'm just not sure how many novels it will take me to get there.

Charlotte Herscher is another Thomas & Mercer superstar. We have worked together on three books now, and she's the brain behind the words—helping me to tighten my plot, improve my storytelling, and heighten the suspense while deepening the characters. In this book specifically, she helped me warm up Lillian, keep Mike in check, and cut out a lot of scenes that were slowing down the action. If you enjoyed the pace and cadence of this book, you have Charlotte and Megha to thank.

More acknowledgments to those who contributed: Kellie Osborne smoothed out the kinks, caught my misuses, and in general kept me from looking like an idiot. Rachael Herbert handled the moving pieces of production and dealt with my delays and questions with patience and grace. This gorgeous cover is courtesy of James Iacobelli, who captured the feel of it perfectly and was open to my ideas and requests. And to the T&M behind-the-scenes staff who I have not yet had a chance to meet, but who played a hand in the formatting, distribution, marketing, and production of this novel, thank you.

Outside of publishing, I would like to thank my family for their unending support and patience. Chances are that you guys will never read this far into the back of the book, so I'll shower you with grateful-ness in the form of poorly cooked beignets, full control of the television remote, and the chance to watch me nod off on the couch only to jerk awake and expect a recap of everything I've missed. I love you all and appreciate your understanding of everything that this author life brings with it.

Also a sincere thanks to Tricia Crouch, for keeping me sane and my social media alive, and for listening to me talk about imaginary people as if they are real.

And last but not least: YOU. If you are reading these words, it is because you spent your hard-earned money on this novel and then devoted your time to read every chapter and into the back matter. Thank you so much for your support. I sincerely appreciate it. If you'd like email updates on my writing, you can get on my list at www.next-novel.com.

BOOK CLUB QUESTIONS

1. Double lives are a common theme in the novel, with almost all of the major characters hiding a secret. Ignoring for a moment the sexual aspects of Mike and Lillian's double lives, do you think that a healthy marriage can exist if a person hides a part of their life from their spouse?

2. Do you think Lillian would have had the relationship with David if she hadn't first discovered Mike's affair?

3. What is your favorite moment in the story?

4. In the first half of the book, there is a countdown to "The Death." Who did you think was going to die? Were you surprised when it was Lillian?

5. Who was your top suspect as the killer? Did your suspect change over time?

6. Did you suspect that Sam was "the other woman" in Mike's life? How did discovering that change your opinion of Sam? Did you, at that point, suspect that he killed Lillian?

7. Do you think that David developed genuine feelings for Lillian, or was she just a mark? Did Mike's finding and destroying the calendar raise your suspicions of David?

8.   If you were Sam, would you have shared the location of the liquor bottle to save Mike's and Jacob's lives, even if it incriminated you to Mike?

9.   Do you think any of the relationships in this book (Sam/Mike, Lillian/Mike, Lillian/David, Sam/Lillian) were genuine, with love?

10. Do you feel like Mike gets off too easily? Where do you want to see Jacob and Mike in five years?

ABOUT THE AUTHOR

Photo © 2013 Eric Dean Photography

A. R. Torre is a pseudonym for *New York Times* bestselling author Alessandra Torre. Torre is an award-winning author of more than twenty-six novels. She has been featured in such publications as *ELLE* and *ELLE UK* and has guest-blogged for *Cosmopolitan* and the *Huffington Post*. In addition, Torre is the creator of Alessandra Torre Ink, a website, community, and online school for aspiring authors. Learn more at www.alessandratorre.com.